# Fulfillment

Sharisse had protested when he lay down beside her, but there was only one blanket. She had to lie next to him, and she'd accepted his arm for a pillow. She was as nervous as a cat.

She was undoubtedly worried about their proximity, but so was he. He was, in fact, amazed by his own restraint. She trusted him to protect her, so he could not take advantage of her. That trust gave him a satisfying feeling, and he wouldn't betray it.

Sharisse was exasperated with herself. She had been lying there staring at the dying fire, sleep impossible. She had never slept next to a man before and had no idea it would be so disturbing. Was this desire? Did she want a man to the point of aching for him?

His expression, and what she saw in his eyes, told her what he was going to do. And dear Lord, she wanted him to do it . . .

*Other Avon Books*
**by Johanna Lindsey**

BRAVE THE WILD WIND
CAPTIVE BRIDE
FIRES OF WINTER
A GENTLE FEUDING
GLORIOUS ANGEL
HEART OF THUNDER
PARADISE WILD
A PIRATE'S LOVE
SO SPEAKS THE HEART

# Tender is the Storm

## Johanna Lindsey

**AVON**
PUBLISHERS OF BARD, CAMELOT, DISCUS AND FLARE BOOKS

AVON BOOKS
A division of
The Hearst Corporation
1790 Broadway
New York, New York 10019

Copyright © 1985 by Johanna Lindsey
Published by arrangement with the author
Library of Congress Catalog Card Number: 84-091630
ISBN: 0-380-89693-1

First Avon Printing, June 1985

AVON TRADEMARK REG. U.S. PAT. OFF. AND IN
OTHER COUNTRIES, MARCA REGISTRADA, HECHO EN
U. S. A.

Printed in the U. S. A.

WFH 10 9 8 7 6 5 4 3 2 1

For Connie and Vicki Lynn, and dreams
that can come true, one for each of
you.

# Prologue

THE cat was large, over two hundred pounds and nearly eight feet long. High up in the mountains, it lay on a boulder, its eyes riveted on a spot thirty feet below, where the slope leveled off to form a wide ledge. There among the tall pines was a small herd of wild horses, roped off. They were nervously stamping the ground, sensing the cat's presence even though there was no breeze to carry his scent.

Suddenly the cat sensed danger. Then he saw the two men winding their way up the mountainside leading a string of horses, seven more to add to the waiting herd. They were quite young, the two men, and looked almost identical. Both had darkly bronzed skin and long black hair flowing loose about their shoulders, and both wore knee-high moccasins and long white breechclothes spanning well-muscled thighs. But one was tall and bare-chested beneath his short black vest. The other was much shorter and wore a long-sleeved white cotton shirt girded with a cartridge belt sitting low on his hips.

When the new horses were added to the herd, the cougar rose from his perch and leaped from the boulder, moving cautiously toward the two young men.

1

One was half-Apache, and the other, taller man wasn't an Indian at all.

The two men stopped, frozen, staring up at the huge cougar. Why hadn't they sensed him? All was still except for the prancing of the horses.

The tall man stuck out his hand, and the cougar closed the distance between them with a thundering purr. The cat rubbed his head into the extended hand and wrapped his body around the man's bare legs. After a moment, he moved the whole tawny length of his body under the open hand, then sauntered off and plopped down on a smooth piece of ground two feet away.

Billy Wolf let out his breath very slowly so the other young man wouldn't hear him. His hands were close to trembling, and it threatened his manhood.

"Sonofabitch!" Billy said in the language his friend had taught him so well, then more loudly when that didn't get the taller one's attention. "Sonofabitch! You hear what he's doin' to the mares, Slade?"

The taller man turned his head and bestowed on Billy one of his rare smiles. "Do*ing,* Billy, *ing.* Get that *g* on there."

"Shit, don't talk to me about grammar now!" But the point had been made, and Billy wouldn't forget again. "Weren't you just a little nervous before you knew it was him?"

"A little," was all Slade Holt said before he went over to quiet the horses.

Billy Wolf followed rapidly. "Will you just look at him lying there like he knows he's welcome, like he never left your side."

"He does know he's welcome," Slade said flatly.

Billy stared at the cougar and shook his head. "You ain't seen him in eight months, and it was a year before that time. How does he remember you? How do you recognize him now that he looks like any other mountain lion?"

"I didn't recognize him," Slade admitted, a grin beginning. "I just knew he wasn't a threat, same way you knew I wasn't a threat when we first met."

Billy thought that over for a moment and accepted it as reasonable. As was his way, he abruptly changed the subject.

"Are you really set on leaving tomorrow, Slade?" When the other simply nodded without answering and sat down next to the giant cat, Billy frowned. "But are you sure you're ready?"

Slade glanced over at a crevice dug in the side of the mountain. The crevice contained a blanket, one set of white man's clothes, boots he'd had Billy trade a horse for last winter, a sack of canned goods Billy had brought him, and the handgun and holster he'd stolen two years before, when Cactus Reed had taught him how to use the gun. It was that gun he was thinking about now. Learning to handle it with a degree of expertise had been the only thing he'd felt lacking in his education. It had taken two years of daily practice before he admitted to himself that he was good—better at least than the man he planned to kill with it.

"Ready?" Slade's light green eyes rested on the cougar, and he reached out to rub the big cat between the ears. "My problem has been a waiting problem for too many years. I was a kid, aching to grow up fast because I couldn't do anything about the pain others had caused me until I was grown up. I was twelve when you finally got up the nerve to approach me."

"Nerve!" Billy interrupted indignantly.

"Admit it, Billy," Slade said, amusement in his voice. "Your people thought I was crazy, and not just because I lived out in the mountains alone. You were only a year older than I was. Even your warriors took a wide berth around the crazy white boy."

"What were we supposed to think, you being a dirty, half-naked kid whose stink could be smelled a mile off? Anyone who got within shouting distance of you, you pulled an imaginary gun and shot them with it. If that's not loco—"

Slade burst out laughing. "I shot you, too, when you first showed up."

"With your finger," Billy grunted, but he smiled. It was rare that Slade Holt laughed with genuine humor instead of bitter cynicism.

"I told you why I stunk so bad back then. It took half a year before that skunk smell wore off."

"It would've helped if you'd availed yourself of a creek."

"Why? Back then, not having to take baths was about the only thing I liked about my freedom."

Billy twitched his nose. "You're of a different mind now. I'm grateful."

Slade shrugged. "Some things change over the years. I don't shoot make-believe guns anymore, either. It was a game I used to play with my twin brother."

Slade's expression darkened. A pain shot threw his head as it always did when he thought of his brother. He rubbed hard at his temples. The cougar realized something was wrong. His ears pricked up, and he stopped purring.

Billy knew about the headaches Slade suffered because he couldn't remember much that had happened after he and his brother ran away from Tucson when their father was killed by a gunslinger, Feral Sloan, eight years ago. Slade witnessed the gunfight, saw Sloan intentionally pick a fight with Jake Holt, Slade's father.

Jake, one of a thousand prospectors, came west looking to strike it rich. He and a friend, Tom Wynhoff, were two of the lucky ones. They found gold twenty miles west of Tucson, a rich find. But their luck didn't last, because others wanted that gold. Slade knew very little about it. His father had told him only that a man had approached him, wanting to buy the mine. Slade's father had said no.

Soon after that, Tom Wynhoff was found dead in an alley, a lead ball in his chest. That same day, for no reason, Feral Sloan picked a fight with Jake and shot him dead in the street. Slade was standing ten feet away. Moments later, Sloan passed Slade and bragged to a friend on the street, *easiest hundred dollars I ever earned.*

Slade's ten-year-old mind grasped that the gunfighter had been paid to shoot his father. The danger to him was made clear when an old man standing near Slade grabbed his arm and warned, "First old Tom, then Jake. You and your brother own that cursed mine now, Slade Holt, but you can bet you won't live to see the profits. I seen it happen a hundred times, the no-good, lazy bastards who want what a man breaks his back finding, and kill to get it. You younguns are next. Get your brother quick and get the hell out of the county. Greedy men don't stop at killing babies."

Slade found his brother, and the two of them hightailed it northeast, away from the mine, away from Tucson, making for the mountains that stretched to the north. They were followed. Slade got a glimpse of Feral Sloan riding fast behind them before a bullet grazed his temple and he fell from his horse down a rocky incline. He remembered screaming before he passed out, but he remembered nothing else.

The rain woke him. He was alone, with no sign of his brother or his horse, and no tracks to follow. He later realized he should have stayed where he was in case his brother had gone for help after leading Sloan away from him. But he wasn't thinking clearly, and he set off to look for his twin. Months later, he finally gave up. It had been a useless search, anyway, because he was afraid to go near towns in case the hired gunslinger found him or that nameless man who wanted him dead heard he was alive.

He learned to survive alone, to reach for manhood, when he would no longer be defenseless. He survived through desperation, learning by trial and error, roaming the regions from the Gila River as far south as an Apache mountain stronghold.

Strangely enough, the Indians never frightened him. They respected him for that and left him to share their domain. Slade feared and avoided all signs of white men. After two years without speaking to a single human, Slade was open to friendship when young Billy Wolf approached, six years ago.

They couldn't speak to each other at first but gradually learned each other's languages. Billy lived with his mother's tribe then, and as they were nomads, long periods would pass between the times Billy and Slade saw each other.

Billy was the only one Slade ever let close to him besides Cactus Reed. Slade had found Reed in the Galiuro Mountains a little over two years ago. The man was half-dead, two bullets in him, claiming he and the fellow he rode with had had a slight disagreement and he'd lost the argument in a big way. Slade patched Cactus up. In return, Cactus taught Slade all he knew. He knew a great deal. The man was an ex-bountyhunter, a breed who lived by their guns and their courage, challenging killers.

Cactus turned out also to be a bit of a thief, for he took off one day while Slade was hunting, taking a dozen of the wild horses from Slade's herd with him. Either he wasn't a man who felt beholden to anyone, even someone who'd saved his life, or he felt he and Slade were even because of all he'd taught the young man.

Slade didn't go after him. Wild mustangs were easy to come by, and he used them only to trade for what he needed, letting Billy take the rest out of the mountains to sell for cash. Over the years he had accumulated quite a stash of money from those horses, but it was money he'd had no use for—until now.

Billy Wolf was feeling sorry for himself. He knew that once Slade began his search he would probably never see him again. He had always known this day would come. He'd expected it last year, in fact, when Slade reached his full height, an intimidating six feet three. His vigorous life made him lean and muscular, and the hot Arizona sun made him as dark as an Indian. When Slade entered civilization again, Billy knew damn well the suspicious townsfolk would mistake him for a half-breed like himself. Slade had one thing on his side, though, and that was his sense of self-possession. Even his quiet manner was intimidating, despite his being only eighteen. And those brightly piercing eyes and finely chiseled features guaranteed him attention from women.

Billy grinned. "What will you do first, get your hair cut or have your first woman?"

Slade glanced up, but his expression gave nothing away. "I suppose the hair will have to come off first if I hope to find a woman who won't run away screaming."

"If you cut the hair and they don't mistake you for a half-breed, you'll have women fighting over you. Maybe you'd better leave your hair long to avoid that. You'll have enough trouble. You do know what to do with a woman, don't you?"

"I reckon it won't be too difficult to manage," Slade drawled, "being as how you showed me how it's done when you and Little—"

"You didn't!" Billy shouted, heat rushing up his neck. "Our camp was miles away when I . . . you mean you followed me back?"

"I was right behind you," Slade said smoothly. "Walked right into your wickiup, and you didn't even sense my presence. She did, though. She looked right at me and grinned. She never told you?"

"No, damn it!"

Slade frowned. "Are you really so embarrassed? Have I made you angry with me?"

"It was a private matter."

"You're right," Slade conceded. "Yet I can't regret it, my friend. It taught me more than I'd expected to learn." He was thoughtfully silent. "It showed me that the man loses nearly all his natural instincts when he takes a woman. He becomes weak. But she doesn't involve herself so fully, so she becomes the stronger."

"Ha!" Billy was glad to be able to recover a little. "That's not always the way it is, Slade. You saw me with my first woman, and I was clumsy and over-eager. I have since learned how to make a woman mindless with passion. It is she who now loses control over herself, not I. But that takes a special technique, and time to learn."

Slade weighed Billy's words, debating whether he was lying to save face or telling the truth. He decided it was a little of both, but gave his friend the benefit of the doubt.

"You've mastered this technique? Every woman you have now falls under your power?"

"I've mastered it," Billy bragged with extreme confidence, then pointed out quickly, "But hell, there are lots of women who don't like it no matter what you do." Billy didn't reveal that in his short experience, those few women were the white whores he'd tried out in towns.

"It might be different for you though," Billy continued. "White women take to half-breeds same as they do to full-blooded Apaches—which is not at all."

"But how do I learn your technique?"

"Hell, if you think I'm going to teach you . . . Get a woman to show you what pleasures her, same as I did."

Slade's response to any subject that made him uncomfortable was to simply walk away from it. He did that now, getting up to move back over by the horses, calling to the gray mare he favored, leaving Billy facing the wide expanse of his back.

Billy couldn't resist a last taunt. "Hell, you're worried about your first time?"

"Only that the woman will know."

Billy had to strain to catch the words. He understood. He vividly remembered how he'd felt the first time.

"Shoot, you can always wait a few more years. After all, you don't know what you're missing yet," Billy offered. "Or better yet, get the lady drunk, and she won't remember a thing."

Slade turned to meet Billy's dark eyes, and Billy grew uncomfortable. Slade was better than an Apache sometimes when it came to controlling his features. It would make anybody nervous. His expression now revealed absolutely nothing of his inner thoughts, but Billy knew from experience that he could be masking a killing fury or total boredom. There was no way of knowing which. And even though they were friends, when Slade turned that certain look on him, the hairs crawled on the back of Billy's neck.

"Well, dammitall, I don't know how we got on this subject, anyway," Billy said gruffly, and turned away from those light green eyes. "Seems to me we ought to be discussing what you aim to do with these horses. If you're leaving in the morning, well . . ."

Slade's gaze moved over the thirty-odd mares. He'd captured most of them in the last three years, a slow process of tracking a stallion's harem, living with them day after day, blending with the land, becoming nearly invisible, and finally singling out one and stalking it. He'd long ago learned not even to try for the stallion, and he had to wait until the male was otherwise occupied before he approached a female. But it was an enjoyable task, even though it required patience, patience Billy had helped teach him, patience that came naturally after three years.

"They're yours now, Billy," Slade said.

Billy's eyes widened. "Damn it! Damn it! I knew you just went on the raid last week to please me. I knew it!"

"Nonsense," Slade scoffed. "I enjoyed the challenge of taking that rancher's stock right from under his nose. His spread was big enough that he won't miss them. And I hadn't been that far east in a good many years. It gave me a chance to see what new towns were springing up. And it gave me an adventure to remember for when I become . . . civilized."

"But all of them, Slade?" Billy protested. "You can use the money they'll bring."

"I have enough money for what I have to do."

Billy didn't express his thanks except with a nod of acceptance. "So where will you begin your search?"

"Where it began."

"You really think Sloan will still be in Tucson? Hell, that's the territorial capital. Characters like Sloan don't find it easy in big towns anymore."

"It doesn't matter," Slade said offhandedly. "There or somewhere else, if he's still alive, I'll find him."

"And after you kill him?"

"I'll have the name of the man who hired him." There was a cold edge in his voice now.

"And after you kill that one?"

Slade turned away before answering. "I'll then be free to find my brother."

Billy changed the subject quickly. "What about your father's gold?"

"What about it?"

"It's still there, ain't it? You said your father and his partner rigged it so there was a worthless mine visible to anyone who wanted to look while the real mine was hidden up the mountainside where no one could find it."

A rare show of anger crossed Slade's handsome features. "That gold killed my father, separated me from my twin, and forced me to live like a wild animal. I want no part of it." Then he said, "What good are riches, anyway? The land offers all a man could want."

Billy grunted, deciding not to point out that Slade was thinking like an Indian. Was that a good thing or not?

Billy Wolf looked hard at the young man he loved like a brother. "Well, if you ever need anything, you know where to find me." Then he grinned, trying to make light of the moment. "I'll be the rich scout with the pretty wife—it shouldn't tax you too hard to find me. I just hope I don't run into your large cougar friend any time you're not around."

Slade laughed.

By early evening the Whiskers Saloon was crowded. It looked no different from all the other saloons Slade had walked into during the last year. By now he was immune to the reaction his appearance caused. Everything always quieted down until he ordered his first drink. Men sometimes moved away from him. Once it had been his quiet manner that made people wary. Now it was the savage look about him.

Slade never appeased the curious or volunteered his name without reason. His name had become a curse, inspiring fear beyond that caused by a stranger who carried a gun like he knew how to use it. The name had become an obstacle only a month after he began his search, and all because some fool cowboy in a small mining settlement had challenged him. Many witnesses saw Slade's gun clear his holster before the other man had touched his. That was all it took. In the next town he came to, they knew about him. Too late he learned about rumors. A man who had never drawn his weapon could be reported to have ten to fifteen notches on his gun. But if he let his speed be observed, he'd be counted as one of the bad guys.

Slade had yet to kill anyone, yet he was a known killer! He had only reappeared in the white man's civilization a year ago, but rumor had it that he'd come up from Texas five years before, after killing his first man. All his killings had been fair and square, it was said, the assumption being that a fast gun didn't have to fight dirty. Yet marshals quickly asked him to leave their towns, and Slade found it impossible to get information out of anyone once they knew his name.

He had changed his appearance. He had let his hair grow again and wore knee-high moccasins instead of boots. It helped a great deal. He didn't have to lie and say he was a half-breed, but he gave that impression, and people thought he was. So after a year of searching, he had finally found Feral Sloan.

He found him in Newcomb, a town of less than two hundred even if you counted the surrounding ranches and their hands. It galled the hell out of Slade when he learned that Sloan had settled in this town seven years ago, soon after it was founded. It galled him most because Sloan was foreman on the ranch nearby that he and Billy Wolf had raided that last time. He had been that close to his father's killer and hadn't even known it. And he was closer now, for Feral Sloan was in the saloon, sitting at one of the card tables with two other men, his back to the wall.

Slade had spotted him immediately. His image had never left Slade's mind. The gunslinger was about thirty now, with slicked-back hair and a chin that jutted aggressively. But the lanky body had gone soft, and his hairline had receded. There were lines of dissipation on his face. But if those years had not been kind to his appearance, they had obviously been profitable years. He dressed in an ostentatious display of silver conchas and diamond jewelry and fancy duds.

Slade concluded that Feral Sloan was either one of the town's main guns or the only one. The latter was likely. There were many cowboys from the nearby ranches in the room, it being Saturday night. Slade had learned to judge a man in the first instant the other fellow looked at him. He could dismiss all the men in the room except Sloan.

It was only a waiting game now, and Slade Holt had become good at waiting. He knew Sloan would come to him, would have to, for the sake of his reputation. Approaching a menacing stranger was a task that always fell to the town gun. The people expected it, demanded he ask questions to appease their curiosity. When the town toughs didn't get the answers they wanted, they either commenced a show of friendliness or walked away grumbling loudly, praying the stranger wouldn't take offense and start a fight.

Slade had only twenty minutes to wait before Feral Sloan joined him at the bar. Those men who had moved to the ends of the bar to give Slade plenty of room now moved over to the tables. If there was to be any shooting between these two dangerous men, the tables offered cover.

"Where you headin', mister?"

He remembered the voice all too well. *Easiest hundred dollars I ever earned.* His head began to ache with the memory, but nothing marred his expression, even as he faced this hated man.

"You talking to me, Sloan?"

Feral was surprised and suspicious. "You know me?"

"Sure. I heard of you a long time back. But that was years ago. Thought you were dead."

Slade was playing his man perfectly. Men like Sloan loved their reputations, and Sloan was quick to defend his absence from the public eye.

"I got such a nice little setup here, I couldn't resist settlin' down," Feral bragged. "But you know how it is. A man's name sometimes gets so big, people just won't leave him alone."

"I know." Slade nodded solemnly. "I hear you're a foreman now on the biggest spread in these parts. Must be a nice job."

Feral chuckled. Here was a man who could appreciate his cleverness. "The nicest—seein' as how I work only when I feel like it."

Slade lifted a dark brow, pretending interest. "You mean you get paid for doing nothing? How is that?"

"I work for Samuel Newcomb, and you might say I know somethin' about him that he don't want to become public knowledge."

Slade whistled softly. "He's rich then, Newcomb?"

"Let's just say he owns half the town and his bank holds mortgages on the other half."

"I guess he can afford to keep you on his payroll then, rather than—"

"—pay someone to get rid of me?" Feral finished, finding this quite amusing. "That might be his style, but he don't dare. I left a confession with a friend, you see. If anythin' happens to me . . . well, you get my drift."

Slade looked down at his drink. "A man that rich must have a lot of enemies."

"Oh, he's well liked around here, but with his past he can't take no chances. He's got himself a small army of men to protect him. And get this," Feral chuckled again and leaned forward as if imparting a secret. "He's even got a special attachment to his will that if he dies by malice, a hundred thousand goes to the man who gets his killer! That's common knowledge, see? Smart, real smart. The man who kills him wouldn't live out the day, and that's a fact. Hell, the only way you could hurt that bastard would be to ruin him financially. But it would take a power-fully rich and clever man to do that."

"You don't sound as if you like your benefactor."

Feral shrugged. "Comes from knowin' a man too well too long. We rub each other the wrong way these days."

"You've been with Samuel Newcomb a long time, have you? He wouldn't have been the man you worked for over in Tucson back in '66, would he?"

Feral's expression changed abruptly. "How the hell did you—? No one around here knows that. Who are you, mister?"

"Is he the one, Sloan?" Slade persisted in a calm voice.

Feral began to sweat. This tall kid had shocked him, and he wished he were anywhere but where he was. Still, he couldn't resist a chance to boast. "I did a few jobs for Sam in Tucson, killed a couple of fellows he wanted out of the way. No big deal, just a couple of nameless prospectors." He shrugged modestly. "Now you tell me how you knew."

"I happened to be there," Slade replied in a low voice. "I saw your work firsthand."

"Did you?" Feral perked up. "But hell, you must have been just a kid then."

"True, but what I witnessed I'll never forget."

Feral mistook Slade's meaning. "You saw me get Hoggs? Yeah, that was a close one. The bastard got what he deserved for daring to challenge me."

"No," Slade said slowly, ominously. "It was the nameless prospector I saw you shoot, the one Newcomb paid you to kill." His conscience needed that confirmation.

Feral turned wary again. "That fight wasn't worth remembering. There was no challenge to it."

"I know."

Feral swallowed. "You never said who you are, mister."

"Name's Holt, Slade Holt."

As he said it, his voice carried to a nearby table. His voice spread in a matter of seconds until the room buzzed with the name.

"You're pullin' my leg, mister." Feral mustered enough bravado to sound almost belligerent. "Slade Holt ain't no half-breed."

"That's right."

The eyes that had seemed light green before now burned with yellow fire. Feral's hands were sweating, and that wasn't good. Couldn't handle a gun well with sweaty hands.

"Didn't mean to offend you none, Mr. Holt."

"You didn't." A single muscle ticked along Slade's smooth jaw, the only sign of the turmoil inside him. "Your offense was committed nine years ago when you killed that nameless prospector. And your mistake was in not killing me when you had the chance."

Feral's eyes widened in sudden understanding, but understanding came too late. He smelled death, his own. Automatically he reached for his gun, but the ball slammed into his chest just as the gun cleared his holster. He was thrown backward with the impact, landing on his back several feet away. Slade's soft moccasins made no noise as he walked over and stood by Sloan's head.

Sloan was looking up into a face that showed no emotion, not even triumph. He was dying, and the man who had killed him was taking it in stride.

"Lousy bastard," Feral managed in a whisper. "I hope you go after him now." His words weren't coming out as clearly as he heard them in his mind. "Then you'll be a dead man. Damn kid. Dead like you should've been . . . you were supposed . . ."

Feral Sloan's eyes glazed over. Slade stared at the dead man for a moment. Though he had meant to kill him and didn't regret it, his stomach churned. Bile rose in his throat. But his expression remained impassive, and the onlookers thought him a cold-

blooded killer, unaffected by death. The legend of
Slade Holt was being confirmed there in the saloon.

Slade wasn't thinking of that. He was remembering two ten-year-old boys racing desperately
away from Tucson with a murderer after them. He
was seeing it all again, and this time his head didn't
ache with the memory. Feral Sloan had shot him and
assumed he was dead. He hadn't bothered to climb
down the rocky gorge to make sure. Now, finally,
Slade remembered all of it. He knew now how to
start looking for his brother.

He left Newcomb without a backward glance.

# Chapter 1

*1882, New York City*

NOT too far north of the hectic business district, Fifth Avenue became a quiet residential area. Trees grew at curbside between handsome street lamps. Elegant mansions lined Fifth Avenue. Brownstones could be found next to houses with mansard roofs in the French Second-Empire style. A Gothic Revival mansion stood next to an Italianate-style mansion with pediments over the windows and a balustrade atop the cornice.

The facade of Hammond House was a mixture of brownstone and white marble, with a high stoop on the first floor and three more stories above the first. Marcus Hammond lived here with his two daughters. A self-made man who was well on the way to wealth long before his first daughter was born, he permitted no obstacles. Few challenged his will, so he was generally good-natured and generous, especially with his daughters.

One of those daughters, the older one, was at the moment readying herself for an outing with her fiancé, a man chosen for her by her father. Sharisse Hammond didn't mind the choice. The day Marcus had told her she would marry Joel Parrington during the summer, she'd just nodded. A year before she

might have questioned his choice, might even have
protested, but that was before she returned from a
tour of Europe and a disastrous love affair so humiliating that she welcomed a safe, loveless marriage.

She had nothing to complain about. She and Joel
Parrington had been friends since childhood. They
shared the same interests, and she found him terribly handsome. They would have a good marriage,
and if they were fortunate, love would come later. It
would have been hypocritical for either of them to
speak of it now, though, for Joel also was abiding by
a father's dictates. But they liked each other well
enough, and Sharisse knew she was envied by her
friends. That went a long way toward keeping her
pleasant if not overly enthusiastic. It never hurt to
be envied by a crowd of women who were forever trying to outdo one another. With her wealth on a par
with theirs and her looks rarely commented on, her
fiancé was the only thing Sharisse was envied.

Her thoughts were not on Joel just then, however.
Sharisse was wondering where in a house of so many
rooms she would find Charley. She had decided to
take him along on today's outing. He would keep her
company if Joel turned absent-minded, as he had
been doing lately.

She left her maid, Jenny, to put away the outfits
she'd been trying on before she'd decided on the
basque top with a skirt trimmed in velvet, a French
style of plain green satin combined with wide moiré-
striped green satin. She carried her Saxe gloves and
plumed poke bonnet to put on just before she left.

She stopped first at her sister's room down the hall
to see if Charley might be with her.

Sharisse knocked once and didn't wait to be invited in before opening the door. She took her
younger sister by surprise, and Stephanie gave a
start and quickly stuffed some papers into her desk
drawer. She glared at her sister accusingly.

"You might have knocked," Stephanie pointed out sharply.

"I did," Sharisse replied calmly, a twinkle in her amethyst eyes. "Writing love letters, Steph? You don't have to hide them from me, you know."

Stephanie's lovely pale complexion was suffused with color. "I wasn't," she said defensively. "But it's none of your concern, anyway."

Sharisse was taken aback. She didn't know what to make of her little sister anymore. Ever since Stephanie had turned seventeen at the start of the year, her whole disposition had changed. It was as if she suddenly harbored resentments against everyone, and all for no reason. Sharisse, particularly, became the brunt of unexpected temper tantrums ending in bursts of tears and followed by no explanation at all. She had given up trying to find out what was bothering her sister.

What was so perplexing about it was that Stephanie had finally come into her own over this last year, turning into a stunning beauty who had beaux at her beck and call. With her full breasts and trim waist, her very petite build, and the added bonus of lovely blonde hair and blue eyes, hers was the beauty that happened to be at the height of fashion. She was envied by every woman who lacked even one of those attributes—including Sharisse, who lacked them all. She couldn't help it, but she did so wish she looked like her sister. Sharisse hid her disappointment well, though, hid it under a guise of self-assuredness that fooled the most discerning. Some even thought her haughty.

Stephanie's perplexing behavior was enough to try a saint. The only one she didn't snap at was their father. But both girls knew better than to show a fit of temper in his presence. Their mother, who had died two years after Stephanie was born, had been the only one who'd dared to argue with Marcus Hammond. She'd had a fierce will, and their fights had

been frequent and heated. When they were not fighting, they had loved just as fiercely.

Neither girl seemed like her parents. Their father
believed both were biddable and sweet-natured.
They were excellent performers.

"What do you want?" Stephanie asked peevishly.

"I was looking for Charley."

"I haven't seen him all day."

Sharisse started to leave, but her curiosity was
piqued. "What were you doing when I came in,
Steph? We never used to keep secrets from each
other."

Stephanie looked hesitant, and, for a second, Sharisse thought she was weakening. But then she stared
down at her hands and said childishly, "Maybe I was
writing a love letter. Maybe I have a special beau."
Looking up, she said defiantly, "And maybe I'll be
getting married soon, too."

Sharisse dismissed all of it as sulky nonsense. "I
wish you would tell me what's bothering you, Steph.
I really would like to help."

But Stephanie ignored her. "I see you're dressed to
go out."

Sharisse sighed, giving up. "Joel suggested a ride
through Central Park if the day turned out to be
nice."

"Oh." Pain flashed through Stephanie's eyes, but
only for a second. Then she said airily, "Well, don't
let me keep you."

"Would you care to come along?" Sharisse asked
on a sudden impulse.

"No! I mean, I wouldn't dream of intruding. And I
have a letter to finish writing."

Sharisse shrugged. "Suit yourself then. Well, I do
want to find Charley before I leave. I'll see you this
evening."

The moment the door closed, Stephanie's face fell,
and her eyes filled with tears. It wasn't fair, it wasn't
at all fair! Sharisse always got everything. Nothing

but roses came her sister's way. She had been the one to get their mother's glorious copper hair and her unusual eyes that could be a deep, dark violet or a soft, sensuous amethyst. She was the one with poise and self-confidence, always their father's favorite. Their governess, their tutors, even the servants looked to Sharisse for approval. Their Aunt Sophie preferred Sharisse because she reminded her of her dear departed sister. She was not fashionable, not at five feet seven with that vivid coloring, but she was the one to stand out in a crowd, fashionable or not, and she did it regally, as if it were her right to be the center of attention.

Stephanie had never begrudged Sharisse any of her good fortune. She loved Sharisse dearly. But now Sharisse would be getting what Stephanie wanted more than anything in the world—Joel Parrington. She ached with wanting him. She ached knowing she couldn't have him. Her sister would have him, and it hurt more because Sharisse didn't care one way or the other.

That was the bitterness she had to bear. Her sister didn't love Joel. And he never looked at Sharisse the way he looked at Stephanie, with an admiration he couldn't always hide. If he were given a choice, she had no doubt whom he would choose. But he had never had any choice. Neither had Sharisse. If only their father weren't so heavy-handed when it came to controlling everyone.

If only Sharisse had married sooner! If only she weren't already twenty and could be given more time to choose. If only she would fall in love with someone else. Sharisse could fight for herself if she had to. She could face Father and argue for her happiness. Hadn't she fought to have Charley stay?

But what was the use of hoping for a miracle when the wedding was only two months away? Her heart was breaking, and there was no help for it. And if she was suffering so terribly now, before the event be-

came an actuality, how would it be afterward? After
the wedding, they planned to move into a house just
down the street. How could she bear to see them so
often, to know that they . . . She wouldn't be able to
bear it.

Stephanie opened the drawer in her desk and took
out the papers she had stuffed inside. She had torn
the strip of newspaper out of *The New York Times*'s
advertisements for mail-order brides. If she couldn't
have Joel, she would marry someone who lived far
away, where she would never have to see Joel again.
She had written three different letters, two to men
who had placed the notices themselves and one to an
agency that handled such things.

Stephanie looked the letters over now. They were
attempts to bolster herself by embellishing her good
qualities and accomplishments. Why had she lied?
There was nothing wrong with her. She would make
some man a wonderful wife. Why shouldn't she send
at least one of the letters? To stay in New York
would be to let her heart go on breaking.

Stephanie picked up the newspaper clipping
again. There was a notice from a rancher in Arizona.
She tried to remember her studies. Yes, the Arizona
Territory was far away. And a rancher would do
nicely. Maybe he was one of those cattle barons she
had heard of.

She read the whole advertisement. She was one
year short of the age requirement, but she could fib
just a little and say she was eighteen. "Must be
strong and healthy." She was healthy, but she had
never had any reason to find out if she was strong.
"Must be able to work hard." Well, she could if she
had to, but she would have to insist on servants, half
a dozen at the least. "Send picture." Ah ha! So the
man wanted to know what he was getting, and he
was hoping for something better than a plain girl.

Stephanie smiled to herself. She withdrew a clean
sheet of paper and began her letter to Lucas Holt.

* * *

Downstairs, Sharisse entered her father's study. A huge portrait of her mother graced the wall behind his desk. She knew he often turned in his overstuffed leather chair to gaze at that portrait. If ever a man grieved, Marcus Hammond did, refusing to marry again because he claimed no other woman could compare. His friends had long since given up trying to matchmake for him, leaving him to the memories he cherished.

He sat at his desk, going over some papers. Sharisse knew very little about his businesses, only that they were diversified, a rubber company, a brewery, a furniture company, an importing firm, dozens of warehouses and office buildings.

Her father had no intention of turning over the reins to her. She hadn't been trained for it. That was the main reason her husband had to be of his choosing. One day that man would control everything Marcus Hammond had built.

Marcus looked up, and Sharisse smiled. "I didn't mean to disturb you, Father. I was looking for Charley. You haven't seen him around by any chance?"

Clear blue eyes sparkled under dark gold brows. "In here? You know he's not welcome in here. He knows it, too."

"I only asked if you had seen him, Father."

"Well, I haven't. And I hope never to again," he replied gruffly. "Just keep him out of my way, Rissy."

"Yes, Father." Sharisse sighed. She left and headed for the kitchen.

A worthless moocher, her father called Charley. A no-good alley tramp. But Charley had come to mean more to Sharisse than she had ever guessed he would after she'd found him, battered and bruised, and nursed him back to health.

Sharisse chose an unfortunate time to enter the servants' domain. She heard soft crying and then a loud wail. She opened the door to the kitchen, and

the cook went back to her pots. Jenny, who had come
down for a cup of tea, gulped the last of it and hurried
past Sharisse to run back upstairs. The cook's assis-
tant began furiously peeling potatoes.

Two people stood near the table, Mrs. Etherton,
the Hammond housekeeper, and a new downstairs
maid Sharisse had seen only once before. It was this
small creature who was crying so loudly. At their
feet was a broken teacup from the cobalt-blue collec-
tion Sharisse's mother had brought with her from
her home in France. She and her sister, Sophie, had
grown up there. It was one of eight that Sharisse had
ordered packed to be taken to her new home, a price-
less treasure she'd intended to give to her own children one day. Sharisse loved the set with its intricate
blue pattern and fine gold rims.

Sharisse bent over to pick up the pieces, sick at
heart. The other seven cups were on the counter, a
packing box next to them. She sighed. If she hadn't
decided to take them to her new house, they would
all still be in the china cabinet in the dining room,
safe and whole.

Seeing her expression, the poor maid began to wail
again. "I didn't mean to, miss. It were an accident, I
swear. Don't let her send me away."

Sharisse looked at the stern-faced Mrs. Etherton.

"I've dismissed her, Miss Hammond," said Mrs. Etherton. "I should have done so sooner. If the girl's not
breaking things, she's daydreaming and not getting
a bit of work done."

"If she is prone to breaking things, she should not
have been told to pack my mother's cups," Sharisse
said sharply.

Mrs. Etherton's face turned a bright red, and the
young maid spoke up quickly. "Oh, it were Molly
who was to do the packing, miss, but she's been sick
these last three days and asked me if I'd help her out
so she don't get too far behind in her tasks."

"So you took it upon yourself to . . . ? My apologies, Mrs. Etherton," Sharisse offered.

The housekeeper drew on her dignity and nodded to Sharisse.

The girl turned her woebegone face to the housekeeper and then to Sharisse. "Give me another chance, miss. I swear I'll work harder. I can't go back to Five Points. Please don't let her send me back!"

"Five Points?" Mrs. Etherton was suddenly outraged. "You told me you came from a farm upstate. So you lied, did you?"

"You wouldn't have hired me if you'd known I come from Five Points."

Sharisse listened with distaste. She couldn't blame the poor girl for being so upset. She had never been near Five Points, but she knew of the area of Manhattan that held the worst slums in the city, including the notorious "old Brewery," where people were packed together in decrepit, filthy buildings. The annual record of murders, robberies, and other crimes was staggering. No stranger could safely walk those streets. To think that this poor child, who couldn't be more than fifteen, had probably grown up there and was trying desperately to escape.

"You will give her another chance, Mrs. Etherton?" Sharisse said impulsively.

The housekeeper's face mottled. "But, Miss—"

"Everyone deserves more than one chance," Sharisse said adamantly. "Just see that you are more careful in the future."

"Oh, thank you, miss!"

"Now, has anyone seen Charley?" asked Sharisse.

"In the storeroom, miss," the cook supplied.

"The storeroom, of course," Sharisse said.

Sure enough, there he was lying on the cool tile next to a piece of pilfered chicken. Without another word to the servants, Sharisse left the kitchen with Charley. The long-haired tomcat was snuggled securely in his mistress's arms.

# Chapter 2

STEPHANIE put down the letter she had just finished reading aloud. She looked defiantly at her closest friend, Trudi Baker. "So now you know that I wasn't just making it up when I said I was getting married. Before the month is over, I will be Mrs. Lucas Holt."

They were ensconced in Stephanie's bedroom, a feminine room with white draperies on the two windows, lavender wallpaper, and pink and white bed canopy and table covers. The settee where Trudi was sitting was rose pink brocade and nearly matched her afternoon dress.

The two young girls were of a similar height and coloring, but Trudi's eyes were green. She was six months older, a great difference in her opinion. She also had a more aggressive personality. Both girls acknowledged that she was the daring one, and that was why she was having such difficulty accepting all of this.

If she hadn't seen the coach and train tickets with her own eyes, she would still have thought her best friend was pulling her leg.

"Well?" Stephanie demanded.

Trudi tried to address the matter she felt was most important. "He won't be handsome, you know. He's probably so ugly that no woman out there will have him. That's why he had to advertise for a wife."

"Nonsense, Trudi. It could be just the other way

around. He couldn't find a girl pretty enough to suit him, is all."

"Wishful thinking, Steph! You sent him a picture of you, so why didn't you ask for one of him?"

Stephanie bit her lip. "I did," she admitted. "But he didn't send one or say anything about it."

"You see! He's old and ugly and knew he would never have a chance with you if you saw what he looked like."

"He probably just doesn't have a picture of himself."

"Steph, why don't you just admit you didn't really think this through?"

Stephanie began to look even more obstinate, and Trudi rushed on, "Why him? There are a dozen men right here who would jump at the chance to marry you, men you know, men who aren't strangers. Just because Lucas Holt sent the tickets and is expecting you doesn't mean you have to go. Send the tickets back. What can he do?"

Stephanie looked miserable. "You don't understand, Trudi. The only man I want is going to marry my sister. I *have* to do this. Sharisse's wedding is next week. I don't intend to be here to see it."

"So you're running away."

Stephanie looked at the floor. "If you want to put it that way, yes, I'm running away."

Trudi's brow creased. "Doesn't it matter that you may be miserable the rest of your life?"

"I have resigned myself," Stephanie sighed.

"Haven't you done anything at all to change things? Have you talked to your father? Have you told your sister? Does anyone know besides me?"

"No, no, and no. What difference would it make except to humiliate me? My father doesn't take me seriously. He still thinks of me as a child. And I can't bear for Sharisse to know. I won't have her pitying me."

"She's your sister, not your enemy. She loves you. She might help you."

"There's nothing she can do."

"How do you know? You might be afraid of telling your father, but maybe she isn't."

"She wouldn't dare," Stephanie gasped. Trudi didn't really know Marcus Hammond.

"She's worldly, Steph, and she doesn't let things get to her the way you do."

"She only pretends she doesn't," Stephanie said knowingly.

Trudi tried another approach.

"What if Sharisse refuses to marry Joel? She doesn't seem to love him."

Stephanie smiled wryly. "Nobody dares defy my father, certainly not Rissy or I."

"Honestly, Stephanie Hammond, you're determined to not even try, aren't you?" Trudi said angrily. "You wouldn't catch me giving up without a fight. I would do anything possible to get what I wanted."

Stephanie just shrugged.

"All you have to do is tell your sister the truth. It's not as if she loves him or would really be giving up anything. You said that she doesn't care, that she's been treating her own wedding as if it were just another party to attend this summer. I've seen her with Joel myself. She treats him like a brother. If she loves him, she hides it very well."

"No, she doesn't love him. I'm sure of that."

"Then why shouldn't she help you?"

"Trudi, stop it. There's nothing she can do."

"Maybe. But what if there is? What if she manages to call off the wedding and you end up with Joel? If worse comes to worst, let her be the one to run away. At least then the wedding won't take place."

"That's crazy, Trudi," Stephanie said angrily, but it was anger at herself because she wished it were

Sharisse who was going away. Lucas Holt was probably ugly and old, and she really would be miserable with him. She had made such a mess of things. She felt tears begin.

"Well, I suppose I could at least tell Rissy how I feel," Stephanie said hesitantly.

"Now that's the first sensible thing you've said all day." Trudi smiled at her, a little bit relieved.


"Good night, Rissy."

"Good night, Joel."

Sharisse closed her eyes and waited for the usual perfunctory kiss, hoping desperately she would feel something this time. She didn't. There was no strength in the hands that gripped her shoulders, no enthusiasm in the lips that brushed against hers. He had never held her close to him, and she realized she didn't know what it was like to be swept into a man's embrace. Antoine Gautier had never held her passionately, either. He had made love to her hands, in the Frenchman's style. Even so, the brush of Antoine's lips against her palm had done more to stir her passions than anything Joel had done.

She couldn't blame Joel. After being humiliated by Antoine, she had sworn never to love again—and her heart had taken her seriously. It was just as well. She could never be hurt that way again. So she told herself to stop hoping for something more than tepid affection.

Sighing, she stood by the front door and watched Joel skip down the stairs and get into his carriage. He was so handsome. His complexion was nearly as creamy white as her own. His little mustache was always neatly trimmed. His slim physique wasn't at all intimidating, like her father's well-muscled form. There was no arrogance in him, either, which was important to her. Her father had supplied all the overbearing arrogance she needed for one lifetime.

Joel was good-natured, with a devil-may-care charm.
What more could she ask for?

Who was she kidding? It wasn't at all flattering
when a man couldn't even pretend he found you desirable. At least Antoine had pretended. No, she
wouldn't compare them. Joel wasn't at all like the
deceitful Antoine. She was just wanting, was all.
Her height put most men off, and her slim, boyish
figure deterred the rest. She just wasn't feminine,
and she didn't have what it took to stir men's
passions.

Oh, some men looked at her with unconcealed lust,
but she was wise to them. They were like Antoine,
men who were merely titillated by the thought of
spoiling a woman's innocence. That was all they
wanted. At least she wouldn't have to put up with
that anymore, once she was married.

Next week. She would be Mrs. Joel Parrington
next week. Yet he didn't love her and she didn't love
him. It didn't matter. She was never going to love
again, so it didn't matter.

# Chapter 3

MARCUS Hammond's blood pressure was rising. He glared across his desk at his elder daughter, but for once his displeasure was not making her cower. There she sat in her night rail glaring right back at him. He couldn't believe it. She reminded him so much of his wife. But he wasn't going to stand for this rebellion.

"Go to your room, Sharisse!"

Her large amethyst eyes rounded even more. "You mean you won't even discuss this with me?"

"No."

Her chin raised stubbornly, and she sat back in her chair as if settling in. "I won't go to bed until this thing is settled."

"You won't? You won't! By God—"

"Will you just listen to me?" Sharisse's voice turned pleading.

"Listen to more nonsense? I will not!"

"But don't you see? I can't marry Joel now. How can I when I know Stephanie loves him?"

"Stephanie is a child," her father blustered. "She's too young to know anything about love."

"She's seventeen, Father," Sharisse pointed out. "Wasn't Mother seventeen when you married her?"

"You leave your mother out of this!" Marcus warned furiously.

Sharisse backed down. "If you'll just listen to what I'm saying . . . I don't love Joel, but Steph does. So why should I have to marry him, when she wants to?"

"This should have been brought up when it was settled that you would marry him, not now, with the wedding a week away. You were perfectly willing to marry the boy before your sister made her ridiculous confession to you. It's too late now, Sharisse."

"Oh, I could just scream!" Sharisse cried in frustration, shocking her father further. "It's not as if we aren't intimately acquainted with the Parringtons. Joel's father is your best friend, has been since before I was born. If the situation were explained to Edward, he would certainly understand."

"Like hell he would," Marcus growled, appalled at the thought of telling his friend he wanted to substitute daughters at this late date. The very idea! "I will hear no more about this."

"But, Father—"

"No more I say!" He rose from his chair to his full intimidating height, and Sharisse paled. "You're not too old to take a strap to, Sharisse Hammond, and by God, that's exactly what I'll do if you so much as mention this nonsense to me again!"

Sharisse didn't answer. Her courage fell, and she ran from the room. At the top of the stairs she stopped, her heart hammering. Had she ever been so frightened before? How she'd got the nerve to defy her father, she didn't know. To go against him after that last horrible threat . . . impossible. She had known it wouldn't be easy telling her father, but she hadn't thought he would refuse her so furiously. And to threaten her with a whipping! She shuddered.

Sharisse found Stephanie in her room, sitting anxiously on the edge of the bed, waiting. "I'm sorry, Steph," was all she had to say.

The younger girl started to cry. "I knew it wouldn't do any good. I told Trudi so, but she was so sure you could do something."

Sharisse moved to the bed and tried to comfort her

sister. "Please don't cry, Steph. Maybe after Father thinks about it awhile . . ."

"If he told you no, he won't change his mind." Stephanie sobbed harder. "I shouldn't have told you at all. I should just have left here the way I planned."

"Leave?" Sharisse wasn't sure she had heard correctly. "What do you mean?"

"Never mind." Stephanie sniffed.

"You don't have anywhere to go, Steph."

"Don't I?" Stephanie said angrily, thinking Sharisse was feeling sorry for her. "For your information, I have a man waiting to marry me—right now, in Arizona. I have the tickets to get there. I might even be married before you are," she added, not knowing how long it took to get to Arizona.

"But where did you meet this man?"

"I . . . I haven't actually met him. We corresponded through the mail."

"What?"

"Don't look so shocked. It's done all the time. There is a shortage of women in the West, you know. How else are those brave men to get decent wives?"

Stephanie was saying whatever sounded logical, defending herself. Actually she knew as little about the West or about mail-order brides as Sharisse did. But she didn't want her sister to know that, or to know that she was dreading going to Lucas Holt.

"You mean you were planning to *marry* some man you don't even know? To travel across the country . . . Steph, how could you even think of such a thing?"

"How could I think of staying here after you marry Joel? I can't. I won't. I'll leave tomorrow, and don't you dare try to stop me."

"But I can't let you go. You're such an innocent, Steph. Why, you'd probably get lost before you even got to the train station."

"Just because you've been to Europe doesn't mean

you're the only one who knows how to travel," Stephanie snapped. "I've gone to Aunt Sophie's. I'll manage."

"You've gone to Aunt Sophie's with Father and me. You've never been anywhere alone. And . . . my God, to actually consider marrying a stranger! No, I can't let you."

Stephanie's eyes narrowed angrily. "You would force me to stay here and watch you marry Joel? You would be that cruel?"

"Steph!"

"I love him!" A new flood of tears gathered. "I love him, and you're going to marry him! You know," she added bitterly, "the only thing that would prevent that wedding next week is if you weren't here to attend it. But would you think of leaving instead of me? Of course you wouldn't. You certainly gave up on Father soon enough. I couldn't expect you to have the courage to defy him by running away."

"He said he would take a strap to me," Sharisse said quietly.

"Oh," Stephanie said, all accusation dying.

"Wait a minute," Sharisse said impulsively. "Why couldn't I leave? It would solve everything. Father would see that I am serious about not marrying Joel, and I would only have to stay away until he gave in."

"Do you mean it, Rissy?" Stephanie asked, daring to hope. "Would you really do that for me?"

Sharisse was thoughtful. Her father would be furious. She might have to stay away for months. But at least she wouldn't be responsible for her sister's misery.

"Why not?" she said courageously. "I can go and stay with Aunt Sophie."

Stephanie shook her head. "That's the first place Father will look. You don't think he's going to let you go without trying to find you, do you?"

"Oh, dear." Sharisse frowned. "Well, let me think for a moment."

"You could use the tickets I have."

"Go to Arizona? That's ridiculous, Steph. I won't have to go *that* far."

"But where else could you stay? At least Lucas Holt will take care of you until I can get word to you that it's all right to come home."

"Take care of me?" Sharisse gasped. "The man is expecting a wife, not a guest. And he's expecting you, not me."

"Well, actually, he doesn't know what he's getting. I did send him a picture, but it was the one of you and me and Father, the one taken after you got back from Europe. I . . . ah . . . I forgot to tell him which of us was me."

If Sharisse was going to be good enough to go away, she wanted her far enough away that their father would have no chance of finding her. Arizona was far enough.

"When I wrote to him," she continued, "I signed my name only S. Hammond. So, you see, he wouldn't know the difference if you went in my place. And he doesn't have to know that you have no intention of marrying him."

"You mean deceive him?"

"Well, he's not expecting to marry me immediately. He said in his letter that he would have to approve me first. After a while, you could just say it didn't work out, you can't marry him."

Sharisse was appalled. "I couldn't possibly take advantage of the man."

Stephanie refused to give up. "You don't have the money to support yourself, do you?"

"I have my jewels. They would last a while."

"Sell them?"

"As many as necessary."

Stephanie began to wonder how she could let her

sister do this for her, but then she thought of Joel and suppressed her conscience.

"You probably won't get anywhere near what those jewels are worth," Stephanie said thoughtfully. "I just don't see why you can't take advantage of Lucas Holt. Did I tell you he was a rancher? I'll give you his letter and the advertisement. You can see for yourself he sounds like a very agreeable fellow. He's probably rich. You could live in style."

"Stop it, Steph. I wouldn't dream of using the man that way. I will make use of his train ticket, though, to get me out of here." Sharisse grinned, excited by her own daring. "Shall we go to my room and start packing? If I'm going to go, I'll have to leave first thing in the morning, just as soon as Father goes to his office. You can cover for me in the afternoon and evening. Father won't have to know I've gone until the following day, and by then I should be far away. You'll have to cancel my appointments for me. I was to meet Sheila for lunch tomorrow, and there's Carol's party—"

"How can I ever thank you, Rissy?" Stephanie cried.

"By becoming Mrs. Joel Parrington as soon as you can. I don't mind disappearing for a while, but I don't want to be gone too long," She smiled wistfully. "After all, nowhere can compare with New York. I love it here, and I hate being homesick."

Stephanie grinned. "You'll be back before you know it."

# Chapter 4

BENJAMIN Whiskers stood behind his bar, slowly wiping a beer mug. His eyes were on Lucas Holt, watching him walk to the swinging doors, look outside, then come back to stand on the other side of the bar. He finished his third whiskey, and that was the fifth time he'd looked outside. Ben was dying to ask him what he was looking for, but he hadn't got up the nerve. He still couldn't get it right in his mind that this was the friendly Holt brother, not the other one.

If Ben hadn't been there the night Slade Holt shot Feral Sloan, seven years ago, then he wouldn't have been so leery of Luke Holt. But he had been there, had seen Slade shoot Feral as cool as you please and walk away without a moment of remorse. Slade Holt was a dangerous man. And this one just happened to be the very image of Slade. They were twins. It gave a man the willies.

A lot of folks in town liked Luke, were real taken with him. It wasn't that they discounted the stories about Slade, it was just that they had met Lucas first, and while the brothers looked exactly alike, they were as different as night and day.

Lucas took something out of his pocket, frowned at it, then put it away. Ben had seen him do that twice now. The man didn't look at all agreeable. Most times, he had a few pleasant words, but not today.

He was downing whiskeys like water and looking agitated.

It had been some shock when Lucas came to town to stay nearly two years ago. Folks wondered why he chose Newcomb, but no one asked. No one came to settle in Newcomb anymore. Since the railroad had passed them by, it was a town everyone was wanting to leave. But Lucas Holt had come, buying the old Johnson ranch three miles out of town. He kept to himself and didn't cause trouble. He was probably a likeable fellow if you got to know him, but Ben would never be friendly with Lucas. He would never be able to separate him from Slade.

Slade Holt had been back since Lucas settled there. He didn't drift through often, but he sure gave people something to talk about when he did come. He always came into town after visiting his brother at his ranch. Folks just weren't the same when he made an appearance. Everything quieted down. All fights were postponed until Slade went on his way again.

Hell, no one even had anything to say about the half-breed Lucas had working for him. Who would dare? Everyone had seen Billy Wolf ride into town with Slade. It wasn't hard to tell they were friends. Slade had brought Billy Wolf to Lucas because the Indian was supposed to be an excellent horse catcher, and that's what Lucas had started, a horse ranch. With all the trouble those renegade Apaches from the reservation were causing, the half-breed would have been thrown out of town if not for the Holt brothers. Because of them, no one even looked crossways at Billy Wolf.

Lucas moved over to the door once again, and this time when he came back, Ben couldn't resist asking, "You waitin' for someone, Mr. Holt? I couldn't help noticin' you keep lookin' up the street."

Lucas fixed his green eyes on Whiskers. "I'm meeting someone on the Benson stage."

"You ain't expectin' your brother, are you?"

Lucas grinned at the anxious note in the saloon-keeper's voice. "No, Whiskers, I'm not expecting my brother any time soon. I've got a bride coming today."

"A . . . bride? If that don't beat all! Well, if that don't beat all!" Ben was too excited to be cautious. "Sam Newcomb will sure be glad to hear that."

"Oh?"

"Don't get me wrong," Ben amended quickly. "But I reckon you know Sam ain't been married too long, and I reckon you also knew his wife can't seem to keep her eyes off you. Not that Sam's a jealous man, mind you, but I reckon he likes to know what's his is his. He'll be mighty glad to know you're gettin' yourself settled down with a wife of your own."

Lucas said nothing, but he was fuming. Ben had hit the mark. The very reason Lucas was here waiting to pick up his bride was Fiona Newcomb. He wouldn't be in this fix if not for her. Oh, they had had some good times together when he first settled in Newcomb and she was still Fiona Taylor, operating the only boardinghouse in town. He had never led her to believe he was looking for anything besides a little fun. She, on the other hand, had wanted to get married! When he refused even to discuss it, she had turned her wiles on Samuel Newcomb.

Sam knew he had got Fiona on the rebound, and it ate away at him. Before Fiona, Lucas had had Samuel Newcomb right where he wanted him, on friendly terms. That was because of Slade. Ironic, but the rich man felt indebted to Slade for getting rid of Feral Sloan. The man had been a thorn in his side.

Things had all gone according to plan until Fiona. Because Lucas was from the East and had more money than could possibly have been obtained by horse ranching, Sam figured Lucas knew what he was talking about when he mentioned those few small investments. Did Sam want to get in on them?

He did. And after those paid off, it was easy to talk Sam into the big investment.

They weren't nearly finished with Newcomb, and now it wouldn't be so easy to clean the man out. Sam's friendly interest in Lucas had cooled because of Fiona. As Billy Wolf pointed out, Sam would never relax and be gullible again as long as Fiona had the hots for Lucas.

Still, Lucas never should have let Billy talk him into getting married. It had sounded sensible at the time, but he'd had a few drinks in him, and just about everything Billy said that night sounded reasonable.

"Newcomb will keep his eye on you as long as he knows she still wants you and there's the chance you might take off with her. But if you get hitched, he'll think you've settled down. He'll quit worrying. As it is now, the way he has you watched, he's going to start wondering soon how come you get so much mail from back East. If he ever gets the notion to find out what your dealings are, well, that'll be the end. You have to get his eye off you right now, and marriage is the way."

He didn't want a wife. So what if, when he watched Billy and his wife, Willow, together, he sometimes got a yearning to have his own woman? It was just that life on a ranch was lonely. He wasn't used to staying in one place, and an isolated place at that. He was used to having women whenever he needed them. When this was all over, he would want to move on, but how could he if he had a wife?

So Lucas had hedged. Instead of looking around the area for a woman who would know what she was letting herself in for, he had written his lawyer and had him place notices in the Eastern papers for a mail-order bride. It was his hope that the Eastern girl would be horrified when she saw what she was up against. He wanted her to insist he send her back—and he gladly would, after a reasonable time.

That was the problem. He had to keep her there long enough to finish what he had started.

Having a preacher who came through town only every month or so would help. Just so long as Samuel Newcomb believed he was getting married, he had solved his problem.

He hadn't told Billy that he had no intention of marrying the girl. With Billy and Willow there, and old Mack, too, the girl would be decently chaperoned, and no one could say anything about her staying at the ranch with Lucas before the preacher had his say. *She* might not like it, but then, Lucas figured, anyone desperate enough to turn herself over to a complete stranger couldn't be too choosy. Besides, he intended to pay her well for her time and trouble. He meant for her leaving to seem entirely her own idea, so no one was going to be hurt by his deception.

He took the picture out of his pocket once more. If he'd realized how often he had done that in the last weeks, he would have been furious with himself. His eyes passed right over his intended "bride" and went to the other girl in the picture. That one posed regally, her shoulders thrown back, her small breasts pushed out. Her height gave her a queenly air, and there was a haughtiness to the set of her features. She looked skinny as a reed, yet there was something about her that had captured his interest from the first time he looked at the picture.

Lucas had just about settled on a girl from Philadelphia when Miss Hammond's letter and picture arrived. He knew immediately that she was just what he was looking for. The clothes had done it, the quality of the clothes the three people in the picture were wearing. Those clothes spoke of wealth, and Lucas knew from experience that pampered rich girls knew absolutely nothing about hard work. Therefore, a rich girl would balk at the life he offered. He wasn't at all disappointed that the girl happened to be the most beautiful of all the applicants he had consid-

ered. He couldn't help wondering why a girl of Miss
Hammond's charms would be a mail-order bride.

He wouldn't mind having a pretty face around for
a while. But he had no intention of taking advantage
of her, lovely or not. If she arrived a virgin, she
would return East that way. Even if she wasn't, he
wanted no entanglements with her that might put
ideas into her head, make her think she was honor-
bound to accept him.

Lucas realized he was staring at the picture again,
and he quickly put it away, annoyed with himself.
He moved to the door again, but there was still no
sign of the stage. He wondered what the city-bred
Miss Hammond was thinking about the Arizona Territory, where the sun could bake you through and
through, where you could ride for weeks without seeing another soul. He grinned. The trip had probably
already decided her on going back. The time of year
was on his side, for it was the middle of summer. The
poor girl had no doubt fainted half a dozen times already from the heat. No, a wealthy, gently bred New
York City girl definitely wouldn't like it there.

# Chapter 5

SHARISSE waved her handkerchief through the air, hoping the wet cloth would cool a little before she brought it to her brow again, but it didn't. She was appalled to be wiping herself with a piece of linen already soaked with perspiration, but there was no help for it. Her underclothes clung to her, as did her long-sleeved blouse, and the hair on her forehead and temples wouldn't fit into the tight bun at her neck, so it clung, too.

She had given up worrying about her appearance. She had meant to tone down her looks anyway, to be sure she wouldn't be accosted on the train, even borrowing a pair of glasses from one of the maids before leaving home. Those had long since been broken and discarded, but it didn't matter, because she looked her worst, anyway.

How had everything gone wrong? She still couldn't credit that she had only two dollars left. That would buy one more meal if this stage stopped again before reaching Newcomb. She had eaten atrocious meals and had lost weight she couldn't afford to lose. Lucas Holt would take one look at her and send her packing.

She wasn't supposed to be in this awful, hot place. She was supposed to be living comfortably in seclusion in some small midwest town with Charley to keep her company. Poor Charley. With his long, thick hair, he was suffering even worse than she was, losing great patches of fur, listless, panting constantly. How was she to know it would be this unbearably hot here? This was land she knew nothing about. But even if she had known, she couldn't have left Charley behind.

She still couldn't believe Stephanie had done this to her. Sharisse was the one taking all the risks, including risking their father's wrath, and all for Stephanie. Why would her sister have wanted to make things even more difficult for her? Yet she had tried to talk Sharisse into going all the way to Arizona. Worse became clear when Sharisse found her jewelry missing. She remembered handing her reticule that contained the jewels to Stephanie while she secured Charley in his traveling basket. After leaving the house, she had not set her reticule down once, tucking it beneath her skirt when she napped on the train that first day. She had found the jewels missing when she searched in the reticule for Mr. Holt's letter. Why had Stephanie taken the jewels? The thought of being stranded so far from home terrified her, and she had no money to get back with. She would just have to wait and see what kind of man Lucas Holt was.

His letter gave her no clue, though he sounded almost arrogant in making the stipulation that he have some time to approve her before they married. Well, that could work to her advantage if she had to depend on him for a while. She could use that excuse to postpone the wedding as long as necessary. She would have to disdain everything about him and his life so he wouldn't be too surprised when she insisted it wouldn't work out. And from what she had seen so far of Arizona and its hardy men, she didn't think she would have to pretend very hard.

The large Concord stage swayed as it crossed a nearly dried riverbed. Only patches of slimy puddles remained of the river. The brightly colored stage had room for nine passengers, but there were just four on

this run. Only Sharisse would be staying in Newcomb. Because of the ample room, no one had minded
when she had brought Charley out of his basket.
They had stared at him, though, as if they had never
seen a pet cat before. Maybe they hadn't. She certainly hadn't seen another cat since changing trains
in Kansas.

There were mountains ahead that actually had
trees on them. This so surprised Sharisse after the
deserts and wastelands and mountains of nothing
but rock and cactus that she completely missed seeing the town until the driver called out, "Newcomb
ahead. A one-hour stop, folks."

Sharisse's stomach twisted into knots. Her vanity
surfaced, and she suddenly wished that she had
changed clothes at the last stop. But that had been
something she hadn't been able to do completely
since leaving home. She realized she had taken Jenny's services for granted and had left wearing a
blouse she couldn't get out of by herself.

Sharisse got hold of herself and remembered that
she wasn't out to make a good impression. It was just
as well if she looked as bad as she felt. Years of
proper behavior, however, made her put her jacket
back on as soon as she got Charley into his basket.
She managed to get the last button fastened just as
the stage pulled to a stop.

A giant appeared out of the scattered dust to assist
the passengers from the stage. Sharisse gaped at
him, then quickly looked away when she realized
she was staring. By the time she accepted his hand
to step down from the stage, she did it absent-mind-
edly, wondering which of the men standing around
was Lucas Holt.

"Well, I'll be damned."

Sharisse turned back to the giant. He wouldn't let
go of her hand. "Will you, sir?" she said haughtily.

He had the grace to look disconcerted. "A figure of
speech, ma'am."

"I know," she replied coolly, and was surprised to see him grin.

Standing on the ground, she was even more amazed by his size, so tall and broad-shouldered. He made her feel downright tiny, something she had never felt before. Her father was tall, but this man would dwarf him. Was this a land of giants? But no, a nervous glance around showed the kind of men she was accustomed to seeing. It was only this man, this man looking her over with a stamp of possessive ownership on his face.

Her heart skipped a beat. This couldn't be Lucas Holt!

"You're not—?"

"Lucas Holt." His grin widened, showing a flash of even white teeth. "I don't need to ask who you are, Miss Hammond."

In her wildest dreams Sharisse wouldn't have pictured Lucas Holt like this, so ruggedly male, so hard-chiseled and powerfully built. She sensed a quiet arrogance about him, and, oh, dear, he reminded her of her father. Immediately she decided she couldn't risk telling him the truth, not if he was like her father.

She tried to look beyond the raw strength that frightened her. At least he was young, perhaps twenty-five or -six. And she couldn't call him ugly. Some women might even find him terribly attractive, but she was used to impeccably clean, fastidious men. He wasn't even wearing a jacket. His shirt was half-open, and he smelled of horses and leather. He even sported a gun on one hip! Was he a savage?

He was clean-shaven, but that only drew attention to his bronzed skin and unruly long black hair. His eyes were extraordinary. The color made her think of a necklace of peridots she owned, with stones of yellow-green, clear and glowing. And his eyes seemed even more brilliant next to that dark skin.

Lucas let the girl look him over. It was her, the girl

he preferred in the picture. She was a bit wilted, but
that only gave her an earthy quality. Damn, but she
looked good. It almost seemed as if he had wished her
here, and here she was.

"I guess I'd better get your things, ma'am."

Sharisse watched him saunter to the back of the
stage and catch the trunk and portmanteau the
driver tossed down to him. He was grinning. Why did
he seem so delighted? She looked a fright. He should
have been appalled.

He returned carrying the trunk on his shoulder
and the small case tucked under one arm. "The buggy's over here."

She looked around, saw the hotel. "But I thought
. . . I mean . . ."

Lucas followed the direction of her eyes. "That
you'd be staying in town? No, ma'am, you'll be
staying out at the ranch with me. But you don't have
to worry about your reputation. We won't be alone at
the ranch."

She supposed it had been too much to hope that he
would pay for her room and board, when he probably
had a huge ranch house with an army of servants.
She followed him to the buggy and waited while he
settled her trunks.

"Do you need anything before we leave town?" Lucas asked.

Sharisse smiled shyly. "The only thing I'm in need
of, Mr. Holt, is a long bath. I'm afraid I haven't had a
decent one since I left New York. I suppose it will
have to wait until we get to your ranch."

"You didn't take lodgings on the way?"

She blushed, but it was just as well he knew the
truth. "I didn't have enough money. I used all I did
have just for meals."

"But your meals were included on your tickets."

Sharisse gasped. "What?"

"The arrangements were made. But it looks like

that was money wasted." He looked at her speculatively. "So you don't have any money at all?"

Sharisse was furious with herself. Why hadn't she looked more closely at those tickets? Why hadn't the conductor said anything? Why hadn't Lucas Holt said something about it in his letter?

Her anger carried into her flippant tone. "Is that going to be a problem? You weren't expecting a dowry, were you?"

"No, ma'am." He grinned. Good, so she was completely dependent on him. She didn't have the wherewithal to leave any time she wanted to. "But then, I wasn't expecting you at all."

"I don't understand." Sharisse frowned.

Lucas dug the picture out of his pocket and handed it to her. "Your letter said you were the girl on the left."

Her eyes widened. So Stephanie had lied about that so Sharisse would have no qualms about coming here. She was mortified. Here he was, expecting Stephanie and getting her instead.

"I . . . I see I should have been more specific. You see, I sometimes get my right and left mixed up. I am sorry, Mr. Holt. You must be terribly disappointed."

"Ma'am, if I was terribly disappointed, as you put it, I would be putting you back on the stage. What's your first name, anyway? I can't keep ma'aming you."

His smile was engaging, his voice so deep and resonant. She had expected to be nervous on this first meeting, but not this much.

"Sharisse," she told him.

"Sounds French."

"My mother was French."

"Well, there's no point in us being formal. Folks call me Luke."

Just then someone did. "Who you got there, Luke?"

It was a squat little man standing in the doorway

of a store, Newcomb Grocery. The building housed only that one store. Most buildings in New York contained dozens of offices and businesses.

Her attention returned to the man as Lucas introduced them. She was surprised when he added, "I knew Miss Hammond before I came here. She has finally agreed to be my wife."

"Is that a fact?" Thomas Bilford smiled, delighted. "I guess congratulations are called for. Will your brother be coming to the wedding?"

"I hadn't planned on any big affair, Thomas," Lucas said. "I'll just catch the preacher when he comes through town."

"Folks will be disappointed."

"Can't help that," Lucas replied, this time with an edge to his voice.

"Well, good day to you, Luke, ma'am," the grocer said uneasily now, and quickly went back inside his store.

Sharisse remained thoughtfully quiet as they drove out of the small one-street town. When the last building was behind them, she finally asked, "Why did you tell Mr. Bilford we knew each other back East?"

Lucas shrugged. "No one would believe you were a mail-order bride. Of course, if you'd rather—"

"No! That's quite all right," she assured him.

Sharisse fell silent again and averted her eyes. A change had taken place in the man sitting next to her. Without that boyish grin he could be coldly unapproachable. He seemed to be brooding. Was it something she had said?

"Why *are* you here, Sharisse Hammond?" he asked abruptly.

She glanced back at him. He was looking straight ahead at the dirt road. Well, she had anticipated the question days ago.

"I am recently widowed, Mr. Holt."

That got his attention, but she paled as his eyes

pierced her. She hadn't thought of that! Was a virgin a requirement of his? Being an impoverished widow had seemed the perfect story, a good excuse for being a mail-order bride.

"I'm sorry if you were expecting a young innocent," Sharisse said softly. "I will certainly understand if you—"

"It doesn't matter." Lucas cut her short.

He looked back to the road, furious with himself for reacting that way. It really didn't make any difference. Hadn't he considered the possibility that she might not be virgin? So why did it bother him?

"Was he the man in the picture?" Lucas asked after a while.

"Was he . . . ? Good heavens, no. That was my father."

"Is your father still living?"

"Yes. But we're—estranged. My father didn't approve of my husband, you see. And, well, he's not a very forgiving man."

"So you couldn't return to him after your husband died?"

"No. There wouldn't have been a problem if my husband hadn't left me destitute. Of course, I wouldn't have married him if I'd known he was so heavily in debt," she added primly. "But . . ." She sighed. "I come from a wealthy family, you see. It wasn't as if I could work to support myself when I saw how bad things really were. When I saw your advertisement, it seemed the very solution."

"You're leaving something out."

"No, I don't think so." She began to panic.

"You're not exactly what anyone could call a plain-looking woman," he told her pointedly. "If you felt you had to marry again, why go so far away? You must have had offers closer to home."

Sharisse smiled at the assumption. Of course there had been offers of marriage, many offers, ever since she'd turned fifteen. But they were all made by men who coveted her wealth or who were otherwise unacceptable.

"Yes, I was approached by several men."

"And?"

"They weren't to my liking."

"What *is* to your liking?"

Sharisse squirmed.

"I don't like arrogance in a man, or rigidity. I appreciate sensitivity, a gentle nature, good humor, and—"

"Are you sure you're describing a man?" Lucas couldn't resist.

"I assure you I have known such men," she said indignantly.

"Your husband?"

"Yes."

Lucas grunted. "You took quite a risk, settling on me. What if I don't possess any of those qualities?"

She groaned inwardly. "Not even one?" she said faintly.

"I didn't say that. But how were you to know?"

"I . . . I'm afraid I wasn't thinking along those lines. I just felt anything would be better than the choices I had at home." She gasped. "I didn't mean to imply . . . I mean, of course I hoped for the best."

"Are you disappointed?"

"You certainly can't expect me to answer that so soon." She was becoming more and more distressed.

There was amusement in his voice. "Honey, your first look at me told you whether you were disappointed or not."

"Looks do not make the man," Sharisse heard herself say primly.

She was appalled to find she had defended him, complimented him without meaning to. She had wanted him to feel her disdain.

There he was, grinning again. And she realized that even though they had talked for quite a while, she knew nothing about him. She dared a direct question of her own. "You aren't arrogant, are you?"

"I don't like to think so."

She went further. "Domineering?"

He chuckled. "Me? Ride roughshod over a pretty thing like you? I wouldn't dream of it."

Why did she have the distinct feeling that he was teasing her? She fell silent, giving up for the moment.

# Chapter 6

WILLOW leaned against the frame of the open door and stared at the cloud of dust in the distance. Her house, a one-room structure, was small by white standards. But she was used to a low-domed wickiup made of brushwood and grass, a home that could be burned when it was time to move on, so this house of sturdy wood seemed huge. She had got used to it in the two years since her husband had brought her here to live, away from her tribe and family.

Willow was only a quarter White Mountain Apache. Another quarter was Mexican. The other half, thanks to a bastard who had raped her mother, was some unknown mixture of white. Yet she appeared full-blooded Apache, and she took a deep sense of pride from this.

"He comes, Billy," Willow said in her soft, melodious voice.

Billy Wolf came up behind his wife to watch the cloud of dust as it got closer to the ranch. He grinned and wrapped his arms around her, over her pregnant waist.

"Do you think he's got her with him?"

Willow sensed Billy's grin. She had seen it too often lately.

"You still think it is amusing that you talked him into getting married?"

"I think it's just what he needed. He's getting fed up over how long it's taking to bring the big man to

57

his knees. Another month and he would have let Slade handle it—Slade's way. Luke needed some kind of diversion. Why not a wife?"

"But he may not like her."

"Like her?" Billy chuckled. "Hell, he can hate her for all I care, as long as she's diverting."

"You had no thought for the girl in this," Willow accused him tartly.

He didn't look at all contrite. "Taking care of friends comes first. That's what I'm here for. Now come inside before they see us. City ladies always get the vapors at their first sight of a real live Indian. You know that." He chuckled again. "We'll give her until tomorrow before we make her acquaintance."

Willow looked at her husband critically. "You're not thinking of frightening her, are you, Billy?"

"Would I do that to a friend's bride?"

No, of course he wouldn't, she told herself knowingly, not her fun-loving husband.

Sharisse closed her eyes, trying to imagine that the ranch house wasn't actually small, only . . . quaint? She couldn't do it. It was a simple square building, not even painted. A cabin. And she was supposed to live there? There was a barn, too, and it was twice the size of the house, but also unpainted. A large corral with a big old cottonwood casting shade over it was behind the barn. Half a dozen horses lazed inside the corral. A hundred feet or so beyond the corral was another cabin, even smaller than the first.

"I imagine you're used to grander accommodations," Lucas said smoothly as he helped her down from the buggy.

Sharisse didn't answer. He wasn't exactly apologizing, so what could she say? That her home on Fifth Avenue was a colossal mansion? It wasn't necessary for him to know that.

Her expression said it all, anyway, and Lucas

grinned, knowing how shocked she was. What had she anticipated? Probably a house like Samuel New-comb had erected as an ostentatious display of his wealth, two stories of grand rooms and luxurious fit-tings. Well, Lucas's house served its purpose, and he had been in worse. In better, too, but all he had needed here was a roof over his head. It wasn't as if he meant to stay. Oh, he supposed he might have fixed it up a little for her. Then again—his grin widened—she didn't have to know that he hadn't.

He watched her covertly as she looked around, holding her basket as if it offered protection. She looked so dismayed. She'd had that same look when she first realized who he was, and she had been as nervous as a skittish colt ever since. Did he really frighten her, or was she always jittery? She might have found his size intimidating. Most women did. On the other hand, she probably considered herself too tall for a woman. But from where he stood, she was just about right.

Lucas opened the front door and waited there for Sharisse to finish her survey. The afternoon sun burned down on the cactus scattered around, the grassland that stretched as far as the eye could see, and the mountains.

He imagined it wouldn't be long before that creamy white skin of hers was a ripe, golden color—once he got her working in the garden out back and wearing less clothing. She had to be baking in that heavy traveling suit. The sooner she got if off . . .

His every thought was stripping her. "Sharisse?"

She started, having almost forgotten his presence. He stood at the open door, waiting for her to enter his house. What would she find inside? The same sever-ity?

With a sigh, Sharisse went inside, careful not to let her skirt brush against his long legs as she passed him. The light inside was muted by closed curtains, and there was no time for her vision to adjust before the door closed and she found herself swung around and caught firmly against Lucas Holt's hard chest. She squealed in fright, or started to, but the sound was smothered by his lips over hers.

Shock struck her system, Charley hissed, and suddenly she was standing alone, shaking, staring wide-eyed at Lucas. It was difficult to tell which of them was the more surprised.

"I always thought it was just a figure of speech," Lucas said. "But I guess a female really can hiss like a cat."

"I imagine it is just a figure of speech, Mr. Holt. It was a male hissing, and he really is a cat. I hope you don't mind, but I couldn't leave Charley behind."

She set the basket down to open it and lift Charley out. Lucas found himself staring at the longest-haired cat he'd ever seen, short and compact, a golden orange color that nearly matched the girl's hair. He'd seen cats by the dozens back East, but never one that looked like this one.

At that moment, Mack came in from the back of the house. "What the hell is that?" he cried. "Not you, ma'am," he was quick to amend. "But that thing you're holdin'?"

Sharisse stared at the little man with a chin full of gray stubble, lively blue eyes, and a hat with a slouching rim. Lucas quickly made the introductions, explaining Mack's many jobs around the ranch. But Mack wasn't paying a bit of attention to Sharisse. His eyes were on Charley.

"What is it?" he repeated.

"My pet, Charley."

"You keep that wild critter for a pet?"

"He's not wild," she assured him. "He's a Persian cat. I saw quite a few of them when I was in Europe. They're rare in America, though. In England, they even hold cat shows where rare breeds like Charley can be shown to the public."

"The only cats we got here is predators," Mack remarked. "This little one don't bite?" He reached out a hand tentatively to pet Charley and received a low growl for his trouble.

"You'll have to forgive him," Sharisse apologized. "I'm afraid he doesn't take too well to strangers. I'm about the only one he really tolerates."

Mack grunted and turned to leave, grumbling, "Better not let Billy come across that feisty little thing. He'll think he's found something new to throw into the stew pot."

Sharisse turned wide, horrified eyes on Lucas. "Did I hear him correctly?"

"Mack's the feisty one, Sharisse," Lucas said, amused. "Just about everything he says must be taken with a grain of salt."

"But—"

"You're not to worry about your pet, not at least as far as Billy's concerned. He works for me, too. He isn't nearly as savage as Mack would have you believe."

Was he teasing her? She supposed she would have to take his word for it, but she decided to keep Charley close to her for a while.

Then she addressed another important topic.

"Mr. Holt, about what you did."

"Greeting my prospective bride with a proper welcoming?"

Sharisse was abashed by the devilishly charming grin that turned his lips soft and made him appear rakishly handsome.

"We were interrupted," he went on. "If you'd like me to continue . . ."

"No! I mean, well, we're not exactly an average engaged couple. What might be allowed after an extended courtship doesn't apply to us. We have only just met."

"And you want to get to know me better first?"

"Exactly." She was relieved. He wouldn't be so difficult to manage after all. Just as long as he understood she wouldn't allow any intimacies.

"But how am I to get to know you if you keep me at arm's length? If you don't like kissing, then we've got a problem."

His approval of her seemed to rest on her answer. She bristled.

"I am not in the habit of letting strangers kiss me," she said stiffly. "And you are still a stranger."

Lucas shook his head. "You're telling me to keep my distance, but if I go along with that, we'll end up being strangers much longer than necessary. It's going to take a few months as it is for me to find out if you can fit in here. Am I supposed to waste that amount of time and *then* find out if you and I are compatible?"

Sharisse was aghast. In his mind, it would be purely a waste of time if, after she passed muster in other ways, he discovered there was absolutely no chemistry between them. True. But what he was suggesting was abhorrent. Was she supposed to let him take liberties with her?

Sharisse drew on her years of contrived confidence. "Mr. Holt, I realize our situation is unique and I will have to make allowances for it. However, I really must ask for at least a little time to feel comfortable with you. After a while a kiss or two might be permissible—if you insist. More than that I simply cannot allow, not before we are wed. And if that is not satisfactory to you . . ."

Lucas knew when to back down. "I guess you can't get more reasonable than that. Your room is right there on the left. I'll get your things now."

Sharisse sighed as he left and turned to look around. There were two doors on the left wall of the room she was standing in. The room was bigger than she had imagined, but it was the only room besides those two doors to the left. Against the back wall was a kitchen of sorts, a wood-burning stove, a sink with a hand pump, some cupboards cluttered with dishes, and a big table. A window behind the sink looked out on the backyard. There was a door to the left of the stove. The rest of the room, to her right, contained a fireplace with a thick rug in front of it and a gray wooden settee without cushions. Next to that, near the front door, were an old arrow-back rocker and a candle stand.

Sharisse felt her shoulders sag. It was such a depressing room. So austere. She shuddered to think what her bedroom would be like. She faced that door and opened it. The two windows inside it were open and the curtains drawn, letting in a cheery light, but also the heat. She couldn't find a single thing to her liking and she didn't try, moving quickly to the other bedroom before Lucas came back. This room proved more dramatic, with dark coloring and a look of being lived in. The bed was unmade, and a wardrobe stood open with dirty clothes slung over the doors. Other articles were scattered around. His room, to be sure. She was rather embarrassed to have looked in.

She closed the door quietly. Then it dawned on her. These three rooms were all there was. No servants' quarters. That meant . . .

"How do you like the place?" Lucas asked as he walked in the front door carrying her luggage.

Sharisse couldn't answer, not with the alarming thought that they would be the only two people sleeping in the house. "You don't have . . . any servants here, do you?"

"Not the kind that see to a house, I don't." He gave her that engaging boyish grin. "Now you know why I need a wife."

He was teasing her again, yet she was insulted. "Wouldn't it be simpler to hire a servant?"

"A lot simpler," he agreed. "But I couldn't expect a servant to share my bed, could I?"

He said it so casually that Sharisse felt a tremor in

her belly. Fear? She stayed where she was as he took her luggage into her room.

"You'll want to get unpacked," he called out, "and I recall you wanted a bath. I'll see about that and some grub for you, then leave you to rest." He came back into the room, and his vivid green eyes probed hers for a moment. "You've nothing to fear here, Sharisse. No harm will come to you as long as you're my responsibility."

He left her standing there, weighing what he had just said against everything else that had been said and done that day. Nothing to fear? If only she could just walk away from the situation! But she had no alternative. Even writing her sister, which she intended to do that very night, would produce no results for some time. She was stuck, she was there under false pretenses, and she didn't have the remotest idea how to make the best of things.

# Chapter 7

SHARISSE'S eyes opened to a blinding glare. She sat up quickly, confused, then saw that the hot light had been caused by the little standup mirror she had set on the bureau yesterday. She hadn't realized that the mirror would reflect the morning sun right onto her pillow. The sun was rapidly heating the house.

Slipping into the thin silk robe left on the end of her bed, Sharisse walked over to the window. The lovely robe, a creation of lime green and white lace, matched the negligee given to her by her aunt when they were in France. Sharisse had brought it along, and another like it, because she had thought she would be alone in some sweet little cottage, not sharing a cabin with a man.

Packing thin summer clothing had been the only sensible thing she'd done thus far. Everything else could be counted as simply disastrous—especially her rash decision to leave home in the first place. When she thought of the safety she had thrown away!

Sharisse sighed, looking out at the sun hiding behind the fat fingers of a giant saguaro cactus in the side yard. She could see part of the corral, and she realized with a start that the window was low to the ground. Just about anyone could have walked by it and seen her lying in bed.

She yanked the curtains closed, her face flushing.

There was only one person she could visualize looking in. She quickly closed the other curtains, too, then went back to sit on the bed, trying to calm herself. Everything in the room made her think of Lucas, the large round tub he had filled yesterday, still full of cold water, the tray of dishes. Her eyes fell on the blouse she had gone through so much discomfort to save, lying now in a torn heap in the corner where she had thrown it in a fit of temper. She had had to rip if off her back after all, something she couldn't afford to do, not with the meager wardrobe she had. But she couldn't very well have asked *him* to aid her, or Mack. Alone with two men—that was his idea of being chaperoned!

On the bureau was the letter she had stayed up late writing. Oh, the things she had packed, including her personal stationery, thinking of a quiet existence in some quaint village! It was laughable. Negligees, linen morning gowns, day dresses, an outing costume complete with gloves, bonnet, and matching shoes. A formal evening dress. She had brought along more toiletries than she needed, fans, hair ornaments, silk stockings, petticoats and bustles, even an extra corset. She had stuffed her trunk and yet found herself in an unwelcoming climate in an uncivilized area with nothing suitable to wear. It really was laughable, or something to cry over.

And she did feel like crying, but she hadn't said that to Stephanie. She had taken hours wording the letter just right so she wouldn't throw her sister into a panic or consume her with remorse. She hadn't mentioned the jewels at all except to say they were missing, and that was meant to explain how she had ended up in Arizona after all. There was a brief paragraph describing Lucas Holt, and she had been charitable in the describing. Yet she had made certain Stephanie understood that she couldn't stay away very long. Something else would have to be arranged, and Stephanie would have to handle it.

Sharisse dressed slowly, delaying as long as possible the inevitability of facing Lucas Holt again. Charley was still asleep in the empty washbowl where he had buried himself during the night. He had made one exploratory trip out the window, prowled around the room until she was ready for bed, then settled in the cool porcelain bowl. She wondered if he would adjust to the heat and stop losing so much fur. She wondered if she would adjust. She sighed, leaving the room braced.

She was relieved to find no one in the outer room, but then she realized she was hungry and there was no food on the table and nothing on the stove, not even a pot of coffee. She set her tray of dishes by the sink and considered a search through the storeroom. She supposed they ate early around there and she had just missed it.

She headed for the back door, but it opened before she reached it, and Lucas stepped in. Their eyes met and held for a moment. Then his gaze swept down her, taking in the gown of beige lawn, heavily trimmed and flounced in white lace with wide lace borders down the back and front bodice, along the collar and high neck, and on the long sleeves. Two brown satin bows were prominent on the bustle and another at her throat.

"You going somewhere?"

Sharisse was surprised. "I'm not dressed to go out," she said, as if explaining to a child. "This is a simple morning gown."

He laughed. "Honey, what you're wearing is fancier than anything the ladies of Newcomb could manage even for Sunday best. And that's not a going-out dress?"

She was indignant. "I'm afraid I don't have anything plainer than this, except my traveling suit."

"Which is too heavy," Lucas stated, shaking his head. "I can see I'm going to have to get you some new clothes."

Sharisse blushed. "I will manage."

"Will you? And will you be doing chores in that fancy gown?"

Chores? "If . . . if I have to," she said stoutly.

"Suit yourself." He would not argue with her. "Where's breakfast?"

"There isn't any."

"I can see that," he replied patiently. "So when are you going to get started?"

"Me!" she gasped. "But I can't *cook!*"

"You can't? Well, I guess you'll have to learn real quick."

"But who cooked before?"

"I managed, Mack managed, and sometimes Willow took pity on us and fixed a big meal."

"Willow?"

"Billy's wife."

"You mean there *is* another woman here?"

"Sure. She's expecting a kid any time now." And he warned in a no-nonsense tone, "She's got enough to do taking care of Billy and herself, so don't even think about asking her for help. I've been taking care of myself all my life, Sharisse. But now that you're here . . ."

Her eyes widened in panic as his meaning sank in. "But I really can't cook. I mean, I never have. There have always been servants." She fell silent. His expression was not the least sympathetic. "I suppose I could learn . . . if someone can teach me."

He grunted. "I guess I can have Billy pick you up a cookbook when he goes to town today." He sighed disagreeably and headed for the storeroom.

"I am sorry, Mr. Holt," Sharisse felt compelled to say, though she didn't know why.

"Never mind," he said over his shoulder. "As long as you've got a strong back for the other chores and are a quick learner."

She was left wondering about those other chores while he searched around, finally coming back with his arms full. The next hour was spent ruining her fine lawn gown with flour and grease stains that splashed beyond the apron Lucas told her to put on. She had her first lesson in cooking, and she didn't like it at all. But she was able to watch Lucas when he wasn't looking at her, and wonder about this man who was from the East yet adapted to this land so well. He was by turns abrupt and to the point, then charming in a rapscallion way.

When breakfast was over, Lucas went outside again and Sharisse sat at the table with another cup of the most atrocious coffee she had ever drunk, worse even than the horrible brews she had tasted at the stage stops. She was contemplating the way Lucas's mood had improved while he ate. By the time he left, he had seemed ready to laugh. Well, her mood dimmed considerably when Charley jumped up on the counter by the stove to investigate the spilled flour and she suddenly realized that *she* was supposed to clean up all the mess!

"Oh, I could just scream!" she said aloud before she caught herself. She groaned as Charley jumped down, tracking flour across the floor.

She didn't *have* to clean it up, she thought rebelliously. Yes, she did. If only she had known there would be no servants, that she would have to work like one herself.

It was a good while before the last dish was put away and Sharisse felt she could seek the sanctuary of her room. She turned in that direction, then screamed at the sight of the half-naked man standing inside the back door. Long black hair flowed to his shoulders, and a faded scarf of some sort was wrapped around his forehead. His bare chest was more visible than covered under a short leather vest. His knee-length soft boots hid more of his legs than the rectangular square of cloth managed to hide.

At the moment it was impossible to say who was more startled, Sharisse, facing a savage, or Billy, who found himself speechless for the first time in his life. Expecting a tiny little blonde who would run screaming to Luke, he faced an Amazon who was taller than he was, for God's sake. Granted, she had screamed, but she hadn't moved a foot.

Lucas rushed in the front door, having heard the scream. "What the—?" He looked between them, taking in the situation, then gave Billy a disgusted frown. "You could at least have put some pants on, Billy, until she got used to you."

Billy relaxed a little. "It was too hot," he said, as if that was enough explanation. "What happened to the yellow-haired one?"

"She wasn't the one," Lucas answered shortly.

"But you showed me the picture, and you said—"

"It was a mistake," Lucas ground out warningly. "Now did you two meet, or were you just standing there staring at each other?"

They were both embarrassed, Sharisse doubly so for being reminded of the deception she was playing and for thinking Billy was a savage when he was obviously a friend of Lucas's.

"I'm Billy Wolf, ma'am, a good friend of Slade Holt's—and now Lucas's," he said with a cocky grin.

"Sharisse Hammond," she responded, her voice a little stilted.

"Didn't mean to scare you none," he added for Lucas's benefit. "I came in to see if you want anything from town, since I'm heading that way."

"After you put some clothes on, I hope," Lucas grunted.

Sharisse spoke up. "As a matter of fact, I have a letter to be posted, if it won't be too much of a bother. I'll just get it."

The moment she stepped into her bedroom, Billy whispered to Lucas, "When you saw how tall she was, why didn't you send her back?"

Lucas grinned. "She's not too tall."

Billy looked him up and down. "Yeah, I guess her

height don't matter much to you. But, Jeez, Luke, she's so skinny!"

Lucas raised a brow. "You think so?"

"Well, I just didn't want you disappointed in her, seeing as how she was my idea."

Sharisse came back into the room and handed the letter to Billy. But Lucas snatched it out of her hand, and she blanched at his arrogance, never having dreamed he might read it before it was safely on its way.

"Trudi Baker?" Lucas read the name aloud, then looked up at her questioningly.

Sharisse imagined his thoughts. When she had said there was no one she could turn to in New York, he must have assumed she had only her father and sister.

"Trudi is a friend of my sister, Mr. Holt. My sister, Stephanie, is only seventeen and still lives at home with my father, so, you see, she was in no position to help me." She grew uncomfortable speaking of this in front of the curious Billy. "I'm sending the letter to her best friend's house, because, well, I did explain to you about my father."

She left the rest unsaid, wondering why it was necessary to explain a letter in the first place. She held her breath while he looked at it again. Finally he shrugged and handed it to Billy.

"See it gets posted, Billy, and don't forget the cookbook I told you about."

Billy saluted with the letter and exited jauntily.

Sharisse continued to watch Lucas warily and was surprised when he smiled sheepishly. "That was rather high-handed of me, and I apologize. I'm afraid my curiosity got the better of me. I wasn't expecting you to be writing to anyone."

"My sister and I are very close." Sharisse relented, explaining that much. "Though I can't correspond with her directly because of my father, she did

make me promise to let her know that I'd arrived
safely."

"She knows what you came west for?" His smile
widened. "And did she approve?"

Wholeheartedly, Sharisse wanted to say bitterly.
And then she felt guilty for even thinking it. She
couldn't blame her sister for all this.

"What could she say, Mr. Holt? Stephanie knows
my circumstances."

He let that pass and said reflectively, "She looked
older than seventeen in the picture. But then I took
you for older than eighteen."

"That's because—"

She stopped abruptly, realizing in the nick of time
that he had to have got the age from Stephanie's letters. What other surprises was she going to encoun-
ter because of Stephanie's correspondence with the
man? She wished she could see those letters before
she blundered badly over something.

"Because?" Lucas prompted.

"Of my height," she finished lamely. "It's always
made me look older."

"You don't like your height, do you?"

She nearly choked. No man had ever been so indis-
creet as to even mention the subject. The very idea!
For this one to presume . . . had he no manners at
all?

"It's not so much that I don't like being tall," she
said defensively, wishing she could upbraid him instead. "It's just that most men find my height discon-
certing, and that can sometimes be an embarrassment."

"I don't."

"You wouldn't," she said dryly.

He laughed. Then he gripped her elbow and
steered her toward the front door. "How about a
walk? The rest of your work can wait a bit."

The audacity of the man, Sharisse thought. He

hadn't even waited to see if she would agree to walk with him. Then she realized what he'd said.

"What work are you referring to, Mr. Holt?" She firmly eased her elbow out of his grip and stopped walking, forcing him to halt and look at her.

"The garden needs tending—weeding and so on. Clothes need washing. My room could use a good going over. Just wifely things, Miss Hammond."

She wanted to balk, but his low tone, the way he addressed her as Miss Hammond after dismissing that formality yesterday, made her hesitate. Was he angry? She wished it were easier to tell, but with him she never knew for sure.

"I hadn't realized . . ."

"I can see that," he said gently. "And I'll make allowances for it. But I did warn you in my letter that life here wouldn't be easy."

Did she dare say she thought he'd been referring to the climate? Never once had she thought she'd be put to work as a servant, yet that was the only way she could look at her situation. And there wasn't a single thing she could do about it, short of having him send her back to New York immediately. What a tempting idea that was. Her conscience pricked her as she thought of her sister. She had to give Stephanie a chance. She wouldn't admit how scared she was of seeing her father.

She managed a smile, though she really felt like crying. "About that walk, Mr. Holt."

He grinned and took her elbow again. She was acutely aware of his touch, his closeness. She was so aware of it that she didn't notice where he was leading her until they reached the corral. She drew back in distaste, and he said, "What's wrong?"

She gave him a look. "I don't like horses. And I dislike even more the smells associated with them."

He grinned. "Honey, this is a horse ranch. You're going to have to get used to those smells."

"I don't see why." Her eyes narrowed suspiciously.

"Unless you expect me to clean the barn. Let me tell you—"

"Hold on, no one said anything about cleaning the barn. But you will be riding."

"No, I won't." She shook her head firmly.

His dark brows shot up. "Are you telling me you don't ride?"

"That's exactly what I'm saying."

"We'll have to correct that, then."

She didn't like his expression at all. He looked forward to the lesson, didn't he? "You brought me here in a perfectly good buggy. I can drive it."

"But I don't own a buggy. That one was rented, and Billy is taking it back to town today."

At that exact moment the vehicle in question charged out of the front of the barn, stirring up enough dust to choke them. Sharisse shielded her eyes and watched the Indian, now dressed in a much more civilized manner, race wildly away from the ranch.

Lucas saw her expression and began to feel terrible. He was overloading her with too many burdens too quickly.

"Do you always look so beautiful after spending all morning in the kitchen?"

She turned back to him in amazement.

"You're making fun of me, Mr. Holt. You must know this morning was the first morning I ever spent in a kitchen." She wouldn't belittle herself by adding that her coloring was too vivid for true beauty.

"Then kitchens must agree with you." He grinned.

Before she could answer, he steered her around the corral to the large cottonwood. The breeze kept the corral smells at bay, and the shade was welcome. There was a bench that just fit two people, but he didn't move to sit beside her. He placed his foot next

to her on the bench and rested an arm on his knee so
that he was leaning over her—looming, actually.

She tilted her head to look up at him. His kiss took
her completely by surprise. She moved back to break
away, but his hands fell on her shoulders, and she
was forced to let him kiss her, forced to stare into
those jewel-like eyes and wonder what emotion she
saw there.

It was only a few seconds before she began to notice the texture of his lips, how very soft they were.
His hands slid along her shoulders to her neck, and a
heady feeling came out of nowhere. Her eyes closed.
Her lips moved under his provocatively until he met
the challenge, his tongue boldly slipping between
them.

Sharisse jerked back, gasping. "Mr. Holt!"

Never had she been kissed like that!

She felt so naive. To think she'd come so close to
making love with Antoine, yet knew so little about
kissing. Even Antoine had never kissed her like
that.

Thinking of Antoine brought a quietly sleeping
anger to the fore. All men were the same. They never
gave anything honestly. They always wanted something in return for their sweet words of flattery.
From her, they had always wanted either her money
or her body. Now she could add another want to that
list—servitude. Lucas Holt was after a lifetime servant, with a convenient body as an added bonus.
There was no kinder way to put it.

"I thought we came to an understanding last
night, Mr. Holt." Water would have frozen at the
sound of her voice.

"Considering . . ." He paused meaningfully, grinning like a rogue. "Don't you think it's time you
called me Luke?"

"I don't. And we have an understanding," she reminded him severely, incensed that he was amused.
"Which you seem determined to ignore."

His eyes twinkled merrily. "No, ma'am. As I recall, you wanted time to feel comfortable with me. But you seemed comfortable enough with me just now, so . . ." He shrugged.

"One day's grace was not what I had in mind."

His expression turned carefully blank. "I don't see what all the fuss is about. Do I frighten you? Is that it?"

"I'm not sure."

"Well, at least you're honest, I'll give you that."

Oh, if he only knew, she thought uneasily, her temper cooling quickly. She watched him turn and move the few feet to the corral fence. One of the spotted horses came over to his extended hand. Presented with his back, she stared at his lean body, the tight jeans and buff-colored shirt that left little to imagine about his physique. His legs were so long, well-muscled, too, and nicely shaped.

"I just don't *know* you," she found herself blurting.

He glanced back at her for a second before returning his attention to the horse. "You want my life story? I guess that's reasonable. Later, maybe. Right now I better get back to work."

Was he dismissing her? Yes, he was. How very autocratic! Just like her father, though not in a blustering way. This man had a very quiet arrogance, nothing showy. The worst kind.

Sharisse knew she was arrogant as well and hated that fault. She laid it at her father's feet. Two arrogant wills would make for war and were not to be considered. It would be just like her parents.

Well, if she were looking for a husband—which she surely wasn't—Lucas Slade certainly wouldn't be her choice. Thank God things were not *that* desperate.

# Chapter 8

SHARISSE placed the last bowl on the table and stood back, wiping her brow. She had done it, cooked her first meal by herself. It didn't look like food she had ever eaten before, but she wasn't going to worry about that. Billy had handed her a country cookbook when he got back from town, and she could only surmise country food was different from city food. She hadn't understood some of the terms in the book so she'd just skipped over those parts. What harm could skipping one or two little things do? She had prepared enough food for three, since no one had told her if Mack would be eating with them or not.

Sharisse moved to the open door, hoping for a cool breeze. There wasn't one, but the brilliance of a flaming red sky mesmerized her. Black silhouettes dotted the land like low sentinels: barrel cactus, yucca trees, the giant saguaro cactus. A small animal scurried across the ground. A coyote howled.

Sharisse had to admit she had never seen anything quite so lovely as the scene before her. On the train, the blinds had always been closed against the late afternoon sun, so she hadn't realized the West offered such spectacular sunsets. If nothing else came of this insane trip, at least she had been able to see this.

"Why didn't you call me?"

Sharisse swung around, startled. Lucas was closing the back door. His shirt was open to the waist, and a towel was wrapped around his neck. His hair was damp, with soft black tendrils curling about his temples. He looked so virile, so overwhelmingly masculine. Her guard went up.

"I hope I'm not expected to hunt you down for meals." The haughtiness in her tone was unmistakable.

Lucas tore his eyes away from her and went to the table. "A yell from the window will do," he said as he looked over the food.

"I don't yell, Mr. Holt."

"Really?" She had his full attention again. "Not even when you're mad?"

"I don't get mad."

He laughed. "Honey, I never met a redhead who didn't."

Sharisse gasped. "I do not have red hair!"

"No, you don't," he conceded, admiring the copper tresses. "But it's close enough."

She moved to face him across the table. "I hardly see what hair has to do with it. My father would tell you I am sweet-tempered and quite biddable. I like to think I am."

"Not a disagreeable bone in your body?" Laughter danced in his eyes.

"I don't like to fight, if that's what you mean," she retorted. "I was witness to more than enough of that when I was a child. I am quite thankful I didn't inherit my parents' volatile natures."

Lucas grinned. "Well, I guess I've had enough hot-tempered females. Having a sweet, compliant wife will be a nice change."

Sharisse blushed. A gentleman would never mention the women from his past.

"If you will be seated, Mr. Holt."

"When are you going to let go of some of that starch, *Miss* Hammond?"

"I beg your pardon?"

"Never mind." Lucas sighed. "I see you have three places set. Are we expecting company?"

"I didn't know if Mack would be joining us or not. You said Mr. Wolf has a wife who sees to him, but you didn't say if Mack would take his meals with us or not."

"He's 'Mack,' but I'm still 'Mr. Holt'?" Irritation sparked his words. "Why is that?"

Sharisse groaned. The man was temperamental. For all his devilish smiles and apparent humor, there was this other side to him. She didn't know what to make of him. He might have a violent temper for all she knew.

"I . . . I suppose I could call you Lucas," Sharisse finally conceded.

"Luke would be even better."

"Lucas is more appropriate."

"I'll wager your father threw in 'stubborn' occasionally when he was describing you."

Sharisse smiled despite herself. He might intimidate her sometimes, but he had an exasperating kind of devil-may-care charm that was quite appealing. Put him in a suit and cut his hair, and the ladies back home would find him a delightful rogue, even handsome. Yes, quite handsome. If she hadn't been so shocked yesterday by his rough appearance and appalled by his size, she would have seen that beneath his darkly tanned skin was quite an attractive face. Still, lily-white was in fashion, not bronze. She would have to remember that. It wouldn't do for her to find the man attractive.

Lucas came around the table to seat her, then took the chair next to her. "You set three places," he observed. "But the amount of food you have here will barely feed the two of us, and that's only because I'm not very hungry."

Her eyes widened. She looked at the roast beef and gravy, the half-dozen biscuits, the potatoes, carrots, and onions. Granted, the slab of beef she had started

with had shriveled to a rather small hunk, but
still. . .

She looked back at Lucas and sighed. She ought to
have remembered all the pancakes he had put away
that morning. A man his size would eat large por-
tions of food, of course.

"I'm sorry," she offered sincerely. "I'm afraid the
men of my acquaintance, well, they're not active
men. And they're not nearly so big, either. I just
didn't realize."

Lucas was grinning at her. "I guess a couple of
spins around a dance floor wouldn't stir up much of
an appetite, not like breaking three wild horses. But
Mack whipped us up a big lunch, so don't worry
about it."

Her cheeks pinkened as she wondered if he had
come in today to look for his lunch. What had she
been doing early this afternoon? She hadn't even
thought of lunch, not after their late breakfast.

"Is that what you did today, break wild horses?"

Lucas nodded as he began filling his plate. "I've
got an order for a dozen horses to be delivered to Fort
Lowell, near Tucson. Breaking them in for the cav-
alry is short work. It's turning wild mustangs into
good cow ponies for the ranches that takes a might
more time. Sam Newcomb wants thirty by the end of
summer, and with the other orders I already have,
Billy and I will have to head up into the mountains
again pretty soon."

"You catch the horses?" Sharisse was surprised.
"But I thought you bred them. Isn't that what's usually done on a horse ranch?"

"It's not quite two years since I settled here, Sharisse. Not a single horse came with this place. I've
started a breeding program, even brought in a thor-
oughbred from Kentucky, but it takes time to build
up stock. I've got a good number of foals pastured up
in the hills, but not one is old enough for sale yet, and
they won't be for some time."

"I see. It's just . . . you fit in so well here, I thought you'd been here longer."

"It doesn't take long to adjust," he said meaningfully.

"I imagine that depends on the background you come from," she murmured.

"You think mine was so different from yours?" He was grinning again.

"I'm waiting to find the answer to that," she said sweetly.

He laughed. "I did say 'later,' didn't I? But how about giving me a chance to enjoy this food before I bore you with my life story?"

"If you insist. Coffee?"

"Please."

When she came back to the table with the coffee pot, Lucas had a mouthful of food. She began to fill her own plate. She kept sneaking peeks at him to see what he thought of her first attempt at cooking, but his expression gave no clue.

She took her first bite of the meat. It was tough and bone-dry. Her biscuit tasted moldy, and when she examined it, she could see splotches of raw flour. Were they all like that? The carrots were hard, but edible. The potatoes were mushy. The onions were just right. Well, how could you hurt an onion? And the coffee, after four attempts, was divine.

She glanced up at Lucas, her face hot. "It's awful, isn't it?"

"I've had worse," he grunted.

She wasn't going to let this upset her, she just wasn't. "I suppose the few things I didn't follow in the book counted more than I thought they would."

"You mean you improvised?" He grinned.

"No, I just left out things I didn't understand. But how was I supposed to know what 'knead' meant for the biscuits? I've never heard the word. And it said to slow-cook the roast, but it didn't explain what slow-cooking is. It said to add water, but not how much, to season to taste, but not which seasoning to use. And all I found was salt, anyway."

"The herbs are in the garden, Sharisse."

"Well, this is a fine time to tell me that."

"I guess I'll have to have Willow pay you a visit after all. You can ask her about the things you don't understand. But before then, in the morning, at least add some coffee beans to the coffee."

"But the coffee is perfect!"

"It tastes like hot water."

"That's because you're used to that thick slop you made this morning. I don't know how you can drink it. It tastes like mud."

"You'll get used to it."

In other words, it *had* to be made *his* way. She fell stonily silent, eating as much of her food as she could stomach, then moved off in a huff to clean up the mess.

Lucas leaned back in his chair. The meal hadn't really been all that bad, for a first effort. He had expected worse. He had also expected to find her completely bedraggled and worn out from the day's load, which was probably more work than she had done in her life, much less all in one day. But she didn't look done in, she looked good, too damn good.

She had changed her dress and now wore a splendid garment of olive-green foulard silk with a dark, myrtle-green leaf pattern, trimmed with ecru Oriental lace. This gown had a square neck, not cut very deeply, and three-quarter-length sleeves. She had found another apron and was wearing two to protect her gown.

His eyes followed her as she flitted from counter to sink to table and back. She had been on his mind the whole damn day, and he had been forced to keep busy just so he wouldn't be tempted to seek her out. He couldn't remember a woman ever intruding on his thoughts like that before. No woman had ever affected him so much. The plain fact was, he wanted her. He admitted now that such had been the case ever since he'd seen her picture. Being there in the flesh, she inflamed him. It was almost more than his body could stand.

There were no two ways about it. If he was this hot for her after having her there only one day, then there was no way in hell he could stop himself from making love to her before he sent her away. It was not what he'd planned, but he wasn't going to fight it. If she were a virgin, he'd have had to give the problem more thought, but she wasn't a virgin.

"Did I tell you how lovely you look in that gown?" he heard himself saying.

Sharisse glanced over her shoulder at him. "This old thing? Good heavens, Mr. . . . Lucas. I look a fright. I intended to change to an evening dress before dinner, but the time got away from me."

Lucas grinned to himself. Pity the man who saw her looking her best, then. Ladies and their endless array of clothing ensembles, each suited to a particular part of the day! With all the changing they did, it was a wonder they found time for anything else. But then, a lady's day did not include work. This one was finding out about that the hard way.

He felt a twinge of guilt over putting her through this. It wasn't as if he couldn't afford servants. But a rich, idle rancher was not the image he was in Newcomb to promote. He was simply an Easterner who had cashed in his chips, yearning for the quiet life the West offered. He wanted no one to suspect how wealthy he really was.

Lucas moved up behind her, the urge to touch her almost overwhelming as he picked up her subtle scent. But he grabbed the dish towel instead.

"I'll help you finish."

He surprised himself with that offer. He didn't want her overburdened, though, not yet, anyway. And her smile of thanks was worth the effort. She was so lovely when she smiled.

The last dish put away, they returned to the table, Sharisse bringing the coffee pot with her. Lucas declined any more of the weak brew and gathered a bottle and glass from a shelf before he sat down.

Sharisse frowned. "Do you do that often?" she asked hesitantly, looking at the whiskey.

"I can safely assure you I'm not a drunk if that thought is crossing your mind."

"I'm sorry." Sharisse lowered her eyes to the table, embarrassed by her own effrontery. "It was an impertinent question."

"You're entitled to know."

Her eyes met his again. "Then perhaps you're ready now to tell me all?"

He leaned back thoughtfully, the glass of whiskey in his hand. "We were born in St. Louis, my brother and I. The family on our mother's side was one of the more prominent in the city. She died, and after that, our father, Jake, wanted nothing more to do with her family. He brought us out here to Arizona. Gold drew him, and the promise of his own wealth."

"He was a prospector?" Sharisse was surprised, though she knew she shouldn't be. Gold had drawn thousands of people west since the early '50s.

Lucas nodded. "My brother and I were stuck in a boardinghouse in Tucson while he prospected the surrounding mountains for gold. The trouble was, he found it. A big strike. It led to his death. That was in '66."

"You mean he was killed?"

"Killed for his claim." He nodded.

"But wouldn't his claim have gone to you boys?"

"By rights, yes, so we had to be disposed of, too."

She couldn't believe how casually he was saying it all. "What did you do?"

"Hightailed it out of town." Lucas looked away, then continued. "Sloan, the man who shot our father, was hot on our trail so he could tidy up the loose ends, you might say."

"My God! What kind of monster was he, to hunt down children? You couldn't have been more than eleven or twelve."

"Ten, actually," he said grimly. "He was a hired gun, a man who kills for money without asking for reasons. The West has quite a few of that indiscriminate breed."

"You got away from him?"

"Not exactly. Shots were fired, and my brother went down a rocky gorge. With Sloan right behind me, I couldn't go back for him. I had to ride on. But after I finally lost Sloan, I was lost myself. It took me several days to find my way back to where Slade had fallen, and by then there was no sign of him. There was nothing left to do but make my way to St. Louis, hoping he had done the same."

"You found him there?"

"He never did show up." There was a silence. "I stayed in St. Louis with an aunt, thinking Slade was dead. It hasn't been all that many years since he finally found me."

"Why did he wait so long?"

"He had a sort of amnesia. He was clear enough on most things but couldn't remember that we had family in St. Louis or what had happened to me. He didn't know if I was dead or alive, or where to begin to search for me. And then, too, there was the problem of Sloan—having to stay clear of towns for fear Sloan would see him."

"What did he do?"

"Lost himself in the wilderness. He shared the mountains with the Apache from here to the border."

"You're joking." She was aghast.

"No. He lived alone in the mountains for eight years. But when he was nineteen, something happened that brought back his memory, and he was able to find me."

Sharisse was listening intently. "You don't sound happy about it."

He smiled sadly. "He wasn't the same brother I remembered. We had always been exactly alike. Now we're not. Those years he spent alone had a profound effect on him." Then he shrugged and grinned. "If we had a large family, which we don't, he would be what's called the black sheep."

"That bad?"

"Some people think so."

He didn't elaborate, and she didn't press him.

"Whatever happened to your father's gold mine?"

"It was never found. Ironic, isn't it?"

"For your father to have been killed for nothing? I should say so! And the man who shot him, was he ever brought to justice?"

"Sloan's dead." A harsh note entered his voice. "But the man who hired him is still around."

"You know who that is?"

"Yes, but there's no proof. There's nothing I can do except call the man out. And he's no good with a gun, so it would be plain murder."

"Oh," she murmured. "It must be terribly frustrating for you, to be able to do nothing."

"You could say that," he replied bitterly.

She switched to another subject before Lucas got fed up with her prying.

"Why did you come back to Arizona?"

"For one thing, I got tired of city life. But it was more than that. Slade wouldn't settle in St. Louis, so I decided to move closer to him."

"He lives in Newcomb?"

"Slade never stays in one place too long, but he passes through Newcomb from time to time. I get to see him occasionally, 'cause he travels near here."

She thought about that for a moment. "You must love him a lot to make such a sacrifice."

Lucas laughed delightedly at her reasoning.

"Honey, I don't look at it as a sacrifice. I happen to like it here."

"I'm sorry. I didn't mean to imply . . . well, anyway, I'm glad for you that you've found your brother and have grown close to him again. It must have been terrible, those years of separation."

"What makes you think we've grown close?"

She was flustered to see him grinning at her. "Well, I only assumed. . . ."

"You can't get close to Slade, Sharisse. No one can, not even Billy, who knew him in those years he lived in the wilderness. We're not as close as we were as children, twins or not."

"You mean you're look-alike twins?"

"That's right."

"My goodness. There were a couple of twins at school who looked alike. They even dressed the same, and it was almost impossible to tell them apart. Is it that way with you and your brother?"

"Well, we don't dress alike, but I guess if you stripped us down you couldn't tell us apart."

"Oh, dear," she said. "I guess I can be thankful then that he doesn't live here. I have enough new things to cope with without having to worry about which of you is you."

His expression turned inscrutable. "Oh, I don't think you'd have any trouble telling us apart. We look alike, but we're as different as night and day."

"I don't see how—"

"If you meet him, honey, you'll know what I mean," he replied cryptically, closing the subject. "Is there any other bit of curiosity I can satisfy for you?"

"Not at the moment," she said, smiling her thanks. She stretched. "After such a long day, I think I'd like nothing better right now than a nice warm bath before I retire."

"The buckets are over there." He nodded toward the sink.

"But—" She was aghast. "You mean I have to carry them?"

"If you want a bath."

"But yesterday—"

"—I took pity on you because you were exhausted after your long trip. But you can't expect me to continue carrying water for you. That's women's work."

Her shoulders sagged in defeat. "I see."

"You might want to move the tub in here," he suggested. "It's closer."

"A bath is no longer quite so appealing," she said in a tiny voice.

It was all Lucas could do to keep a straight face. She looked so forlorn. He almost took pity on her again, but it would defeat his purpose to pamper her, even if he wanted to.

"I think I'll just heat some water for the washbowl and go on to bed," Sharisse sighed. "Can I heat some for you, too?"

"I washed up in the barn. But I'd appreciate some hot water in the morning, if you get up early enough."

Another of her chores? She nodded woodenly, then rose and went to the stove. Lucas finished another shot of whiskey, his eyes following her thoughtfully.

"You know, Sharisse, there's a pool up in the mountains about four miles from here. The water there should still be pleasantly warm. We've got a full moon. Care to go for a moonlight ride?"

How wonderful that sounded! But it was cruel of him to suggest it.

"I told you I don't ride," she said.

"Not even double?"

"Not any kind of way. I've never been on a horse in my life."

"It was just a thought. It's still early, after all. But you'll have to learn eventually, you know. There's no way out of this ranch except on a horse."

"You could purchase a buggy."

The hopeful note in her voice touched his heart-strings. But he held firm. "I'm not known to waste money, and it would be purely a waste to buy a buggy when I've got half a dozen mares all gentle enough for you to ride."

"I'll think about it."

She turned stiffly and flounced off into her bedroom with the kettle of water. Lucas was waiting at the stove when she returned with the kettle.

"Good night, Lucas."

"Just good night?" He quirked a brow. "Surely a good-night kiss is in order?" He added with a grin, "You might as well get used to it. I like kissing."

"So I gather," she replied dryly. Resigned, she sighed, "Oh, very well."

She leaned forward, intending to bestow on him the kind of kiss she would give her father. But the moment her lips touched his, his arms wrapped around her, keeping her from pulling away.

He kissed her with incredible tenderness, his lips moving softly over hers, bringing a delicious languor to her limbs. She felt ridiculously weak. Strangest of all, she didn't want to pull away. She was enjoying the sweet exploration of his lips. Even the tangy taste of whiskey on his breath was enticing.

His hands began to move along her back, sending tingles down her spine. Then he was suddenly caressing her neck. The hand moving slowly downward. Her heart began to hammer. She knew what he intended, but she couldn't find the will to stop him. When his hand finally pressed boldly against her breast, she thought she would faint from the sheer wickedness of it.

It was madness. She knew she couldn't let him continue, but the sweet sensations he was stirring overtook her completely. When his lips moved along her cheek to her neck, she was finally able to find her voice.

"Lucas."

It sounded like an endearment, but she meant to admonish him. Her hands had no strength to push him away. His lips were at her ear, and excitement intensified until she could hardly bear it.

His tongue slipped inside her ear, and she thought she would faint.

"I want you, Shari. You know that, don't you? Let me make love to you." His voice became even huskier. "If we were married now, it's what we would be doing for the rest of the evening. It will take hours to love you properly, and I intend to love you properly, Shari."

His words were intoxicating. She had to fight him. Even the way he whispered her name made her tingle, pronouncing it as the French *chéri*.

"You can't . . . we aren't . . . Lucas! Please!" She was pleading for his help because she had lost the strength to resist.

He leaned back so he could gaze into her eyes, but his arms still pressed her close. There was a smoldering heat in his eyes that pierced right to her soul.

"You're not an innocent anymore. Why do you resist? You know it will be good. Now or later, it doesn't matter. And even if we don't marry, it makes no difference. Don't fight it, Shari."

It was the wrong thing to say. He knew it instantly, seeing in her amethyst eyes the sparks that turned them a deep, dark violet.

"Only a man would say it makes no difference. It obviously means nothing more to you than a moment's gratification. But for a woman there has to be more."

"You talk like a virgin," he said accusingly. "Who does it hurt if you and I make love?"

Sharisse stopped breathing. How could she answer when all she had were a virgin's answers? Was it permissible for a widow to be promiscuous? How could she know?

"I don't know why I'm even discussing this with

you," she said defensively. "There will be no marriage rights before the marriage."

"Will you force me to fetch the preacher then just to ease my pain?"

Her belly tightened. "What pain?"

He frowned. "Don't play with me, Sharisse. You can't have been married and not know any more about men than that. You feel this." He pressed her hips firmly to his, and she gasped. "You think that doesn't hurt if I can't do anything about it?"

"I . . . I . . ." Her face flamed red, and she tried with all her might to push away from him. "I'm sorry, I—"

"All right." He cut her off sharply and let her go. Then he cursed himself, seeing the fear in her eyes. "I'm the one who's sorry, Sharisse. I know I'm rushing you, and I apologize. But you're so damn desirable."

"You . . . you're not going for the preacher, are you?" she asked hesitantly.

Is that what had frightened her? "How the hell should I know?" His voice rose again. "Damn, you frustrate me, woman!"

He turned on his heel and left the house. Sharisse ran to her room, slamming the door behind her.

What was she going to do? She couldn't go through that again. What on earth was she going to do?

# Chapter 9

LUCAS tied his horse outside the saloon and sauntered inside. Only a few men looked up, but those who did watched curiously as he moved to the long bar and ordered whiskey. It wasn't often that Lucas Holt came to town, even less often at night.

Lucas finished a glass of whiskey, and when Ben offered him another, he grabbed the bottle without a word and moved to an empty table. He surveyed the room slowly, but it was just the usual crowd that hung out at Whiskers's place—expect for Leon Waggoner, sitting in on a card game. Lucas watched the Newcomb Ranch foreman, and, as he watched, he drank from the bottle.

He had never liked Leon. The man just rubbed him wrong. Too, Newcomb was a king in the town he had founded, so anyone who worked for Newcomb was treated with near-reverence, and it had gone to Leon's head from the start. Now he was what you might call the town tough, and he had the weight and build to carry it off. No one messed with Leon. Too bad he always managed to make himself scarce whenever Slade came to town, Lucas thought cynically.

Leon was blissfully unaware of the cold green eyes boring into his back. He was on a winning streak, and the three regulars he was playing with weren't taking it too kindly. Yet not one of them dared protest. They knew his temper and weren't likely to provoke it. He was in a good mood, but it would just take one of them trying to leave the game to put Leon in a bad mood. It had happened before. Will Days had got a broken nose once for doing just that.

Henry Foster, sitting across from Leon, was getting desperate. He had already lost more than he could afford to. In another hand or two he would be dipping into the mortgage money, and his wife would kill him. They owned the only gun store in town, but the town wasn't big and business had never been good. They had ended up getting deeper and deeper into debt with the bank, and it didn't look like they would ever get out. And there he was, gambling. Would he never learn? If only Leon would decide to call it a night.

Henry had seen Lucas Holt come into the saloon. It wasn't to his credit, but Henry had always been intimidated by men of Holt's caliber. The quiet ones were worse than the braggarts like Leon. He didn't know Lucas personally and didn't want to. It was enough that he had sold ammunition to his brother once and liked to sweat a bucketful before that man left his shop. That was the kind of man, well, you just stayed out of his way, period. Who was to say Lucas wasn't just like him? He certainly didn't look friendly.

A thought occurred to Henry. Anything to get this game over with without looking like he meant to get out.

"You know, Leon," Henry began, clearing his throat nervously, "Mr. Holt has been showing a mighty keen interest in you ever since he came in."

"Which Holt?" Leon swung around until his eyes met Lucas's. Then he turned back with an audible sigh of relief. "Oh, that one." He raked in the pot, but without much enthusiasm.

Henry persisted. "I wonder why he keeps staring at you?"

"Maybe he admires the cut of my clothes," Leon growled. "Shut up and deal."

It hadn't worked. Henry swallowed hard. He just couldn't go on. He had to risk Leon's anger by bowing out. Better now than later, after he was really broke.

"You've cleaned me out, Leon," he said. He rose, hoping for the best. "I've got to call it a night."

Before Leon could tell him to dig deeper into his pockets, the other two men both rose quickly and chimed in with the same excuse.

"What kind of chickenshit is this?" Leon demanded belligerently. "Just because I won a few hands . . . oh, go on then," he finished testily. He began stuffing his winnings into his pockets.

All three men were quick to leave the saloon. Leon Waggoner didn't give them another thought. It had been a good night. He was glad he had decided to come into town instead of waiting for Saturday night, when he joined the ranch hands for their weekly hellraising. He planned to stay the night, making use of Sam's private suite at the hotel. He might even get one of Rosa's girls to spend the night with him. They shouldn't be too busy on a week night, and they would appreciate the luxury of Sam's suite as a nice change from the whorehouse.

He got up to leave and caught Lucas Holt's eyes on him again. What the hell? Half the town might be leery of this man because of his brother, but Leon wasn't. Lucas was just another greenhorn from the East as far as Leon was concerned. So what if he had some dealings with Sam? Sam didn't exactly trust him anymore, not after the way Fiona had carried on around the man.

He was still staring, damn the man. Leon moved casually over to his table, plopping a boot up on the empty chair next to Lucas and leaning forward.

"I hear you're gettin' married, Holt. Hear tell she's a real looker."

"So?"

Leon chuckled nastily. "You don't usually come to town at night. What happened? You and your fiancée have a little spat?"

Lucas set his half-empty bottle aside. Leon didn't match him for height, but he was brawny, so he ought to give a good accounting of himself, Lucas was thinking.

"I don't think I like you discussing my future bride, Leon," Lucas replied in a softly menacing voice.

"Hell, everyone's discussin' her," Leon said, unperturbed. "A new gal in town is news. One who's come here to get married is even bigger news. Tell me, is she as good lookin' as I heard?"

"Perhaps you didn't understand me."

"Oh, I understood you, Holt." Leon grinned wryly. "But I don't give chickenshit what you like or don't like. You may have a brother who's pretty fast with a gun, but that don't mean you are. I'm pretty fast myself—or ain't you heard? I figure I can take you any day."

Lucas smiled a most unpleasant smile. "You think so, Leon? As it happens, what I know about guns I learned from Slade. I don't think you want to find out firsthand what all he taught me. But take your gun off, and I'll make it clear to you that I won't have you discussing my bride."

Leon's eyes narrowed furiously. "Hell, you came here lookin' for a fight, didn't you, you bastard? Well, I'm game. If you want to take a battered face back to your precious bride, you came to the right man."

Leon began unbuckling his holster belt, and Lucas stood up to do the same. But before he'd finished, Leon's belt, gun in place, whipped against the side of his head, sending him staggering to the side. His hand came away from his ear smeared with blood. His eyes lit with a smoldering fury. He growled as he charged into Leon's midsection, sending them both crashing to the saloon floor.

Several hours later found Lucas whistling cheerfully as he led his horse home. His jaw was tender, his knuckles were swollen, and his rib cage hurt like the dickens, but it had been worth it. Now maybe he could get some sleep without thinking about her.

# Chapter 10

LUCAS was surprised to find breakfast waiting for him. But he wasn't surprised at Sharisse's tight-lipped expression. She served him silently and kept her eyes averted even after she sat down beside him. She remained stonily silent all through the meal.

Lucas was half-amused, half-worried. Was it only because of his amorous advances? Or had she heard him slip into her room last night when he got back from town? He could have sworn she'd been asleep then, though. He had only wanted to make sure that she was all right. Well, not only that. He had also wanted to assure himself that she hadn't panicked and flown. And it wasn't as if he had seen anything he shouldn't see. She'd had the sheet pulled right up to her neck. She even slept with her hair in a bun, so his curiosity over how long it was hadn't been satisfied.

Sharisse took her time with the dishes, hoping Lucas would leave before she finished. What she had to say to him took a strength of nerve she hadn't quite built up yet. If he had only said something, she would have had an opening. But he had sat there at the table and matched her silence.

Something had to be said, however. She wasn't going to risk a repetition of last night's outrageous behavior. That thought gave her the courage she needed.

"We have to talk, Lucas."

"About last night?"

"Yes."

She sat down again, but before she could begin, he reached over and took her hand.

"You'll let me apologize first?" he said.

Sharisse was unnerved by his touch, and by the husky timbre of his voice. She couldn't meet his eyes, so she stared at the hand gently squeezing hers. She was startled by the swollen, scraped knuckles.

"You've been hurt." Her eyes flew to his face. His left cheek was swollen.

"It's nothing," Lucas replied with a measure of embarrassment. "I just got into a little scrap with the Newcomb Ranch foreman."

"Here? Or at his ranch?"

"In town."

"Oh. I didn't realize you had left the ranch." Curiosity prompted her. "Who won?"

"Neither of us won." Lucas gave her a sheepish grin. "I'm afraid I didn't give it my best effort."

"Why not?" She quickly amended, "I mean, if you were forced to fight in the first place, I would think you'd try to win. Or at least avoid getting injured."

"I wasn't out to hurt the man, Sharisse. And besides, I'm not injured. It's nothing. But I appreciate your concern."

His grin was too cocky all of a sudden. He seemed almost conceited. She looked away, infuriated that he had mistaken her curiosity for more than it was.

"About last night, Lucas . . ."

"I know," he said. "You're angry with me. I don't blame you."

"It's more than that," she said uneasily, remembering not only his boldness, but what she had felt for him. "What you did was—"

"—unforgivable, I know," he said.

Sharisse glared at him. "Will you let *me* say it? Yes, it was unforgivable," she continued. "You had no right to press your advances on me so ardently,

and no right to get angry when I resisted you. On top
of that, you tried to make me feel guilty about it,
when I did absolutely nothing to encourage you in
the first place."

"I think you're forgetting something," he said
quietly.

She eyed him warily. "What?"

"You came out here to marry me. Most mail-order
brides get married the day they arrive, and now I understand why. The only reason you didn't was that
I'm allowing us time to get to know each other first."

"You said it was to see if I would fit in here," she
reminded him stiffly.

"That, too. But the fact is, I could have insisted we
marry that first day."

She was uncomfortable, but she wasn't going to be
squelched. "It's just as well you didn't."

His brows narrowed. "Is it?"

"Yes, because I . . . I've changed my mind about
marrying you, Lucas. I must ask you to send me
home."

"Boy, when you carry a grudge, you really carry it
all the way, huh?"

"That's not it."

"Then what is it?"

"Simply a matter of taste," she said. "You are
much too forceful for me."

His laugh cut her off. "Honey, if I were all that
forceful, you'd have slept in my bed last night, not
yours. Don't you know that?"

She stood up nervously and moved over to the open
window. She kept her back to him. "I'm not used to
discussing this kind of subject." He could barely
hear her. "I don't know what kind of women you are
accustomed to, Lucas, but I didn't come here to be
your mistress. It is unreasonable of you to ask that of
me. I simply cannot stay here another day, not when
the same thing could happen again."

He said nothing. Her nervousness grew with the

continuing silence. At last she risked a glance at him and found him staring down at the table. Why didn't he say something?

"You do understand, don't you, Lucas?" she ventured.

The eyes he turned on her were unreadable. "You can't leave, Sharisse," he said simply.

"Can't?" she echoed. "What do you mean?"

"I can't send you back to New York right now."

"Why not?" Her voice rose with nervousness and fear.

"It takes more than a few pennies to travel across the country, Sharisse. What money I have is tied up in this ranch. It took all my available cash to get you here. There isn't any left to send you back."

She was too stunned to say anything.

He was getting good at lying, Lucas thought disgustedly. But damn, he hadn't thought she would confront him like that. And he couldn't start over now. People already knew about her. It was too late to bring in another girl.

She was staring out the window, her back rigid. "You know, we could just forget your hasty decision and start again," Lucas proposed. "I may have come on a bit too strong last night, but I wanted you badly and you can't blame a man for trying to get what he wants. If I frightened you, I'm sorry. But I didn't do you any harm, did I?"

Sharisse took a long, deep breath. "No, I suppose not. But I can't go through that again, Lucas."

"If my wanting you disturbs you so much, I'll keep it to myself."

"But couldn't you just . . . not want me?" she ventured timidly. It seemed such a good idea.

The question amazed him. "Just how long were you married?"

"Why?"

" 'Cause you know damn little about men."

"Actually, I wasn't married very long." She

couldn't meet his eyes, but he assumed she was simply embarrassed.

"Didn't your husband ever explain to you that sometimes a man has no control over his body? He can become inflamed by the sight of a beautiful woman, and there isn't a damn thing he can do to stop his body from reacting."

"No, I didn't know that," she confessed. "That's what happened last night?"

"I'm afraid so. But you were in no danger of being ravished, honey. I have never hurt a woman, or taken a woman who wasn't willing. I wouldn't force you, Sharisse. You do believe me, don't you?"

"I don't know," she admitted frankly.

"Well, come here then, and I'll prove it to you," he said.

"What?"

"Just come here. For God's sake, I won't hurt you."

She walked toward him slowly. He could only hope it wouldn't take too long for her to trust him.

When she reached the table, he stood up and gathered her in his arms, ignoring her startled protests. He kissed her long and hard and didn't stop until he felt her resistance ebbing. Then he let her go.

"There you see?" Lucas said. "It's not easy to walk away from you, but I'm going to do it."

And he walked away. Sharisse wanted to stamp her foot, watching him go, for he had flamed those feelings in her again and she hadn't wanted it to end.

# Chapter 11

THE invitation to dinner at Samuel Newcomb's ranch that evening put Sharisse into a dither. It came in the late afternoon, and she wanted to refuse. It was unheard of accepting an invitation that allowed for only a few hours' preparation. But Lucas had accepted for them both, informing her after the messenger had gone.

And what could she say? Samuel Newcomb was the richest man in the area. She had seen his name all over Newcomb, on the meat market, the grocery, a saddleshop, the bank, even the newspaper. As long as she was going to be there for a while, it wouldn't hurt to meet the town founder. He might be able to help her if things got any worse.

It had been a terrible blow to find that Lucas couldn't afford to send her home. Not only was she stuck there, it also heaped additional guilt on her. The man had used all his money to get himself a wife, and all along she'd never intended to marry him. If Stephanie didn't send her money, she would have to ask Lucas to pay for her trip back as soon as he could, and that would mean he'd have to wait that much longer to get another mail-order bride. How despicable, using him this way! She was beginning to wonder if her sacrifice had been worth it.

One good thing about the dinner invitation, she didn't have to cook. Lucas wasn't too delighted about going to the Newcombs', but he had fought with Mr.

Newcomb's employee last night and was probably
uncomfortable because of that.

Sharisse was late getting ready. She had to prepare everything herself, including a bath. But when
she was finished, she was pleased. Her evening gown
was unwrinkled, and she had copied one of Jenny's
simpler coiffures, finishing it with a flower garni-
ture of small white roses. The gown was one of her fa-
vorites, a combination of lampas and surah silks in
blue and ivory. The neckline was deeply rounded,
the sleeves short. Her long ivory gloves looked bare
without bracelets, and a simple velvet ribbon around
her neck had to suffice for ornament, but she felt
the ensemble was complete with an ivory pelerine
trimmed in mink.

She was just fastening that short cape when Lucas
knocked. She opened the door, waiting apprehen-
sively for him to say something. His eyes swept over
her. He was freshly shaven and wearing a jacket. It
was of fringed buckskin, hardly a dinner jacket, but
it was clean. His white shirt was silk. He wore gray
pants tucked into burnished black boots. And he
wasn't wearing his gun.

"Well?" she broke the silence.

"Fiona will be green with envy," he said.

Sharisse frowned. "Please don't tell me I'm overdressed. This really is just a simple dinner gown. I
usually wore it only at home."

"Not even good enough for going out, huh?"

"Lucas!"

"You're beautiful, honey. And no, you're not overdressed for one of the Newcombs' get-togethers. The
fancier the better as far as Sam's concerned."

"Who is Fiona?" she asked as he escorted her outside to the carriage Sam had sent.

"Sam's wife. Bride, I should say. They've been
married less than a year."

"Is there anything I should know about them before we arrive?"

"Just that Sam has an eye for pretty ladies, so you'll have to watch yourself."

"But he's married," she said indignantly.

"So?"

The blunt response brought to mind her own experience with a married man, and she fell silent as the Mexican driver whisked them away from the ranch. Her memories assailed her, and none of them were pleasant.

She had met Antoine Gautier at a party she and her aunt had attended a week after their arrival in France. Antoine was so gay, so dashing, so handsome and debonair. He was the first man ever to sweep her off her feet. She thought she had fallen in love. He later confessed that he had fallen in love with her, too. She was just barely eighteen, and Antoine was a man of the world.

Love does not inspire logical thinking. She should have realized something was wrong when the man never tried to kiss her, kissing only her hands. She should have wondered at the speed of their courtship. Fool that she was, she believed he loved her. She let him maneuver her into an empty bedroom at one of the parties.

Antoine had told her often enough that he wanted her, and she was oh-so-willing to let him have her. He had not asked her to marry him, but it was a natural assumption that he would. Marriage went with making love. Of course he would marry her—there was no doubt about it.

She realized later that he had counted on just that assumption.

She undressed herself that night timidly, while he sat on the bed and urged her to hurry. When she joined him, he had removed only his pants, but she didn't dwell on the fact.

108 *Johanna Lindsey*

There were no tender endearments, no gentle words anymore. Antoine seized her and tumbled her beneath him, ready to take her virginity without a moment's delay. Thank God the door had been thrown open just then, and a woman had entered.

Antoine was furious. "Two minutes, Marie! You could not wait two minutes more?"

"But I thought you would be finished by now, *mon cher,*" the lovely brunette replied sweetly. "How long does it take to win your wager?"

A wager! All her illusions were based on a wager. How she had wanted to cry, to pretend the three of them weren't in that room and she wasn't lying there naked. But she didn't cry. She even managed to get out of the room with a measure of dignity.

Later she had learned that the brunette was his wife. After everything else, it almost didn't matter. She had learned her lesson: men could not be trusted.

Lucas's mood was just as gloomy. That was always the case when he was forced to endure Samuel Newcomb's company. He had to endure it, though. It was why he was there at all. But he hated the pretense, having to put on a friendly demeanor, when what he wanted was to kill the man. But Sam was still protected in his will, and the reward he offered for the capture of his murderer had gone up over the years.

Lucas knew tonight's invitation was simply a matter of Sam's curiosity about Sharisse. It was just as well, for this would give Lucas the opportunity to get the crucial part of his plan in motion. He would just have to get Sam alone to break the news to him.

The end was in sight, after all this time. It should take only another few months before Samuel Newcomb discovered he was destitute. He had to take the bait tonight, that was all.

Fiona had unwittingly helped, for she was costing Sam a pretty penny. Sam wouldn't let her know that his capital was mostly tied up, and he had sold off his smaller properties in Newcomb to buy whatever she wanted. In order to keep her happy, he had to keep buying.

# Chapter 12

SHARISSE was having difficulty remembering all the names. The dinner party had turned out to be a party in her honor, and half the town had been invited.

Mr. Newcomb himself took her around and made all the introductions. His wife, Fiona, had greeted her, then promptly ignored her with appalling rudeness. Samuel Newcomb seemed to find this quite amusing.

"She's jealous, but don't you worry none," he whispered to Sharisse. "She used to be the prettiest gal around, but now you have that honor. I must say, Miss Hammond, Lucas is to be envied."

She blushed prettily, liking the man instantly. He was quite distinguished, in his early forties, with sandy brown hair and gray eyes that were perhaps a bit too revealing. He was a man who enjoyed the finer things in life, and his house was impressive. He was also, as Lucas had warned her, a man with an eye for the ladies.

She didn't mind his admiring glances, however. She felt quite comfortable with Sam, not taking him at all seriously when he suggested he could find a cozy little place for her if she ever got tired of Lucas.

The very idea! Samuel Newcomb was old enough to be her father. But he was just teasing her, she knew that. It was obvious he was devoted to his wife, for his gaze searched her out when she got too far away from him. Fiona was a lovely woman with blue-black hair and pale blue eyes. She was a good deal younger than her husband, not much older than Sharisse, in fact.

Dinner was informal because there were so many people. Folks found a place to sit where they could rest their plates on their laps. Sharisse was enjoying herself. The food was simple, but there was lots of it, and champagne flowed freely.

Lucas left her alone to talk with the ladies. He was kept busy accepting congratulations and repeating again and again the story of how they'd met. She listened carefully to that story so she wouldn't get it messed up if asked the same questions.

The people she met were friendly and seemed genuinely happy for her. But what really put her at ease was that Lucas was never out of sight. It was hard to analyze why she could feel uncomfortable alone with him yet find that his presence at the party gave her comfort. She had only to glance around whatever room she was in to find him somewhere in it. She wasn't aware how often she sought him out with her eyes.

He stood out, and it wasn't only because of his height. Where other men's clothing fit loosely, Lucas's was stretched tautly over his muscular length. He exuded an aura of rock-hard strength and raw masculinity. And she couldn't help noticing that the townspeople treated him with a good deal of respect.

"He's far more good-lookin' than any man has a right to be, don't you think?"

Sharisse had been staring at Lucas again, and she turned back to Naddy Durant. "Who is?" she asked.

"Why, your husband, of course."

"Oh." Sharisse found herself surprised at the young girl's frankness.

Naddy was only sixteen. Her mother, Lila, sitting next to her, didn't seem to find anything strange in

the statement. Lila was nodding in agreement, and
so were the other ladies gathered there.

"But he's not my husband yet." Sharisse made
that point clear.

"Honey, you're as good as married," Mrs. Landis
said. "Why, back in the old days, when a preacher
didn't get around as often, young couples weren't
expected to wait. As long as they were willin' and
able, they set up house and saw to the blessings
later. Now most towns got their own preachers. We
had one for a while, but since he passed away, no
one's come to take his place."

"I see," Sharisse replied politely.

"I don't mind confessin' I was hopin' Luke would
notice me." Naddy leaned forward as if speaking in
confidence, though all six of the women present
leaned forward too. "Either him or his brother,
Slade. They're both so—"

"Nadine Durant!" Lila gasped. "It's one thing to
admire a nice respectable man like our Luke, but
quite another to be thinkin' about a man like Slade. I
thought I taught you better, gal."

Naddy didn't look in the least chastised. "Have
you met Slade yet?" she asked Sharisse.

"No, I'm afraid I haven't," Sharisse replied.

"Then you're in for a treat."

"More like a fright." Lila corrected her daughter
again, displeasure written all over her face.

"Oh, the boy's not that bad, Lila," Mrs. Landis put
in.

"He is, too." Another woman took Lila's side.

"Well, we shouldn't even be discussin' Slade."

"And why not, Lila?" Her husband, Emery, came
up behind her with John Hadley. "It's not every
town that can boast of bein' the home of a famous
gunslinger."

"Now you know very well Slade Holt isn't from
Newcomb," Lila argued with her husband.

"No, but since his brother's settled here, Newcomb is as close to bein' his home as any place is."

Sharisse was staring curiously at Emery Durant. "What is a gunslinger?"

"A fast gun."

"You mean he hires his gun out?" Her eyes were wide.

Emery shook his head. "Don't know that he hires out. Never heard of him workin' for anybody. You mean to say Luke ain't told you about his brother?"

"Not much," she admitted.

"You don't say!" Emery's face lit up like a child's at Christmastime. He took only a second to make sure Lucas was clear across the room before he sat down next to his wife. "Well now, let me tell you about the day Slade Holt first came to Newcomb."

The women sighed collectively, for they had all heard this story countless times. Sharisse wasn't sure she wanted to hear it at all.

"Dressed like an Indian he was," John Hadley said before Emery could open his mouth again. "Looked like one, too, with his hair clear down to his shoulders and—"

"Will you let me tell it, John?" Emery said, exasperated.

"Well, I was there," John grumbled. "You weren't."

"What exactly is Slade supposed to have done?" Sharisse interrupted the start of what looked to be an argument.

"Why, he killed Feral Sloan. Sloan was a tough one, a former hired gun as mean as they come."

"Sloan!" Sharisse gasped, the name still fresh in her memory.

She glanced toward Lucas, wondering why he hadn't told her, but she only caught a glimpse of him as he left the room with Samuel Newcomb. She turned back to Emery Durant, hoping she had misunderstood.

"You mean Slade Holt is a killer?"

"Well," Emery replied, "the only one he's killed around here is Feral. That was close to seven years ago, and he was just a youngun then. It was rumored he'd already put a dozen men in their graves, though. No tellin' how many he's added since then."

Sharisse was getting paler. "Why hasn't he been arrested?"

"What for?" Emery asked.

She blinked. "But you said he killed a man right here."

"It was a fair fight, Miss Hammond. Ain't no one can say otherwise." The others around her were all nodding. "Slade even let Feral draw first. Slade was just faster. Ain't never seen anyone as fast as him."

Did these people know that Sloan had killed Slade's father? she wondered. She needed a drink. What she didn't need was to hear any more about Lucas's brother. "Black sheep" he had called him. Indeed!

In Sam Newcomb's study, Slade was again the topic of discussion, Sam mentioning him as he and Lucas took chairs at his desk. "Have you seen your brother recently?"

"Not for some time," Lucas replied, having difficulty keeping a poker face.

It never failed. Sam asked about Slade every time they met. He liked having fast guns working for him, and they both knew Leon Waggoner wasn't all that fast.

"Well, my offer is still open. Tell him that when you see him."

"I'll do that."

"Now what was so important we had to discuss it in private?" Sam asked as he prepared a cigar for lighting.

"Bad news, I'm afraid." Lucas came right out with it. "That railroad line we were financing has run into some difficulty. It looks like it's a good thing you didn't put more into it than you can afford to lose."

"What do you mean?"

"They underestimated what it would take to complete the line. It seems they've run out of funds with only three-fourths of the track laid. All work has stopped, and they can't manage to interest anyone else in investing so they can finish the job. The banks just aren't interested. It's wiped me out, but at least I still have the ranch. It will start paying off soon, I hope. I'm just glad I warned you not to invest too heavily, because it appears we're not going to get anything back."

Sam was speechless. Lucas knew why. He had known very well that Sam wouldn't take his advice when he first mentioned the railroad deal, and Sam hadn't. He had invested heavily to try and gain the controlling stock, and he hadn't told Lucas what he was doing. Sam had sold all his investments outside Newcomb, even most of the assets of his bank, with the dream of becoming a railroad tycoon. He had never even gone to check on the work in progress after his one visit to the site, accepting the statements the company lawyers sent him as perfectly legitimate. There had been no need to waste any money on actually laying down track, except for the original setup.

"There . . . there must be some way . . ."

"Not unless you know someone who would like to own part of a railroad," Lucas replied offhandedly. "They're asking the original investors to come up with the rest of what's needed, and it's a tidy sum. But I'm broke. I can't do it. Didn't you get a letter yet?"

"No," Sam said.

"You will. It will explain in more detail what went wrong—although a lot of good that does us. Well, I should be getting back to Sharisse, I guess. Good night, Sam."

Sam simply nodded. He felt sick, sick in his gut.
All he had built up over the years was gone unless he
could come up with a little more cash. He would have
to wire that lawyer from St. Louis, the one who had
written about some European clients looking for a
large ranch in Sam's area. Maybe one of those clients
would also like to buy a hotel. That would be putting
everything on the line, but what else could he do?

He would have to do it. There was no other way.
And he was too old to start over again. Times had
changed. It was no longer so easy to steal claims for
quick riches. The law had come to the Arizona Territory.

He sat alone in his study, gazing off into space. He
knew what he had to do. He knew there was nothing
else to be done.

# Chapter 13

SHARISSE was drunk. She handled it beautifully, carrying herself with such dignity and quiet reserve that no one guessed. Even Lucas wasn't aware of it until she burst into giggles as soon as they entered the carriage, then fell asleep on his shoulder.

Lucas was amused. He wouldn't have thought the haughty city girl would have succumbed to the weaknesses of drink. He was surprised and a little delighted to find she could let her hair down after all. But then, nothing could have disturbed him tonight, not after his meeting with Sam.

Sitting across from Sam in his study, he had been able to smell the man's panic. How long he had waited for this!

He almost laughed aloud, thinking of the small herd of horses Newcomb had ordered. When the time came for delivery, there would be nothing left with which to pay for them. But Lucas would have to capture the horses and train them just as if he weren't aware of that fact.

Sharisse stirred at his side, throwing an arm across his chest and nuzzling her head into his neck. Her short cape parted, giving him a view of her deep décolletage and the gentle swell of her breasts. His hand on her waist moved gently over her curves.

Whatever was he going to do with her? She was proving to be much more than he'd bargained for. He desired this girl sleeping so contentedly against him.

And that desire was so strong, it seemed like it had built up over years, not just the three days she had been there. Three days, and he was already plotting her seduction.

He shook his head, disgusted with himself and what he couldn't control. She was going to turn out to be a regret. He knew it, yet what could he do? He had lied to her left and right, and there would be more lies before he was done. It was bad enough that he had worked her into Newcomb's downfall, was using her to help accomplish it.

She feared him, though he couldn't understand why. Because of that she had already said she didn't want to marry him. If he bedded her, would she still feel that way? Was she the type to equate making love with total commitment? He wished she were more predictable. And he wished she didn't fear him.

The carriage stopped in front of the house, but Sharisse was still sound asleep. Lucas sat up slowly, drawing her with him.

"Sharisse?"

She frowned, gripping his jacket. "But I don't want to marry him, Father. Stephanie loves Joel, I don't."

Lucas grinned, wondering what this was all about. "Sharisse, wake up."

She opened her eyes, disoriented. "Who—? Oh, it's you." She looked around the carriage. "What are we doing here?"

"The party, remember? We've just arrived home."

She started to sway and caught herself by holding on to him. Lucas lifted her to the ground.

"Can you walk, or do I have to carry you inside?" he asked in amusement, hoping for the latter.

"Carry me? Don't be absurd!"

Sharisse preceded him to the door, walking in a remarkably straight line. Lucas intercepted the driver's grin and returned it, saluting him on his way. He caught Sharisse just as she stumbled in the door.

"I thought there wasn't a step there," she said indignantly, glaring behind her at Lucas.

"There isn't," he chuckled.

"Oh."

The room was flooded with moonlight, so he didn't light a lamp. He swept her up into his arms, amazed at the effect this had on him. He was holding her, had her just where he wanted her. Yet he was as powerless as she was, unable to resist the sweet parting of her lips.

He wanted only a taste, but her lips moved beneath his, warm and alive, igniting a fire in him. He groaned. Sharisse sighed, resting her head on his shoulder, quite unaware of what she was doing to him.

He realized he could have her right then. There would be no resistance in her condition. But this was not how he wanted her. She had to be willing, wanting him, not incapacitated by drink. If he took her now, she might not even remember. If she did, she might be sorry later and despise him for taking advantage of her. He wanted no guilt, no recriminations. And for some reason, it was important that she remember.

Hell, where did all these noble sentiments come from? He still had every intention of seducing her. If he was going to be unscrupulous, he ought to do it right.

Sharisse sighed, having fallen asleep again. Lucas smiled wistfully. Not tonight, honey, but soon. His lips brushed her forehead, and he carried her to her room.

She woke when he laid her on the bed and began to remove her shoes. "I can do that," she protested.

She sat up too quickly and, overcome with dizziness, fell back. Lucas grinned.

"Just think of me as your lady's maid," he told her, dropping her shoes on the floor. "I'm sure you had one."

"But you don't look anything like Jenny." She found that very funny and giggled. She didn't notice the removal of her cape but leaned forward so he could get at the buttons down her back. "I'm glad she's not here now, or I would really be in for an earful. She doesn't approve of drinking, you see, and—" She gasped. "Why didn't you tell me your brother was a killer?"

"Because he isn't."

"But he's killed hundreds of men!"

"Hundreds?"

"Well, dozens, but what's the difference?"

"You've been listening to gossip, Sharisse." He grinned as he lifted her off the bed so he could slip the gown out from under her. She didn't notice.

"I couldn't help but listen. My God, to think you called him a black sheep! *That's* putting it rather mildly, isn't it? You could have warned me."

"That he killed a man?"

"Many men!"

"He's killed only one man, Sharisse. All the others he's supposed to have killed don't exist. It's just rumor. It's what people want to believe about him."

"Really only one?"

"Yes." He began unlacing her corset.

"But—"

"He was a cold-blooded killer who deserved to die."

She had forgotten that the man had ridden after Lucas and Slade when they were only children, after killing their father. If the law had been unable to bring him to justice, was it so wrong for Slade to do it?

"They said it was a fair fight," Sharisse said quietly.

"So it was. Slade could just as easily have been the one to die."

"I'm sorry."

"Forget it." He had the corset off and moved to the pleasurable business of removing her silk stockings.

Sharisse sighed, stretching. "I'm glad he's not as bad as they made him out to be."

Lucas sighed too, wondering how he was enduring all this, undressing her so she could sleep comfortably, when his body had something entirely different in mind. Damn her for drinking herself into such a state.

"Slade is what he is," Lucas said gruffly, refusing to put himself through any more.

"That's nice."

Lucas shook his head. She hadn't even heard him. She was drifting off to sleep again.

He pulled the sheet over her and kissed her brow gently. "Good night, Shari."

"Antoine . . . my love."

The mumbled words were barely discernible. Antoine? Her husband? It was the first time he had heard the name. She had said she loved her husband. He hadn't given it much thought but now he found he didn't like it at all.

Damn! She was messing up his mind. Should he and Billy take off for the mountains sooner than planned? The sooner the better, he told himself grimly.

# Chapter 14

TICKLING on her face woke Sharisse. She opened her eyes to stare into Charley's large copper-colored ones. He was purring loudly. He moved his head, and his long whiskers tickled her cheek again. She smiled, having been wakened this way on many mornings. It was his impatient way of letting her know he was hungry.

"Good—oh—morn—ing."

She had sat up too quickly, and the throbbing started. She put her fingers to her temples to ease it, wondering if she were sick. But no, last night came back in a flash. She should never have drunk those last three glasses of champagne. Now she knew what Jenny had always meant by the evils of drink. What a devil of a headache. The pain was bearable only as long as she stayed still.

Vague memories were nagging at her. She recalled tripping as she came in the door last night, and Lucas picking her up and kissing her. How clearly she remembered that. And they had spoken of Slade, but why couldn't she remember that clearly? What had they said?

"Miss Hammond?"

"What?" she snapped, then realized it was a woman calling from the other side of the door. "Is that you, Willow? Come in."

Sharisse moved to draw the sheet up over her nightgown, then gasped to see she wasn't wearing

one. She was still in her chemise and muslin petticoat. Her eyes widened in horror as more memories
flashed through her mind.

"Are you all right?"

"What?" Sharisse managed a smile for the Indian
girl. "Yes, I'm fine, really. I was just remembering
something . . . distasteful. So you are Billy Wolf's
wife?"

The girl nodded. She was quite exotic looking,
with almond-shaped eyes in an oval face, straight
black hair that fell just below her shoulders, and
smooth, dark skin. She wore a faded blue skirt that
just reached her bare feet and a loose long-sleeved
blue shirt. Sharisse had not expected her to be quite
so lovely or gentle looking, not with that heathen for
a husband.

"Luke said not to wake you, but I began to worry.
It is nearly noon," Willow was saying.

"Good heavens, I had no idea."

She saw the sun streaming in through open curtains, curtains she would have closed. That confirmed that Lucas had put her to bed and then left.
He *had* left, *hadn't he?*

"Are you sure you're all right?" Willow ventured
in a soft, melodious voice, soothing Sharisse's raw
nerves and hangover.

"Yes, really. I . . . I just have a little headache."

"If you like, I will make you something for it,"
Willow offered.

"Would you? Oh, I would appreciate that. I'll just
get dressed and join you in the other room."

When the door closed, Sharisse searched her memory frantically. Lucas had left after he'd undressed
her. Or hadn't he? She didn't feel as if her virginity
had been taken, but then she might not know the difference. Oh, she had to remember!

A short while later Sharisse opened her door hesitantly, afraid she would find Lucas in the other
room. But there was only Willow.

"My goodness." Sharisse smiled in greeting. "I didn't notice before, but you really *are* expecting a baby soon, aren't you?"

Willow patted her extended belly lovingly. "It will be soon, yes."

"Is there a doctor near here?"

"What for?"

"But . . . surely . . ." Sharisse fell silent, not knowing what to say.

Willow was smiling at her. "What do I need with a doctor? I know what to do."

"You mean you don't want any help?"

"It is a private time. I will even send Billy away if he returns before the baby comes."

"Returns? He has gone away?"

"To the mountains. He and Luke have gone to find the wild herd for Mr. Newcomb."

Sharisse managed to hide her surprise. "Lucas mentioned something about that. I just didn't realize he would be . . . leaving this soon."

"Ah, I see he did not tell you. It is just like a man to avoid saying good-bye when he is not yet used to a woman. Billy was the same when we were first married. He thought nothing of going off without telling me that he was leaving or where he was going."

"Surely it was because he was used to living alone?" Sharisse suggested.

"No. He was married before. Of course, his first wife was a shrew, and he avoided her as often as possible. Perhaps you are right and it was only what he was used to. Now he likes his good-byes, for he uses that as an excuse . . ."

She smiled, and Sharisse found herself shocked at the frank insinuation. She also found it extremely difficult to imagine the savage-looking Billy as an amorous male.

"Is this for me?" Sharisse indicated the glass on the table. At Willow's nod, she sipped some of the powdery liquid, found it only slightly bitter, and drank the rest of it.

"Sit," Willow offered, taking the glass. "I will make you breakfast."

Sharisse was appalled. "I won't hear of it. You should be in bed, with someone waiting on you, not waiting on me. And lunch is in order now, anyway. You sit, and I'll make it."

"Why should I be in bed?"

"Why? Because of your condition."

Willow laughed softly. "I am not sick, only having a baby."

"But you can't be expected to do everything you would normally do. Why, the few women I have known who had babies wouldn't leave their houses once they began to show their pregnancies. They took to their beds the last few months. My own mother insisted she be waited on hand and foot when she was expecting my sister."

"Perhaps she was truly ill."

"No, she bloomed with good health as I recall." Sharisse frowned thoughtfully. "You mean it isn't necessary to pamper yourself?"

"An Indian woman would be ridiculed if she let such a little inconvenience stop her from caring for herself and her family. To lie about, doing nothing, can only make the body weak, when strength is needed for the baby's birth."

"I never thought of it that way."

"When you have your own child, you will see that it is a pleasure, not a burden. There are herbs that will ease the sickness in the beginning, and after that it is only a joy, knowing you will bring new life into the world. The pain in the end is only a small sacrifice for the wonder of that life."

How on earth did this subject get so out of hand? Her own baby indeed! That was something she had yet to think about, and she didn't want to start now.

"Well, I'll still make us lunch, but perhaps with

your supervision. I suppose you've heard I can't cook?"

Willow giggled, a delightful sound. "Billy thinks it is funny. He envisions Luke wasting away to nothing."

"Does he?" Sharisse said tartly. "Well, perhaps I'll fatten him up instead."

# Chapter 15

IT was a delightful week. With Lucas gone, Sharisse was able to relax. She found she was actually enjoying herself despite the work and the heat. Willow's company was responsible. It was nice being friends with another woman without any rivalry involved. Rivalry, no matter how subtle, had always been present with her friends back home.

Once she got used to Willow's open and frank nature, she began to realize what a prude she really was and to admire the Indians' way of looking at life. Willow had never given birth, but she wasn't worried, and her serene attitude put Sharisse's fears to rest.

They spent a day making candles and soap, and another day making preserves. Sharisse learned how to can vegetables. She put away her cookbook, finding it easier to make her own notes from what Willow told her. The results were good. She surprised herself by having fun learning things, and she began to wish Lucas would just stay away. She wasn't looking forward to a return of the tension his presence caused.

She tried not to think of him at all. That was easy while she was busy during the day. At night, however, when she was alone in the house, she was too aware of being alone. The slightest noise disturbed her. Then she wished Lucas would hurry back, but only then. Then, too, she could picture him clearly, and she was strangely disquieted by what she saw and the thoughts that followed. She found herself remembering the delicious sensations he had aroused in her.

One night Sharisse fell asleep with those thoughts moving through her mind. A pleasant dream followed. But when Charley yowled, she was instantly awake, sitting bolt upright.

"What is it, Charley?"

Then she saw the answer. With Lucas away, she had felt safe leaving her curtains open. The room was just light enough that she could make out the shape of a man standing near the foot of her bed. So Lucas was back. Well that was a fine way to let her know.

"I think I stepped on the cat." He supplied the reason for Charley's cry. Just then, Charley jumped into her arms for comfort. She held him protectively, enraged by Lucas's boldness. "Just what do you mean by coming in here while I was asleep?"

A match flared, and Sharisse shielded her eyes against it. A moment later the candle on her bureau was lit and she was able to see Lucas staring at her, a strange look on his face.

"I think I should be asking what you're doing here." he said in a colorless voice.

A horrible foreboding crept over her. The heavy stubble on his chin, the wild disarray of his hair, even the coating of dust covering him, were all to be expected of him. But the clothes were so different from anything Lucas had worn before: black pants tucked into soft-soled moccasins that were fringed at the knee and dyed black. The navy blue shirt was worn outside the pants. A black hand-tooled holster slanted from his waist down his right hip. A shining pearl-handled gun was strapped to his thigh. A black silk bandanna knotted on the side of his neck completed the darkly menacing look.

It had to be Lucas, it had to be.

"Lucas?" Her voice was an embarrassing squeak.

He shook his head slowly back and forth, a corner of his mouth turning up in a caricature of a smile. He walked deliberately to the bed, his footsteps making no sound at all.

"You can't belong to Luke, or you'd be in his bed, not here." He was looking her over with interest. "So who are you?"

The color fled from her face. My God! My God! It *was* Slade! She was hypnotized by the eyes that locked with hers.

"No answer?" He unknotted the bandanna and let it drop to the bed, then reached for his gunbelt. All the while he kept his eyes fastened on hers. "Suit yourself. I don't need to know your name to share a bed with you."

Her heart began a hammering beat, but still she couldn't move. This just wasn't happening. She wasn't watching Lucas's brother undress.

His shirt fell to the bed, and then he sat down next to her to remove his moccasins. Sharisse leaped off the other side of the bed, taking Charley and the rest of the sheet with her. But it was the wrong side of the bed. The door was on the other side—where he was.

She stared at him, her eyes darkly violet. She had no idea how ludicrous she looked, clutching Charley to her breast with one hand and the sheet with the other. The sheet barely covered her, and the blue negligee only revealed what the sheet failed to hide.

Slade had not moved.

"If there's some problem about you and me sharing this bed, you better spit it out now."

Sharisse pointed a stiff finger at the door. "Get out!"

It was the wrong thing to say. She realized it immediately. He came around the bed toward her, his expression menacing, his near-nakedness even more so. She backed away until the wall stopped her.

"Why?"

He was so close that his broad shoulders blocked her view of the rest of the room. That one word, uttered so forcefully, echoed in her mind. She didn't dare meet his eyes, and that left her staring at the smoothly corded muscles across his chest, which was just as frightening. She squeezed Charley tightly, so tightly that he squirmed to get out of her hand, and she had to let him go or risk dropping her sheet.

"I . . . I didn't mean to . . ." She forced it out. "You had no right to come into my room."

"This is my room, honey," he said. "It's the room I use whenever I pay Luke a visit."

"Then you didn't intentionally . . ."

She was staring at his lips, which turned up in a wolfish grin. "Honey, you were as much a surprise to me as I'm sure I was to you. A pleasant surprise, though, I admit."

A finger touched her cheek, making her tremble. She couldn't muster the courage to slap his hand away.

"I . . . I must ask you to leave, Mr. Holt."

"You can ask me, but you'll have to have a good reason." He tilted her chin up, forcing her eyes to meet his. "I'd rather stay."

"You can't!" she gasped. She tried to slip past him, but he wouldn't let her. "Please, Mr. Holt."

"Perhaps you'd better tell me who you are," he suggested.

"I'm your brother's fiancée."

"You can do better than that."

"But it's true!"

"Oh, I'm not doubting that, honey," he replied huskily. "I just need a better reason than that to find myself someplace else to sleep."

"You can't be serious!"

"Why not?"

"He's your brother!"

"And you're the most beautiful woman I've ever come across," he stated plainly. "So what has Luke's being my brother got to do with what I feel right now?"

"I am going to marry him," she said. Was there something wrong with Slade?

"You're not married to him yet." He shrugged.

His hand slipped behind her neck, exerting a gentle pressure that drew her forward. "No," she whispered. "No. Please." She could hardly breathe.

His mouth closed over hers, hot and demanding. Fear shivered down her backbone. A knee parted her legs and pressed against her groin, and she couldn't stop him. An ardent shock followed that reverberated through her system, and she moaned despite herself.

It was so easy to imagine that he was Lucas. The same sensations Lucas caused were being aroused in her. How was it possible that they could both do this to her? But this was Slade, not Lucas, and he was proving to be as dangerous as she had been warned he was.

She managed to push him away. "No!"

He stepped back. Hard passion smoldered in his glittering green eyes. Her sheet had fallen, and those eyes were ravaging her body through the sheer negligee.

"You shouldn't wear such flimsy little nothings. I could rip that thing off you in a second."

"Don't touch me."

"I could make you my woman, you know."

"Don't," she repeated in a whisper.

He considered her thoughtfully for a moment, apparently debating with himself. She held her breath.

His hand shot out, his fingers sliding along the curve of her neck, then down the deep V of her gown. His fingers were warm, making her knees ridiculously weak. But it was that look in his eyes that sent sparks through her belly.

"I'll scream—Mack will hear."

He smiled, his voice so very husky. "Mack has a

hearing problem, or didn't you know that? But why do you mention the old man? Won't Luke come to your rescue?"

"Must I be rescued?"

"Depends on how you look at it."

He obviously thought Lucas was in the other room. "You could just leave," she suggested hopefully.

"I already told you, honey, I'd rather stay."

"But Lucas—"

"—doesn't have to know."

"I'll tell him." Her voice was barely a whisper. "You won't get away with this."

"Scream then and get him in here. I'll fight him for you if that's what it takes." When she didn't answer, he laughed. "You won't call him? Maybe you don't want him in here after all."

She was getting close to hysteria. "He's not here. He's off hunting wild horses with Billy Wolf."

"So we're alone here? Then why are we wasting time talking?"

He leaned forward, but Sharisse brought both hands up hard against his chest. "I'm warning you, Slade Holt. I *will* tell Lucas, and he'll hate you!"

"Is that supposed to bother me?"

"You're despicable!" she gasped. "If you're so desperate for a woman—"

"—find one somewhere else?" His eyes moved to her breasts. "You don't really want me to do that." Those eyes came back up to taunt her. "You're trembling."

"Well, you frighten me."

"That's not why you're trembling."

"Stop it!" she cried.

He gave her a measuring look. "Why are you fighting it?" His brow wrinkled. "Or is Luke the only one you want?"

"Yes," she said, and then with more emphasis, "yes!"

He stepped back so suddenly then that she fell right into his arms. She jumped back.

She thought she heard him sigh, but she wasn't sure. He turned and walked back to the bed. She kept her eyes glued to him, aware of how wobbly her legs were.

"What's your name?"

He was picking up his things from the bed.

"Sharisse Hammond."

"How long have you known my brother?"

"Not long." She wanted desperately for him to leave. "Perhaps Lucas can satisfy your curiosity, Mr. Holt."

"Do I make you that nervous?"

"Yes, you do."

He laughed. "All right, I'm going." But he stopped at the door, turning to pierce her once more with those bright green eyes. "I'll stick around until Luke gets back." Then he added softly, ominously, "It's not finished, beautiful. Give me time. You'll find I will do as well as Luke. Before I leave here, I'm going to prove it to you."

The door closed, but Sharisse remained rooted where she stood until she heard him close the door to Lucas's room. Then she ran and locked her own door.

# Chapter 16

SHARISSE crawled out of bed at dawn, slipped on her silk robe, started the coffee, then went back to bed. That was the most she would do for Lucas's brother. She wasn't about to cook for him, and the less she saw of him the better.

The second time she awoke it was late morning. She decided to treat the day as any other, to ignore the fact of there being an unwelcome guest prowling the ranch.

The door to Lucas's bedroom was open, but there was no evidence that Slade had slept there last night. The bed was made. She hoped he'd slept in the barn.

There was no sign that he had been in the kitchen, either, not even a dirty coffee cup. But the pot was nearly empty, so she couldn't hope that he had left the ranch during the night.

She put fresh water on to weaken the coffee for herself. But before she could pour it, a pair of hands slipped round her waist, pulling her back against a hard body. A smooth chin nuzzled her neck. She nearly jumped out of her skin, she was startled so. She hadn't heard a single sound. But a hasty glance to the side revealed that smoothly shaven face, and she sighed with relief.

"Oh, Lucas, you scared the life out of me. I thought you were—"

He laughed wickedly. "I told you it wouldn't make

any difference, beautiful. You don't even have to close your eyes to imagine I'm him."

She gasped and pushed him away from her. "You! You may look like him, but you're nothing like him. You're offensive, unscrupulous, ruthless—"

"I know, a real mean *hombre,*" he said smoothly. "So I guess you should learn better than to rile me."

"You do not frighten me, Mr. Holt," she replied haughtily.

"Well, I'll be damned." He whistled. "You've got some spunk after all."

He pulled a chair away from the table and straddled it, facing her. Cleaned and shaved, he bore an uncanny resemblance to Lucas. They were truly identical, even to the bronze tint of their skin. But Slade didn't have Lucas's boyish grin or exasperating charm, which made a great deal of difference. This was a cold man, sardonic, perhaps even cruel, certainly unprincipled. Yet . . . she had seen this man in Lucas in a way. There were times when Lucas looked just as cold and unfeeling. Still, Lucas was human. Slade didn't seem to be.

She turned her back on him and finished pouring her coffee.

"I bother you, don't I?" he ventured softly.

"Yes."

"You'll get used to me."

"I very much doubt that, Mr. Holt."

"You might as well call me Slade, since you'll be marrying into the family."

She turned around and glared at him, remembering last night. "I'm here to marry your brother, not you."

"The Apache keep it all in the family," he told her. "When a warrior dies, his widow is expected to marry her husband's brother."

"I'm not an Apache, and neither are you." But she wasn't forgetting that he had lived like one.

"You're not from around here, are you?" he asked.

"No, I'm from . . . St. Louis," she said nervously, remembering the tale Lucas had made up.

"How did you meet Lucas? He hasn't been back East for a couple of years."

She looked away. "Lucas can explain better than I."

"Was it love at first sight?"

"Mr. Holt!"

"Don't tell me it's none of my business. After all, he's my only brother and my only family."

"I wish you had remembered that fact last night," she said harshly.

There was a very slight shrug to his shoulders. "One's got nothing to do with the other as far as I'm concerned. Like I said, you're not married to him yet."

It was too much to hope that he might regret his deplorable behavior. She should have known that. He stood up, his eyes growing brighter. She felt the same curious constricting in her chest she had felt last night, and she had to breathe deeply to get any air at all.

He started to approach her. "Stay away from me, Slade." She held the steaming cup of coffee in front of her, the warning clear.

He stopped. "You're going to put up a fight?"

"Every time," she said.

"But you can't win," he told her plainly. "If you were holding a gun it would make no difference. Don't you understand?"

His hand snaked out and took her wrist in an iron grip. He forced her hand to the counter, exerting enough pressure that she had to let go of the cup.

"I give you credit for trying, honey." Was that amusement in his voice? "Just don't try it again. And wear that pretty blue nightgown tonight."

He kissed her hard and fast, then let go of her and walked out the door without a backward look.

# Chapter 17

"MACK?"

"Back here!" he called.

Sharisse walked through the barn uneasily, covering her nose against the odor. She found Mack in a large stall at the rear, where two young foals were nudging each other out of the way to get at the sweets Mack was offering them.

She was amazed at her daring in being there, but she had no choice. Slade's threat was real. If she stayed, he would have her.

Lucas was the only one who could protect her. But it was too late in the day to send Mack after him, for it might be very late by the time Mack and Lucas arrived back at the ranch. She couldn't take the risk.

"Can you prepare a horse for me, Mack?"

He eyed her skeptically. "Luke mentioned somethin' about you never havin' been on a horse."

"That's true, but he also said I would have to learn sometime."

God, let him tell her there was an old buggy or something around. She was terrified of getting up on a horse.

"That's the truth. You plannin' to practice, or was you goin' to town?"

"Actually, I want to find Lucas. I was hoping you could take me to him."

"Shoot. They're a good three, four hours' ride from here!" he exclaimed. "And there's no tellin' where

143

they made camp. It would take me days to hunt 'em down. I can't be away from the ranch that long." He gave her a probing look. "What's so all-fired important that it can't wait a day or two? He should be back soon."

She couldn't very well explain, and her nerves were getting worse. "Will you just get me a horse, please?"

"Not if you're gonna do somethin' foolish. Now if you was to ride to town first and get you a tracker who could find 'em in less than a day . . ."

She brightened. "Yes! I'll do that." She didn't know what she would pay a tracker with, but she would worry about that later.

"So that's what you aim to do?" he asked, suspicious.

"I'm not a complete fool, Mack. I just didn't know that I could hire someone to take me to Lucas. Now that you've explained that . . ."

"All right then, I'll get you Sally. She ought to give you an easy first ride."

She watched him amble off to the back corral. She wrung her hands, wishing he would hurry.

She was wearing her heavy traveling skirt, the only thing she had that she could possibly ride in, and every petticoat she possessed under it for padding. She no longer had a blouse to wear with it, and rather than borrow one from Willow and have to explain, she had taken an old shirt of Lucas's that she could button to the neck. The cuffs had been rolled up several times, She had found an extra wide-brimmed hat of his, too, and had bound her hair into a tight bun beneath it. To put it mildly, she had never looked more ridiculous. But that wasn't important, in light of the way things were.

"You running away from me, beautiful?"

Sharisse jumped, turning to face Slade.

"I . . . I was just . . ."

"She wants to see Luke about somethin'," Mack

volunteered as he came back. He was leading Sally, a small sorrel. "I told her she oughta just wait, that he'd be back soon enough, but the gal's stubborn. Gonna find someone in town to take her to him."

Slade was looking at her with an unreadable expression.

"It's none of his business where I'm going," she snapped at Mack.

"I don't see why not, him bein' Luke's brother," Mack grumbled. "And shoot, he knows the mountains better'n anyone. He could find Luke before the sun set. Why don't you ask him to take you?"

Sharisse paled, shaking her head wildly. "That's out of the question."

"Why?" Slade asked smoothly. "I've got nothing better to do. I wouldn't mind at all."

"I couldn't impose."

"You wouldn't be."

"But—"

"There's no use arguing, Miss Hammond." Slade cut her off. "I couldn't let you ride out of here alone. There's just no telling who you might run into between here and town. Of course," he added with a grin, "you can always stay put and wait for my brother to come to you."

The insinuation was clear. Stay put, and wait for Slade to come to her bedroom. He was trapping her. If she stayed, she was lost. But he wasn't going to let her leave without him. He could just as well carry out his threats on the trail. Which was the lesser danger?

He took her silence for agreement and moved off to get his horse.

She followed him until they were out of Mack's hearing. "You know *why* I was leaving," she hissed. "Why can't you just leave me alone?" He didn't answer, didn't even look up. "I want you to leave me alone. Can't you understand?"

As if he hadn't heard a word she'd said, he glanced

over his horse, shouting to Mack, "No need to ready
that one for her, Mack. She'll ride with me."

"I won't!" Sharisse said.

"You can't ride astride in that tight skirt, not unless you're willing to bare your legs, which I'm sure
you're not."

"I won't go with you at all," she whispered furiously.

She turned to leave, but he gripped her waist, and
in a moment she was deposited sideways on his
horse. Before she could even attempt to slide off, he
was up beside her, his arms holding her in front of
him. He gathered the reins in his hands.

"Don't scream, beautiful," he breathed softly.
"The old man will only think you're frightened of the
horse."

By the time she had reasoned that out and realized
that Mack might be smart enough to guess otherwise, it was too late. Slade was galloping out of the
barn, and her frightened gasp truly was because of
the horse. She couldn't help herself. She heard him
laugh, but she didn't care. Her first ride on a horse
was everything she'd imagined it would be—horrible. Yet when he slowed the horse to a trot, it was
even worse. The jarring was so bad, her teeth rattled.

Several miles from the ranch, Slade stopped. "I
don't mind you holding me tightly, honey, but it
really isn't necessary. I'm not going to let you fall
off."

She loosened her grip to lean away from him a
ways, but didn't trust her position enough to let go of
him completely. The ground seemed terribly far
away.

Keeping one arm firmly across her middle, Slade
turned in the saddle to get something from the back
of the horse. "Lift your butt," he said as he turned
back.

"What?"

His expression was as bland as ever. "Brace yourself on the horse's shoulders and lift up so I can stick this blanket under you. It's going to be a long ride, and you might as well be comfortable."

"Oh." She dared to ask then, "You mean you really will take me to Lucas?"

They rode at a steady pace for the rest of the day without another word. Could she trust him? Would he really take her to Lucas?

The land rolled by, with rusty-hued buttes and red-rock cliffs and the ever-present yellow-green of towering cactus. The flowers were a marvel in that sun-baked land. The golden baeria and purplish-pink owl's clover dotted the mesas, and higher up in the mountains grew violets, veronica, and gentian.

The air was cooler, too. After they had ridden some hours, the vivid blue sky began turning violet in the east and bright orange-gold in the west. She worried over whether they would find Lucas before the light was gone—and whether Slade was taking her to Lucas at all. Just then he surprised her by saying, "We're here."

"Where?"

There was nothing to see. They had been following a twisted path up the mountainside, the path strewn with boulders and thick mesquite shrubs. Steep rock walls hampered the view.

"You don't think they would leave a herd of horses out in the open, do you?" he said. "The San Carlos Reservation isn't that far from here. Renegade Apaches scout this area."

"Renegades?" she said fearfully, turning to glance over her shoulder at him. "But I thought all the Indians were confined."

"Some don't like to be confined," he replied smoothly. "Arizona has been plagued by discontented warriors for more than twenty years. We are in the path of the forays they make across the border."

"Then we could have come across a band of Indians at any time?"

"Does that scare you?"

"Of course it does."

"No reason," he said casually. "The only Indian around here at the moment is Billy, and he's as harmless as they come."

She looked around. "How could you know? And where is he?"

"Should be on the other side of that narrow passage up ahead," he said, ignoring her first question. He got down from the horse and held his hands up to her. "Come on."

She gripped the pommel of his saddle. "How do you know? Was their trail that easy to follow?"

"Billy knows enough to cover his tracks."

"Then how could you—?"

"I lived in these mountains for a time. I used to track the wild herds myself. Billy and I have used this spot, among others."

Of course he knew his way around. Lucas had told her about the eight years Slade had spent in the wilderness. And the renegades he had spoken of? He probably knew them personally!

She slid forward, bracing her hands on his shoulders, and let him ease her to the ground. But he didn't let go of her. Before she could lower her arms, he jerked her against him and fastened his mouth hungrily to hers. She couldn't think clearly. There wasn't even time to struggle before her body betrayed her, delighting in the sudden rush of heat that made her reel. Her arms circled his neck of their own accord.

A muffled groan escaped him, and he abruptly let her go. She stumbled back against the horse. What had stopped him this time? His eyes were glowing dangerously, but was it desire, or anger?

Wordlessly he grabbed her wrist and dragged her along behind him through a rock-walled passage.

She couldn't break his hold. She couldn't control him—or her own fate. Either Lucas would be in that passage or she was about to be ruined by his notorious brother.

# Chapter 18

THE sight of horses roped off against the side of the cliff made Sharisse giddy with relief. Billy was squatting by a fire, roasting meat. He glanced up with surprise as Slade pushed Sharisse through a narrow opening and into this small area.

The rock walls ended abruptly on both sides of the improvised corral, the steep mountain slope continuing on from there. Huge boulders marked another level exit nearby. The whole rugged scene was bathed blood-red by the setting sun.

Billy stood up. He was dressed exactly as he had been when she'd first met him, looking every bit as savage.

"What'd you bring her here for?" Billy asked belligerently.

"She wanted to find Luke," Slade replied tonelessly.

Sharisse moved quickly away from him, closer to Billy. Billy made her just a little less nervous than Slade did.

"Where is Lucas?"

"You're crazy," Billy told her plainly. "We'd have been on our way home tomorrow."

"Well, how could I know that?" Sharisse said defensively. "Please, where's Lucas?"

Slade came up beside her before Billy could answer.

"It's good to see you again, Billy."

"I was beginning to wonder if you were ever going to come around again." Billy was relaxed, grinning now.

Slade shrugged. "Luke seems to be doing all right by himself. With your help, of course," he added, looking at the corralled horses. "How many are his?"

"More than half," Billy chuckled. "You taught him well before you took off."

"Billy, where is Lucas?" Sharisse demanded sharply.

"Back yonder somewhere." He nodded toward the exit opposite the opening she had entered through. "I ain't seen him all day," Billy explained. "He caught a young buckskin that was sniffing around the herd while the stallion was away. We couldn't keep him with these mares. He was stirring them up too much. And with so much horseflesh to choose from, he wouldn't settle down." He grinned, thinking this subject awfully delicate for her ears, unaware that she had absolutely no idea what he was talking about. "Had to move him away from their scent. I guess Luke's decided to keep him company."

Sharisse was staring at that passage. It was growing darker by the moment. What if Lucas stayed away from camp all night?

She glanced hesitantly at Slade and found him watching her with dark amusement in his eyes. She moved away from him again, circling around the fire. His laugh sent shivers through her.

"Get my horse for me, will you, Billy?" Slade asked, his eyes following Sharisse. "It's been a particularly trying day."

Sharisse caught her breath. And leave them alone? No thank you.

"I think I'll just go and find Lucas myself, rather than wait," she said quickly.

"Well, hold on." Billy stopped her, bending to scoop a large chunk of meat into a piece of rawhide.

He wrapped it thickly, then tossed it to her. "As long as you're going, you can take him this and save me the trouble—in case he was thinking of bedding down with the stallion all night."

"He'll join us, once he knows I'm here," Slade said. "I'm looking forward to seeing him, so don't keep him too long, beautiful." His eyes held hers. "He and I have something to settle, and I don't want to put it off."

Sharisse nearly ran through the dark passage between the boulders. She didn't feel safe at all, not even after leaving Slade behind. The narrow trail widened, but the light was nearly gone and she could barely see. Everything was dark, frightening shadows, especially on the side of the path that was a steep drop down.

She slowed, taking each step carefully. She had, of course, no idea how far ahead Lucas was, and she prayed the feeble light would last until she found him. She nearly ran into a tree as the path turned sharply. To the left was the beginning of a thick pine forest. Ahead the path continued through more walls of rock. She kept moving, then stopped. The path divided suddenly, one trail leading back the way she had come, or so it looked.

"Lucas?" Please let him answer. "Lucas?"

She waited breathlessly, but there was no sound at all. The sky was cut off behind her, and rather than move into the darkness to her right, she turned toward the forest. At least, up ahead, the sun was still visible.

But after some time, she still hadn't found him. She turned back, but when she finally got back to the place where the trail had divided, she hesitated again. Should she risk getting completely lost or take the path she knew? It was a matter of finding Lucas or spending the night alone with Slade and Billy.

She moved into the unknown. The path veered to

the left, apparently straight into the heart of the mountain. But no sooner was Sharisse enclosed in darkness than she saw firelight. She ran toward it. Next she saw the horse, tied with a rope staked to the ground. There was a small round area enclosed by large boulders, a dead end unless you were agile enough to climb smooth rock.

Lucas apparently was. He lay flat on top of the huge rocks with a gun trained on her. Sharisse froze.

"Sharisse? What the hell are you doing here?"

He jumped down from the rock in one easy movement, walking to the blanket by the fire. He returned the gun to the holster lying there next to his saddlebags. The sight of him gave her pause. He wasn't wearing a shirt. His blue pants were tucked into knee-high black moccasins, just like Slade's.

"Lucas? It *is* you, isn't it?"

"What kind of question is that?"

"More important than you would believe," she said raggedly, beginning to feel all the effects of the last few hours.

"Have you met my brother?" he asked. "Is that why you're not sure it's me, Shari?"

Shari. That was all she'd needed to hear. Slade wouldn't know that way Lucas shortened her name and added the French pronunciation.

"Oh, Lucas!" She ran to him and threw her arms around him, bare chest or not. "I can't tell you how glad I am to see you!"

"I can see that," he murmured, holding her tightly. "Maybe you better explain."

She held him, marveling at the sense of safety he gave her. "It was awful," she told him in a rush. "I hope it doesn't distress you, but I have to tell you I don't like your brother at all."

He set her away from him so he could look at her face. "What did he do?"

"He . . ." She paused. Now that she was safe, she felt almost foolish to have been so frightened. Would

he ridicule her if she told him? "Oh, must we talk
about it now? I think . . . I've brought you your dinner, see?" She handed him the meat she had been
clutching in her hand. "Billy wasn't sure if you
would be joining him tonight, so he sent this."

"But how did you get here?"

"Slade brought me."

"You mean he's here? Why didn't you say so?"
He moved away and doused the fire with dirt.

"Lucas, wait!" she cried, and he swung around to
face her, waiting. "Must we join them? He . . . he'll
still be here in the morning."

He looked puzzled. "You mean you want to stay
here?"

"Yes."

"I've only got one blanket."

She missed his warning completely. Her mind was
on postponing a confrontation, and she wasn't listening carefully. "It's not really cold," she replied
carelessly.

Lucas hesitated. Did she know what she was
letting herself in for? It appeared she had trans-
ferred her fears from him to Slade. He had hoped
that would happen. He owed his brother a debt of
gratitude.

"You might as well make yourself at home then."
He grinned and tossed the meat back to her. "Help
yourself to that, and you'll find some biscuits in my
saddlebags."

Sharisse moved over to his blanket and settled
herself. She removed her hat. Then she blushed,
realizing he had probably recognized the hat and
shirt as his.

"I borrowed a few of your things to get here," she
said. "I hope you don't mind."

"The shirt looks better on you than it ever did on
me."

He built the fire again, concentrating intently.
She spread the food out beside her, hesitating only a

moment before breaking off a piece of meat with her fingers. She was starved.

"You want to tell me about it now?" he asked quietly, sitting near her.

"What?"

"About what got you up on a horse to come here. I could've sworn you were dead set against riding."

"Oh," she hedged.

She really didn't want to tell him what a despicable man his brother was. He might not even believe her, and then what?

"The ride wasn't as bad as I thought it would be," she said. "But then, I didn't have to control the horse. I . . . I rode in front of Slade."

"Did I mistake you? I thought Slade was why you're here."

"Well, yes."

"Yet you agreed to let him bring you, and even rode double with him?"

"Lucas," she said, "he didn't leave me any choice. He saw that I was leaving the ranch to find you and took it upon himself to join me. He even sat me on his horse and took off before I could do anything about it. I didn't *want* him to bring me. Heavens, the very reason I had to leave was . . ."

She hesitated, and Lucas grinned. "Was to get away from him?"

"You find that amusing?"

"Slade's like that, honey. He very seldom asks permission before he does something. You're just not used to Slade."

"I don't intend to *get* used to him." She was beginning to feel put-upon.

"Aren't you being a bit hard on him?"

"No!"

"He didn't hurt you, did he?"

"Well . . . no."

"All right, Sharisse." He was annoyed over her evasiveness. "What exactly *did* Slade do?"

She couldn't bring herself to meet those probing eyes. "He kissed me."

"That's all?"

"Lucas!" She cried, her voice bouncing off the walls. "Isn't that enough? He knew I was your fiancée and he kissed me anyhow!"

"Honey, I can see where it might have upset you, but I can't really blame Slade for trying. Maybe you don't know what a temptation you are," he said bluntly.

She looked away. She had expected him to be angry, not amused. Had she reacted hysterically? The threat had seemed so real. Still, Slade had brought her to Lucas, and he hadn't forced himself on her, only threatened to.

"I still don't like him." Agitation sharpened her tone.

"Not many people do, honey."

Was that bitterness in his voice? He sounded so sad. "I'm sorry. You're not angry with me, are you?"

"No."

"I wouldn't have come if he didn't make me so nervous. You see, I just couldn't stay there alone with him."

"It's all right, Shari." He smiled reassuringly. "You're not to worry about it. He won't bother you again."

Not as long as I'm with you, she added to herself. "I'm glad you're not like him," she said impulsively. She couldn't read the look he gave her.

# Chapter 19

SHE wasn't asleep, and he knew it. She was rest-less, turning toward him, turning away. Lucas lay there, fighting with himself, wondering what was wrong with her.

Sharisse had protested when he lay down beside her, but there was only the one blanket. She had to lie next to him, and she'd even accepted his arm for a pillow. But she was as nervous as a cat. She was un-doubtedly worried about their close proximity, but so was he. He was, in fact, amazed by his own restraint. He had her where he wanted her, was even reason-ably sure he could make her respond to him, yet he kept away.

She would have to come to him. She trusted him to protect her, so he could not take advantage of her. That trust gave him a satisfying feeling, and he wouldn't betray it.

Sharisse was exasperated with herself. She had been lying there staring at the dying fire, sleep im-possible. She had never slept next to a man before and had no idea it would be so disturbing. Was this desire? Did she want a man to the point of aching for him? From the moment Lucas had joined her on the narrow blanket she had felt this strange disquiet. What would end this awful wondering? She had been willing to give herself to Antoine when there hadn't been any of this restless yearning, so why was she re-sisting so hard now? It wasn't as if anyone would

find out. Her friend Sheila had said there were ways
to make a man believe you were a virgin when you
were not. But what about the other way around? To
make a man think you weren't a virgin when you
were? She couldn't give herself to Lucas and take the
chance that he would be able to tell, for then he
would know she had lied about being married. It was
too late now to admit the truth.

"Shari, you're not asleep."

It was not a question.

She stayed as she was as long as possible, then
slowly turned around to look at him.

"Lucas? Is something wrong?"

How inane that sounded. She knew very well what
was wrong. He didn't bother to answer.

"Shari." He said that and nothing more.

His expression, what she saw in his eyes, told her
what he was going to do. And dear Lord, she wanted
him to do it.

His eyes were moving over her face, caressing
each feature. His gaze settled on her lips, and then
his mouth descended to claim hers. The taste and
smell of him was intoxicating, filling her. Time stood
still. There was only his mouth, working magic. The
pins fell from her hair, releasing it to a glorious fall,
and she felt his fingers running through it. Her
hands moved up to encircle his neck, letting him
know it was all right. His tongue slipped between
her teeth, and she welcomed it, teased it, hesitantly
following with her own tongue.

He groaned, his lips moving along her face to her
breasts. She clasped him tighter. He was beginning
to undress her, and soon her shirt was open, then her
skirt. Her many petticoats were untied, and even the
hooks on her corset gave way under his deft fingers.

He pulled her to her feet in a sudden, swift movement, and half her clothing dropped to the ground.
He caught her to him with one arm and finished
disrobing her with the other. By the time she

thought to say no, she was entirely naked and he was lowering her to the blanket again. His fiery kisses dispelled the last of her resistance, and she gave way with all of her being.

He stroked her wonderingly, making her quiver with urgent desire. He stopped suddenly and moved away from her, and she nearly cried out to him. He shed his clothes and moved across her again.

His eyes raked her, burning with a passion that mesmerized her. This was, she knew, her last chance to stop him. No words came. There was only the glorious feeling of him, the hard, masculine body. She reached up to draw him closer, and he hesitated for just a moment, then let himself be drawn by her until his weight covered her. His mouth captured hers in a heated kiss.

He entered her slowly, savoring her. But his tender care allowed for a steady build of pain as he pressed against the membrane that would not give. Sharisse pushed against him a little, but he continued kissing her breasts and moving inside her. His lips worked their magic, and when he suddenly thrust deep inside her, the stab of pain was over before it began.

It was done. Sharisse felt a terrific relief. An incredible burden had finally lifted. He filled her deeply, touching her in a way that brought surge after surge of renewed desire. Fire grew in her loins, and soon there was only the pleasure, increasing with every thrust. The pleasure became nearly unbearable, frightening in its intensity. Waves rushed through her, sweet shocks flooded her, and she was left weak and trembling. Lucas tensed, clasping her to him for a final plunge. She felt his throbbing, and a tender feeling for this man consumed her. She held him to her as tightly as she could.

# Chapter 20

SHARISSE woke with a start. As she sat up, one of her petticoats fell away, the only covering she had. She had been draped in her petticoats. She blushed furiously, for Lucas must have done it. He had watched her while she was sleeping. How embarrassing!

"Good morning, beautiful."

She gasped, and whirled around to face him, clutching the blanket to her. "Lucas?"

"You mean you're still not sure?" He chuckled.

"Well, don't call me that!" she snapped, irritable because of the fear that had washed over her.

"But you *are* beautiful."

He came to her and knelt down beside her. Swiftly he stole a kiss. But just as her heart picked up its beat, he sat back, fingering a lock of her hair. He watched it float through his fingers until it fell back down to her waist. His eyes met hers. She remembered all of last night with vivid clarity.

"Lucas?"

He shook his head, sensing her serious thoughts. "I was damn curious about the length of your hair," he said in an exasperatingly casual way. "Why do you hide it in a bun?"

"I'm too old to wear my hair loose."

"Too old? What do you mean, too old?"

"It's not at all fashionable, Lucas."

"And you must stick to fashion, even out here?"

The teasing light in his eyes unnerved her. That, and feeling how naked she was behind the blanket.

"Lucas, this isn't an appropriate time to be discussing my grooming habits. I would like to get dressed, if you wouldn't mind making yourself scarce for a few minutes."

"Ah, that's another thing," he said, picking up her corset from the pile of clothes. "Why do you wear this grim contraption? You don't need it."

"Lucas!" She grabbed it, thoroughly embarrassed. "What I wear or don't wear is none of your concern."

"It is when you smother yourself beyond any good sense. Western women—"

"I don't care to hear about Western women right now, Lucas. Please, just let me dress."

"All right, honey." He stood up, amused. "I was just thinking of your comfort."

Was he going to leave? The very idea of not wearing a corset! Whatever was the matter with him?

"There's water in the canteen and a towel in my bags if you want to wash up," he said. "I'll give you ten minutes, so don't dawdle. It's going to take all day to get the mares to the ranch. Billy can handle it on his own, but he won't get started until we join them."

"Them" meant that Slade hadn't left. How could she face him after last night? Would he be able to guess what had happened?

A rush of heat spread up her neck, but fortunately Lucas had sauntered off through the passage and around the bend, giving her the privacy she wanted. He hadn't mentioned last night, had even prevented her from mentioning it. Here was the most incredible experience of her life, and he acted as if it hadn't even happened! Well, that wasn't really true. Wasn't his manner more intimate, possessive even?

And then she realized that his saying nothing meant he didn't know she'd been a virgin. She had worried for nothing.

Her relief was tremendous, and not just because he was unaware of her deception. There had also been the possibility that he might feel honor-bound to marry her after taking her virginity, but now she didn't have to worry about that.

She refused to think about it anymore and quickly made use of her ten minutes. But it was not long before she was thrown into another quandary on discovering dried blood on the towel. She dropped it with a gasp and hastily ground it into the dirt. But no sooner did she feel the evidence was safely camouflaged than the blanket caught her eye. There was no time to wash out the telltale signs there. She would just have to keep the blanket with her.

She was putting on her boots when Lucas came back. "All ready?" he asked.

"Yes."

She hastily grabbed the blanket roll as he moved to gather his things. He looked at her questioningly, and she said, "I thought I'd use it as a cushion for the ride back."

"Slade teach you that trick?"

"Yes."

"Thoughtful of him, wasn't it?"

"I suppose," she muttered grudgingly.

"You're not worried about seeing him again, are you?" he asked gently, holding her by the shoulders.

"I . . . " She stumbled over the words, his closeness confusing her. "No . . . not as long as you'll be with me."

"Good." He patted her and went for his things again, strapping on his gunbelt and tossing the saddlebags over his shoulder. "His visits are short and infrequent," he added. "So you'll never have to put up with him for long."

The fact that he apparently found nothing wrong with what his brother had put her through made it worse. "That's encouraging."

He either didn't detect the sarcasm in her voice or

chose to ignore it. He untied the stallion and didn't
speak again until the horse felt the slack on the rope
and reared up, backing away from Lucas.

"Follow well behind me, Sharisse," Lucas warned.
"This fellow could try to make a bolt for it and I
might not be able to hold him."

As it happened, the stallion held back and had to
be dragged and coaxed along the path until they
neared the other horses. Then Lucas had to hold him
back.

By the time Sharisse reached the camp, Lucas had
given the stallion over to Billy, who would have to
manage him while herding the mares as well. She
and Lucas would ride Lucas's own horse.

It was Lucas who asked the question. "Where's
Slade?"

Billy didn't even glance up. "He got mad when you
didn't come back to camp last night. I don't think he
took too well to your staying with her when you
might have visited with your brother." He looked up
then, revealing that he found the whole thing highly
amusing. "No, I don't think he liked that at all."

"Is that what he said?"

Billy grinned. "No. But that's what I figured was
bothering him. Actually, he didn't say much of anything. You know how he is when he gets all quiet
and closed off. It's easier talking to a mule."

"Watch it, Billy."

The Indian laughed, delighted. He tossed Lucas a
rawhide pouch. "Here, you can eat this on the trail. I
had nothing better to do while I was waiting for you
to get down here."

He was rubbing it in, and Lucas wasn't amused.

Billy went to his horse and mounted. In another
few moments Lucas had the rope untied that had
confined the herd, and Billy started leading the
horses through the passage. Sharisse sat down on a
flat rock out of the way and waited. No more words
had passed between the two men. Was Lucas angry?

When the area was empty except for her and Lucas, he came to her, offering his hand to help her up. His expression reminded her of Slade, and she didn't like that at all. She felt compelled to say something. "I'm sorry he didn't wait, Lucas."

His expression didn't change. "Are you?"

Her back stiffened. "I'm not a hypocrite. I'm not at all sorry I don't have to see him again. But if he left because of me, then I'm sorry that I kept you. I mean, I'm sorry you didn't come down to see him."

*"Did* he leave because of you, Sharisse?"

"How should I know?" she asked, exasperated by this.

"Maybe you neglected to tell me everything that went on between you two?"

She became very uncomfortable. "I told you that he wanted me. And, well, he did give the impression that he . . . might fight you because of me. Perhaps he changed his mind and left so the two of you wouldn't end up fighting."

"My brother? Fight me over a woman? What the hell did you do to make him want you so badly?"

"How dare you accuse me? I'm not at fault here!"

Her dark amethyst eyes flashed in anger, and it was all she could do not to slap him. But Lucas was amused by her show of temper and wrapped his arms around her, pulling her resisting body close to him.

"All right," he conceded. "I guess you didn't have to do anything. I know how easy it is to get carried away by you, Sharisse."

She was amazed how abruptly his manner could change, almost as if his antagonism had been feigned, a deliberate attempt to provoke her. She was thoroughly confused.

"Lucas . . . shouldn't we leave?"

"I told you Billy could handle the horses once he got started. There's no hurry."

The husky timbre of his voice warned her. She knew what was on his mind. The thought of making love in the bright light of day was something she couldn't even allow herself to imagine. Yet the way he was pressing her against his body stirred her. She finally managed to find her voice.

"Lucas? Shouldn't we . . . go?"

He sighed and stepped back. "I suppose you're worried about your cat?"

Sharisse was surprised by the question but latched onto the excuse gratefully. "Yes, I've never left him alone this long."

"Well, come on then. It's a long ride. And you never know. Slade might have gone back to the ranch to wait for me."

He settled her in front of him on the horse so that he could steady her, not, as Slade had done, so that he could touch her and frighten her. Oh, it was such a relief to be riding home with Lucas. And, yes, despite everything, the small house was beginning to seem like home.

They rode in silence, still a little wary of each other but enjoying each other's company nevertheless.

# Chapter 21

SHARISSE held the baby in her arms, rocking it gently. How this infant fascinated her with its full head of black hair and tiny, perfect features. He had been born the night they returned from the mountains, as if Willow had waited until her husband was home.

Billy Wolf had been no help during the delivery, however. Sharisse heard him confess to Lucas that he had slept through the birth. He wasn't awakened until he heard the baby cry.

That was amazing in itself. And that Willow was up and about the very next day was equally amazing. Willow disproved everything Sharisse had ever heard about having babies. She made it seem so normal. And the baby boy was strong and healthy, a delight just to watch.

Sharisse had ignored her own work these last three days to spend time with Willow and her baby. Lucas didn't seem to mind if his meals were late or his clothes weren't washed. He seemed tolerantly amused, in fact, that Sharisse wanted only to talk about the baby.

Lucas was very busy, breaking in the new mares. It was a blessing, because he was exhausted by evening, and so far he had made no amorous advances. But how long would that last?

The problem was she didn't know what to expect from Lucas. At first she had worried because he was

so attentive and desirous. Now she worried because
he wasn't making advances. They were still sleeping
alone in the house, yet he didn't suggest they share
the same bed. Was he just exhausted? If only she
could ask him, but she could hardly broach the subject!

To worry her further, she hadn't heard from Stephanie. Oh, what a little communication wouldn't have
done for her peace of mind!

Lucas had gone to town for supplies that morning,
but he still wasn't back and it was the middle of the
afternoon. She was beginning to fret when she heard
the buggy approaching. She reached the front door
just as Lucas pulled the buggy to a stop.

"What are you doing with this?" she called to him.

"Taking you to town. I thought you might like to
dine at the hotel."

What a delightful idea. Oh, she had a suspicion as
to why he suggested it, and she couldn't blame him.
It was her cooking.

He jumped down from the buggy, flashing her a
wide smile as he handed her two wrapped parcels.
"These are for you, but not for now," he told her.
"For tonight, dress yourself in your fanciest city
gown. There's someone in town I want you to meet."

"And who is this someone?"

"A friend of mine from back East—St. Louis actually. He just arrived today."

"But," she said uneasily, "you've already told me
my simplest dress is too fancy for around here. I
don't want to look overdressed, Lucas."

"You won't."

"Is it your intention to show me off?"

"What's wrong with that?" He grinned. "It's not
every man who can claim he's got the best-looking
woman around for a fiancée."

"Lucas, be serious!"

"I am serious, beautiful."

"I've asked you not to call me that."

"Are you going to stand here and argue, or are you going to get ready? I thought you'd enjoy an evening in town. It's a weeknight, so the place won't be crowded. And Emery Buskett is a city man himself, so he'll be utterly charmed by you."

"Did you tell him I was from St. Louis, like you've told everyone else? Good Lord, Lucas, am I supposed to talk confidently about a town I've never even been to?"

"Now don't go panicking before you have to." He was grinning again. "As a matter of fact, he doesn't know a thing about you. We had other things to talk about today."

"That's why you're so late?"

"Good Lord, Sharisse, you sound like a wife already," he complained.

"I do not!" she gasped indignantly. But she knew he was only teasing her.

"Actually, it was a surprise to see Emery," he explained. "I didn't know he was coming."

"And now you want to surprise him—with me?"

"You don't like surprises?"

What could she do with him when he got into a rascally mood? He must have had a pleasant reunion with his friend, and perhaps one drink too many.

"I'll go and get ready, Lucas."

"Good girl." He gave her a quick peck on the cheek. "You can have the house to yourself if you want to bathe in the kitchen to save time. I'll clean up in the barn."

"You won't come in until I call you?"

"I can't make any promises, beautiful."

He laughed, and she watched him saunter away. Why did he persist in calling her "beautiful" when he knew it annoyed her? And how could she stay annoyed with him when he was such a rogue?

# Chapter 22

THE Palace Hotel was a pleasant surprise, nothing like she had expected. It was narrow and only three stories high, and the top floor was one large suite belonging exclusively to Samuel Newcomb. But its plain wooden facade hid luxury. With chandeliers, and crystal lamps on each of the tables in the dining room, she felt at home. Of course, a fine New York restaurant would never be so empty, nor would she have worn a simple outing dress, which she decided was elegant enough.

There was only one other couple in the dining room, and only one waiter to serve them. She watched Lucas covertly while they sat waiting for Emery to join them.

She hadn't mentioned the parcels he'd brought from town. The plain calico dresses were obviously for her to work in, and the boy's pants and cotton shirts were probably for riding. The clothes told her that, as far as he was concerned, she wasn't leaving any time soon.

While they waited for Emery, Lucas watched Sharisse, too. She took his breath away. He had told her to dress up, and to his mind that meant something flashy. But she had dressed in sheer elegance, in a black and red lampas basque. There were three flounces of Chantilly lace on the skirt, draped to reveal the rich black satin beneath. The dress brought out her rich, vibrant copper-colored hair. She looked exquisite. But then she always looked good to him. He shook his head. If only he hadn't discovered what a little liar she was.

He still didn't know what to make of it. Damn, she was as good at spinning tales as he was. And he had been just as gullible as she was, believing everything she told him. He'd never guessed that she really might be a virgin. A virgin! He ought to have known. She sure acted like one.

That fact delighted and enraged him. He certainly hadn't got any sleep the night of the big surprise. He had spent hours trying to figure what could have motivated her to claim widowhood, when the simple truth would have been much more appealing. It didn't make sense.

The next morning, she had managed to hide the evidence of her recently-lost virginity. The little innocent really thought her ruse had gone undetected, and she meant to keep it that way. But why? What was her real story, anyway? Was she running away from someone? From the law? Did she really have no intention of marrying him? Was that also a lie? He was consumed by curiosity.

Those splendid amethyst eyes turned his way, and she smiled shyly at him. Hell, there was no reason he couldn't keep her as long as he needed her. Five minutes later Emery walked in, but he wasn't alone. Lucas groaned at the sight of the Newcombs. He was puzzled. Emery had told him that Sam insisted no one learn about the sale of his ranch, not yet. How would Sam handle being caught in the lawyer's company? For that matter, Emery looked quite uncomfortable. Handling things from afar was one thing, but being thrust to the forefront of a colossal swindle was another. It had taken Lucas a long time to find a lawyer whose scruples wouldn't be a problem for what he had in mind. He hadn't considered that Emery and Sam Newcomb might meet face to face.

Just then, Samuel Newcomb was wishing he were

anywhere but where he was. It had been Fiona's idea
to come to dine at the hotel with his business associate, which was what he had told Fiona Emery Buskett was, merely an associate. And wouldn't you
know, she had spotted Holt and his fiancée and was
making her way to their table. Of all the rotten luck.

Damn. He hadn't wanted Luke to know that the
man who was handling their mutual investment was
in town. He would certainly wonder why he was
there, and he might put two and two together and
see what Sam was up to. Sam was buying the new
block of stock in Fiona's maiden name so none of the
original investors would know he was after the
controlling interest. If that fact were known, someone else might get the same idea and go for the
controlling interest himself. Sam had been so careful, and now this. He wasn't worried that Holt would
come up with a very large investment, but there was
the possibility that he might know some of the other
investors and tell them what Sam was up to.

When the time came for expansion, Sam would direct that expansion to Newcomb. His dream of the
town he had founded being a huge city one day was a
possibility. And with profits pouring in, he could buy
back all his properties pretty soon.

That would be the easy part, once the absentee
buyers that Emery was coming up with found out
that Newcomb was at present on its way to becoming
a ghost town. Sam had promised Emery a sizable
profit to keep that information to himself. That was
why he had insisted on Emery coming to Newcomb.
He wasn't going to broach such a delicate matter
through the mail. If he hadn't been able to buy the
lawyer, Sam would simply have got rid of him and
dealt with someone else. But Emery had gone along
with everything. He had assured Sam that he and
Luke weren't close friends. Besides, Holt's investment would be salvaged by the deal Sam was mak-

ing, so he couldn't very well complain when he finally heard about it.

"What a pleasant surprise," Fiona was saying. "We certainly didn't expect to find you here, Luke—and of course your charming fiancée," she murmured. Her pale blue eyes lit on Sharisse with unconcealed contempt. "What *is* your name, dear?" She dismissed her, smiling at Lucas. "You poor man. I suppose the hotel is the only place you can get a decent meal these days."

Sharisse was shocked by the blatant insult. The proper thing she wanted to do was to be icily polite. That was proper. But the way Fiona Newcomb was devouring Lucas with her eyes rubbed Sharisse the wrong way, and what was proper went right out of her mind.

Fortunately Lucas found his voice before she could bare her claws. "I don't need an excuse to bring my fiancée to dinner here, Fiona, but if you're curious about her skills in the kitchen, you might as well know she puts your imported cook to shame."

"How delightful," Fiona replied dryly.

Sharisse beamed at the sweet lie. "Actually, Mrs. Newcomb, Lucas promised me an evening of hearing the latest news from St. Louis. A friend of his is in town."

"Not our Mr. Buskett?" Fiona asked. She looked over her shoulder to see him approaching with Sam.

"How did you know Emery was in town, Luke?" Sam asked suspiciously.

"I happened to see him when I was here today. But you know how lawyers are when they're on a business trip—all work and no socializing. And since he's only passing through, I figured if I didn't bring Sharisse to town tonight to meet him, she wouldn't get the chance. But how did *you* know he was in town?"

"He, ah, came by the ranch to pay a courtesy call, introduced himself. After all, I'd never met the man, and he is handling some affairs for me."

"Is that right, Emery?" Lucas admonished in a friendly tone. "You wouldn't accept my invitation, but you went to see Sam?"

Emery was too flustered to find an answer, but Sam had a ready response. "I'm sure he would have gone out to your ranch if he hadn't seen you in town already, Luke."

"Well, of course." Emery found his voice. "Lucas, you didn't tell me you were getting married. If I had known, I certainly would have gone to see you to offer my congratulations."

Lucas smiled at the lawyer's quick recovery. He made the introductions. Fiona stood there, bristling, as Emery kissed her rival's hand.

"Hammond?" Emery said thoughtfully. "I have just recently heard that name, but where?"

Sharisse tensed. He couldn't possibly have heard of her, but she changed the subject anyway.

"I suppose I must be disappointed, if you've made a prior commitment for dinner, Mr. Buskett." She glanced briefly at Sam and Fiona. "But perhaps you will be coming through Newcomb again, and we can meet?"

"In order to enjoy your company, I will be sure to return," Emery replied smoothly.

"Why wait?" Fiona interjected, seeing an opportunity to have the whole evening to use her wiles on Lucas. "There's no reason why we can't all dine together, is there?" Fiona took the seat next to Lucas before Sam could say no. "After all, we don't want to deprive the dear child of hearing all the latest gossip from home. There's *so* much that might have happened in the two weeks she's been here."

Fiona's sarcasm was apparent to all, but Sharisse decide to feign ignorance. "You're too kind, Mrs. Newcomb, and not just for sharing Mr. Buskett with us." She laughed. "Why, it's been simply ages since anyone's called me a child. And I was beginning to feel quite old."

"It must be your ungainly height that deceives people," Fiona said snidely. "But of course *I* was able to see how young you are. A woman can tell."

"Ah, Mrs. Newcomb, you must stop flattering me. Really, twenty is not so young." She didn't dare glance at Lucas for fear he was choking on what he would think was a lie. "But perhaps when I am as old as you are I won't have this problem of being thought younger than I am. You don't have that problem, do you?"

Sam almost laughed as he watched Fiona clamp her mouth shut. He and Emery pulled another table close to make places for themselves. He knew what his wife was up to. She had been a regular bitch since meeting Sharisse Hammond. She just couldn't stand it that she was no longer the prettiest belle in the territory. On top of that, the new beauty had the man Fiona hankered for. Now if Luke would only hurry and marry the girl and put an end to Fiona's hopes once and for all, Sam's life might be a little easier. He signaled the waiter for a round of drinks, bracing himself for the evening.

On the short side of thirty and considered quite the ladies man by his friends, Emery Buskett completely forgot the reason for his being there and took the chair next to Sharisse. To find a woman of Miss Hammond's style and breeding in this small town was an unexpected delight, and he fully intended to monopolize her during dinner if Mrs. Newcomb would stop baiting her long enough so that he could.

He was out of his league, he knew that. Sharisse was undoubtly from one of those rich St. Louis families he had only read about in the papers. He couldn't recall ever hearing the name Hammond, though. Not in St. Louis. But where *had* he heard that name recently? Damn, he hated it when something eluded him like that.

The drinks came, whiskeys for the gentlemen and a bottle of fine white wine for the ladies. Sam took it upon himself to order dinner for everyone, and the meal progressed amiably enough while Fiona fixed her attention on Lucas and Sharisse managed to fool the engaging Emery Buskett into believing she knew exactly what he was talking about as he told her this and that about St. Louis society.

She didn't know that Lucas was paying more attention to her conversation than to Fiona's. He was amused by her performance, but Emery's unconcealed admiration of her was more than he'd bargained for. The man wasn't half bad looking, and he presented a dandified air that she probably felt right at home with. He would remind her of everything she had left behind. Damn, why the hell had he ever thought of getting Sharisse and Emery together? What a dumb thing to do.

"Marcus Hammond!" Emery exclaimed suddenly, embarrassed when everyone stared at him. "I'm sorry. You know how it is when something gets on the tip of your tongue but won't go any further? That was the name I couldn't remember earlier."

"Well, don't stop there, Mr. Buskett," Fiona said dryly.

"Oh, it was nothing," Emery replied.

"Any relation to you, dear?" Fiona asked Sharisse, obviously without any interest at all.

"No," Sharisse said, a bit too loudly. She had been able to mask her expression, but her voice was another matter. She kept her eyes lowered as she added, "I'm afraid I've never heard of Marcus Hammond."

Emery decided to tell the story. It might be entertaining. "This is some rich eccentric from New York. A friend of mine from there and a host of other men are all in peril of losing their jobs if they don't find the eccentric's daughter. My friend, Jim, works for one of the larger detective agencies in New York, you see. The reward for this girl is so ridiculously large that his boss wants results *or else.*"

"New York?" Lucas said thoughtfully. "What's the girl's name?"

Sharisse wanted to crawl under the table.

"I'm afraid I never asked the daughter's name," Emery answered.

"Was the girl kidnapped, Mr. Buskett?" Sharisse ventured, realizing that if she didn't show some interest, Lucas would wonder why not.

"No, a runaway, actually, which was why Jim could do nothing but complain about his assignment when he came by to see me last week. He has four states to cover, and little hope of success. It's just too easy to get lost in a country this size, too easy to change your name or your appearance. They know the girl left New York by train with a fortune in jewelry that would take her just about anywhere she felt like going. But Jim figures she doubled back and is hiding out in one of those fancy hotels in New York. That's his theory."

"Why?" Fiona asked.

"She was born in New York and lived there all her life. Aside from a trip to Europe, she's never been out of the state. Why would she leave the only home she knows just because of a disagreement with her father? That's what made her take off. Jim's complaint is that he thinks the girl will return by herself and no one will collect that huge reward, so he was sent west for nothing."

"This is all fascinating, Mr. Buskett," Fiona said innocently. "Especially when we have our own Miss Hammond sitting right here. If Luke hadn't told us that she was from St. Louis, why, I would wonder if she weren't this spoiled little rich girl running away from her father."

Sharisse forced herself to appear calm. She wanted to scream. The woman was only being bitchy, but she was doing more damage than she could ever know. Lucas's expression indicated that.

Her eyes darkened to violet, but her lips were fixed

in a smile. "Why would you say a thing like that, Mrs. Newcomb? Such a fanciful notion I might expect from the senile, or from someone who had imbibed too much. But you're not *that* old, and you've barely touched your wine. So what excuse do you have for making a ridiculous speculation like that?"

Fiona came half out of her chair. "Why you little—"

"Now, now," Sam interrupted, chuckling. "Why don't you call it a draw, Fiona?"

"But—"

"Forget it," he said forcefully. "Go powder your nose or something while I order you a dessert to cool you off."

She left in a great spurt of indignation. But Sharisse rose immediately afterward.

"My nose could use a little powdering as well. If you will excuse me, gentlemen?"

"Sharisse."

She deliberately ignored the warning note in his voice. "Don't worry, Lucas, I won't get lost. I'll just follow the sound of the door that just slammed."

With a brilliant smile, she left the table and was gone before he could call her back. Now to see how Mrs. Newcomb handled herself in a private confrontation.

Lucas sat there scowling, drumming his fingers on the table. Sam, on the other hand, could barely contain his amusement. Emery was simply perplexed.

After a moment, the noise coming from around the corner in the ladies' retiring room, though muffled, was still loud enough to make Lucas jump to his feet.

"Oh, let them be." Sam stopped him, his good humor increasing. "What harm can a couple of women do to each other?"

"That's hardly the point," Lucas snapped.

"Have a heart, for my sake," Sam cajoled. "If Fiona doesn't get this out of her system, she's going to be pure hell to live with. And, really, what harm can they do to each other? Women don't resort to violence. Shouting abuse is their specialty."

He was right, Lucas reasoned. Slowly he sat down again. The shouting died down. The sound of a door slamming signaled that whatever had happened was over with. Yet neither woman returned. Lucas's anxiety mounted again.

He was about to rise once more when the desk clerk brought Sam the message that Mrs. Newcomb had retired to their suite.

"Without any more explanation than that?" Sam demanded.

The clerk knew his boss well enough to grin. "Well, sir, I don't think you'd care to hear the rest of what Mrs. Newcomb had to say."

Sam cleared his throat. "No, I don't suppose I would." He dismissed the man, turning to Emery and Lucas. "Please forgive my wife, gentlemen. She's not usually so rude."

"So you're staying here at your hotel tonight, Sam?" Lucas commented.

"Yes. I'm thinking seriously about moving into town permanently," he replied. "Maybe that's what's wrong with Fiona. She's been so bored at the ranch, she doesn't know what to do with herself."

Lucas silently congratulated Sam on coming up with that plausible excuse. He had been wondering how Sam would explain the move without admitting that he had sold the ranch.

"You could always dismiss your servants," Lucas chuckled. "That would give Fiona something to do."

"Ha! She'd leave with them. No, I'm afraid I've spoiled that women terribly. Make sure you don't make the same mistake, Luke, with your pretty little gal."

"Spoil Sharisse? I'd have to take her back East to do that. She's not exactly suited to this kind of life."

"You thinking of moving away then?" Sam's interest perked.

"I thought you just advised me not to spoil her."

"So I did." Sam couldn't manage to hide his disappointment.

The clerk was back again, his message for Lucas this time. "Your intended sends her apologies, Mr. Holt, for not returning. I don't think she's feeling well."

"Where is she?"

"Waiting for you out front in your carriage."

"Hope it wasn't anything Fiona said," Sam offered, and the three men stood up to leave.

Lucas was just angry enough to say, "Undoubtedly it was, and you and I both know why. I'm sick and tired of it. She's your wife now. Whatever she and I had once is over. See that she finally understands that, Sam. Because if I have to, I'll damn well wring her neck—especially after tonight."

Lucas left Sam to explain that to Emery any way he chose to tell it.

# Chapter 23

SHARISSE couldn't stop crying. It was such a silly thing to do, something she hadn't done since her disastrous affair with Antoine. But wasn't her behavior tonight just as stupid? Never in all her life had she acted like that. She was afraid she didn't know herself anymore, afraid this impetuous adventure was changing her in ways she couldn't stop. Certainly that was the reason for these tears that wouldn't stop.

Lucas found her like that, her face hidden in her hands and her shoulders shaking. She was crying soundlessly. If she had been wailing loudly he might have thought it was a female ploy for attention, but this silent suffering disturbed him. A feeling long dormant rose up to overwhelm him, the instinct to protect and defend his own.

"Sharisse?"

Her head jerked up at the sound of his voice. She had hoped to hear him, to have time to compose herself. Why had he come upon her so silently? She was mortified. She'd meant to keep her face averted, too, and conceal her left cheek. Yet here she was facing him, and what she hadn't wanted to happen was happening. His expression changed from concern to unmistakable fury as he saw the vivid mark on her cheek.

For a breathless moment, Sharisse wasn't sure

who his anger was directed at. Then he exploded. "I'll kill her!"

"But I'm not hurt, Lucas," Sharisse assured him.

"Then why are you crying so hard?"

"Because of what I did. Oh, it was just awful!" Fresh tears erupted. "I shouldn't have followed her. I should have listened to you. But I never thought she would attack me."

He sat down next to her and pulled her into his arms. "Fiona lives by a different set of rules than you do, honey. I thought you realized that."

"How could I? I'm accustomed to civilized women. I only meant to find out why she was baiting me and to let her know my tolerance was at an end. But when she slapped me, oh, I don't know what came over me. I . . . I hit her back, Lucas. I'm so sorry."

He set her away from him, amazed. "Your instinct was only natural," he told her softly. "It's nothing to cry over and certainly no more than Fiona deserved."

"But you don't understand," she cried. "I think I broke her nose!" Shocked, he burst out laughing. "Lucas Holt, it's not funny!"

"God, yes, yes it is," he laughed. "She insulted you, hit you, and you're crying because she got more than she bargained for. It's funny, believe me."

"But a broken nose, Lucas."

"Did you hear the bone break?"

"Well, no. But she was bleeding. And she looked at me as if I'd killed her."

"Well, of course," he said. "She wasn't expecting the civilized city girl to fight back. Stop fretting over it, honey. If she was hurt that badly, she'd have screamed the hotel down."

"Do you really think so?" she asked hopefully.

"Yes. I think so."

Sharisse brought out her handkerchief from her reticule. She was calmer.

"I'm sorry I left so rudely. I hope you extended my apologies."

"I did more than that where Sam was concerned. The man should have more control over his wife," he said roughly. "Why'd she slap you?"

Sharisse considered all that had been said leading up to the fight, and her back stiffened. But her expression was innocent when she looked at Lucas.

"All I did was suggest that if she had been as satisfying a mistress as she believed, then you would have continued the relationship instead of looking for a wife."

Lucas flinched. "So she told you?"

"Actually, what she said was that she had *had* you first, and she could *have* you again if she wanted you. She's rather . . . coarse."

"Did you believe her?"

"I saw no reason to doubt such a blatant claim." The iciness in her manner was becoming more pronounced.

"I'll be damned." Lucas grinned. "You're jealous, aren't you? That's why you socked her."

"Don't be absurd," Sharisse declared hotly. "But you could have warned me, Lucas. Where I come from, a man doesn't force his fiancée to dine with his ex-mistress."

"Damn it, she was never my mistress, Sharisse. I saw her occasionally, not on a regular basis, and not exclusively. She made it clear she was available, and we had some good times. That's all there was to it. When she married Newcomb, that finished it. Her boasting that she can have me again is wrong. I don't mess with other men's wives."

"And if she weren't married?"

He smiled. "Why would I want her when I have you?"

Sharisse blushed and looked away. But her voice was firm as she ventured, "If she gave you such a good time, why didn't you marry her?"

"If a man married every woman he fooled around with, he'd end up with a passel of wives, honey. Are you really going to make me account for everything I did before you got here?"

"You didn't answer my question, Lucas. Why didn't you marry her when you had the chance?"

"I could say that I thought she wouldn't make a good wife, but the fact is I simply wasn't looking for a wife back then. Now, does that appease your jealousy?"

"I wasn't jealous," she insisted.

"Of course not," he said smoothly, enjoying himself.

She gasped. "Oh, I could just scream! Take me home, Mr. Holt. I've had too much of your stimulating conversation this evening."

"Yes, ma'am." He chuckled and whipped the buggy into motion.

The ride took place in silence. When they reached the ranch, he turned the buggy over to Mack and escorted Sharisse to the house. She waited only long enough for Lucas to get a lamp lit so she could see her way to her room. His blunt question, just as she entered her room stopped her in her tracks.

"Who is Joel?"

She stopped, then swung around. "Where did you hear that name?"

"From you."

Her mind raced. "I don't talk in my sleep, do I?"

"No, but you mumble a lot when you're drunk."

There wasn't any humor in his voice. And his expression was somber. She was instantly wary.

"Joel is a friend, Lucas. Someone I grew up with. Why? What did I say?"

"You told your father that you didn't want to marry him. That Stephanie loves him, not you." He walked toward her as he spoke, stopping too close to her, forcing her to meet his eyes. "Is that why you ran away from your father, Sharisse?"

"No," almost slipped out, but then she realized what his question implied. "You think I'm that girl Mr. Buskett was telling us about, don't you?"

"Aren't you?"

"I believe I answered that question earlier tonight," she replied stiffly. "But before you doubt me any more, I should tell you that my father's name is John Richards. Hammond was my married name." How adept she was becoming. "I suppose I should have made that clear before, but it didn't seem important."

"Antoine Hammond?"

"Certainly not! I despise Antoine!" she said forcefully, losing her temper. Then she caught herself. "I suppose I mentioned Antoine, too, that night I drank too much?"

"You did."

"What exactly did I say to make you think he was my husband?"

"You called him your love."

"Oh," she said. How was she going to explain that?

"Which is it, Sharisse?" he asked softly. "Did you love Antoine, or despise him?"

He ran a finger along her jaw, down her neck, to her shoulder, resting his hand there with just enough pressure to prevent her from turning away. He meant to hold her there until he got the answer. Maybe it was time for the truth, or part of it.

"Antoine was a man I met a long time ago, Lucas. I was young and naive, and he was worldly, romantic, and terribly handsome. I thought I was in love, when actually I had simply reached the age where I was ready to fall in love. So I was susceptible to the first man who extended any effort to win me. I realize that now, but at the time I was too enchanted to question anything." Bitterness crept into her manner, and her eyes darkened with memory. "Antoine turned out to be a scoundrel of the worst kind, a liar, a deceiver. He . . . "

Sharisse blanched as she realized she had just described what she herself had become. If Lucas ever found out how she had lied to him, deceived him . . .

"He what?"

She lowered her eyes. "He . . . he wanted only one thing from me. Luckily I learned of his perfidy in time."

"You mean you saved your virginity in time."

Her eyes flew back to meet his.

"Yes," she replied softly.

"But you gave your heart away freely. I was under the misconception that your husband was the only man in your past. How many others did you fancy yourself in love with besides Antoine?"

Her temper was ignited by his teasing. How dare he make light of that humiliating experience? She was reminded of Fiona and how casually he treated his past dalliances. Yet he dared to question her?

She smiled sweetly and gave a little shrug. "You can't expect me to answer such a question, Lucas. I'm not the sort of woman who keeps count."

"That many, eh?" He chuckled.

She gritted her teeth in exasperation. The rogue. He knew very well what she was up to. But it was too late to change her tune now. And she still wanted to get his goat.

"Yes, that many. Can I help it if I'm fickle?"

He shook his head in mock sympathy. "So many loves, and only one husband to show for it—so far. So who do you love now, Shari?"

His lips closed over hers. He didn't expect an answer. Love had nothing to do with them. He was the kind who wouldn't care if she loved him, as long as he got what he wanted. But she wasn't going to let him—not again. She didn't want . . . him to . . . make love . . .

The moment her arms closed around his neck in

surrender, Lucas swept her off her feet and carried her to her bed. His little virgin. She might not love him—and she might be an exceptional liar—but her body didn't lie. She was his. For now, anyway.

# Chapter 24

SHARISSE stretched languorously and opened her eyes. It took her a moment to realize that the bare male chest she was looking at wasn't alien to her anymore. She knew she should be appalled, devastated. To have shared her bed with a man all night, to wake up beside him just as if they were married when in fact they were not! He was not obliged to marry her just because he had taken her virginity. Why, he didn't even know the truth about that.

Truly, she ought to have been a little indignant that he was still there in her bed, that he was getting all the benefits of a wife without actually binding himself to her, but the truth was that she would have been terribly disappointed if he had left after making such glorious love to her. And she rather liked having him there to snuggle close to.

She knew it would be dangerous for her to analyze why she felt the way she did. If she thought for a minute that she might be falling in love with Lucas, she would panic. No arrogant man like her father was going to control her for the rest of her life, even one whose arrogance was as subtle as Lucas's.

No, it was safer to think she was perhaps immoral. Oh, not really in a bad sort of way. Good heavens, she was twenty, a woman with a mind of her own. Why should she have to wait until she found a husband to experience the ecstasy that Lucas had shown her? Why should she deny herself that pleasure just because they weren't married?

Sharisse smiled at her rationalizations. She was really becoming corrupt. But just then, looking at the broad expanse of Lucas's chest, she didn't care.

How different he looked when he was asleep. It was the first time she had seen him sleeping, the first time she'd been able to look and take her time about it. She liked what she saw, the corded muscles running along his chest and bare arms, the way his chest hair curled down to a point on his stomach. Even relaxed, he was powerful. His chin was slack, with a slight shading of whisker growth, his brow smooth, with an unruly lock of coal-black hair falling across it.

She was disconcerted to suddenly realize that without the usual grin curling his lips and the laughter in those jewel-like eyes, he could very well be his dangerous brother lying there.

Now why had that thought occurred to her? She hadn't thought about Slade since she and Lucas had returned from the mountains. She'd been relieved not to find Slade waiting for them at the ranch. But it was true. With the eyes closed and the face relaxed, there wasn't a single difference between them.

Twins. Remarkable what different experiences could do to two brothers, making one as dangerous as a coiled rattlesnake and the other a loveable rogue. One took her feelings into consideration, the other arrogantly disdained them.

Sharisse quickly looked away, afraid to continue with that train of thought. She caught sight of Charley in his porcelain bowl, and she grinned at his expression. He actually looked disgruntled. Well, Charley had never taken to Lucas, always growling softly when Lucas got near her. She supposed he wasn't too pleased to find Lucas in what he no doubt considered his personal domain.

At that moment Charley jumped out of his bowl and then out the window, as if he had only waited until he got her attention so he could make his displeasure felt, and now he was showing her what he thought of her promiscuous behavior. Well! To be snubbed by one's own cat.

"Good morning, beautiful."

Sharisse turned to Lucas with a start. "How many times must I ask you not to call me that?" she said, exasperated.

"Don't scold, honey, not so early in the morning." He pulled her down, and in one quick movement he was on top of her, grinning devilishly. "And why can't I call you beautiful?"

"Because your brother did, and it reminds me of him," she retorted with as much dignity as she could muster.

His lips brushed hers teasingly, and then he kissed those tender, perfectly shaped breasts. "Well, I don't want that, at least not when I'm making love to you. I don't care to be jealous of my own brother."

"Are you a jealous man, Lucas?"

Between soft kisses, he murmured, "Don't know."

"Then why did you say that?"

"Let's just say, when you're with me, I want to be sure you're with me completely. Understand?"

"I can barely think at all now, Lucas," she whispered.

Her eyes closed and she moaned softly as he moved lower, his lips nuzzling her belly, his hands gripping her sides, raising her off the bed so that her head fell back. She was lost in sensation, whirling inside a tide that he deftly stirred.

She nearly cried out as he stopped. When she opened her eyes, he was looking her over in a way that made her feel worshiped, adored, and wanted, definitely wanted. This man was not after her money or her virginity. There was no ulterior motive behind his lovemaking. He simply wanted her—for herself. The feeling thrilled her, striking a chord of warmth in her that had never been touched before.

"God, you're beautiful."

"I'm beginning to think you really think so," she said breathlessly.

His eyes locked with hers. "But you don't think so?"

"Oh, Lucas, stop talking," she moaned. She reached for his head and pulled him down to her.

He laughed deeply. She wanted him now, but he wanted to savor her, explore her. He wanted to make her pleasure the sweetest yet.

His lips claimed hers in a searing kiss, while his hands found her most sensitive places. He learned what delighted her most as he brought her to one exquisite height after another. He also learned that where Sharisse was concerned, there was as much pleasure in giving as in taking. Before the morning was over, he had broken down the last of her inhibitions. It was an experience neither of them would forget.

# Chapter 25

SHARISSE dropped the petticoat she had been washing as Lucas came around the side of the house into the backyard. He was carrying Charley curled in his arms. He was grinning, and Charley was purring. Sharisse had to wonder if she weren't imagining things.

But the moment Charley got a whiff of her scent, he let out a terrible howl and fought like a demon to get out of Lucas's arms. Once loose, he jumped through her bedroom window.

"I had a feeling he'd do that," Lucas said as he straddled the rug-beating rail near her. "I couldn't figure out why he and I didn't hit it off. See, I usually have a way with animals. It runs in the family. But I finally figured out what was wrong."

"What?"

"When was the last time Charley had a female?"

"Lucas!"

He laughed. "I'm serious. He's a male and needs a female just like all males do. But with none available, he's been using you as a substitute."

"Don't be absurd."

"That cat sees me or anyone else who gets near you as a rival."

"Nonsense," she insisted. "I told you he just doesn't like strangers."

"Then why did Charley just come up to me in the

barn as friendly as can be? Because you weren't there for him to fight over."

"You mean he really came to you?"

"You saw for yourself that he let me carry him."

"But if what you say is true, where am I going to find a female for him out here?"

"I don't think Newcomb has any other cats, but I can send wanted notices to the nearby towns and see what we come up with. I need to take the buggy back today, anyway, so go change clothes and come with me."

"But then how will I get back from town?"

"You'll ride a horse. It's time you had a riding lesson, anyway."

She turned away from him and went back to scrubbing her petticoat. "I think I'll stay here. You don't need me with you to place those notices."

"But I want your company."

"I've got too much work to do, Lucas."

"Go put on those pants I bought you, Sharisse."

Her head shot up. "I will not wear those pants, especially to town!" How dare he order her?

"I didn't buy them for you not to wear them. You're going to put them on."

"I won't," she replied adamantly, shaking her head.

He got up slowly and started toward her. She jumped back, bringing the soaking petticoat with her, holding it out before her as if it were a weapon.

"You want to make a little wager, honey?" he asked softly. "You want to bet that you will go to town with me, and wearing those pants? You want to bet that I'll put them on you myself if you won't do it?"

Her eyes widened. "You wouldn't."

When he took another step toward her, she dashed for the house. Before she reached the back door, he caught her.

"All right!" she cried. "I'll do it, but put me down!"

He did, and Sharisse was enraged to see him grinning. "Don't be too long about it, or I'll think you still want my help."

"Lucas Holt, you're a tyrant!" she snapped.

He walked away, calling back over his shoulder, "No, I'm not. I just can't bear to be parted from you today."

"Oh, I could just scream!" And she did.

Two hours later they returned the buggy to Pete's Livery and Corral and stabled the two horses that would take them back to the ranch. Sharisse was wearing her traveling suit, the jacket over the shirt Lucas had bought her, the horrid pants concealed beneath the skirt. Lucas laughed at her compromise, the loathsome brute.

But she hadn't been able to stay angry with him. That was one thing about this rogue that was different from any other man she knew. She could be utterly furious, but he had only to grin and tease and cajole and she would forget what she had been angry about.

Lucas left her at the mail dispatch office while he went to see if Emery's stage had left on schedule that morning. "There was something I forgot to tell him yesterday," he explained, "and if the stage is late as usual, it will save me having to write him about it."

"What am I supposed to do while I'm waiting for you?"

"Make three copies of the notice, and I'll pay to post them when I get back. You know better than I do how to describe the kind of feline Charley will like. Wilber will give you paper and pen. And check to see if we've got any mail while you're there."

"But wouldn't the mail have been delivered to the ranch?"

He shook his head. "You have to pick the mail up here."

"You mean I could have had a letter sitting here and not even known it?" She was horrified.

Lucas gone, she quickly went inside the office and spoke to Wilber at his desk. As quickly as her hopes had risen, they were dashed. No letter from Stephanie. There were two letters for Lucas, one from Monsieur Andrevie, New Orleans, and the other from Emery Buskett in Newcomb. She grinned. She supposed Emery had forgotten to tell Lucas something, too.

She composed her inquiries carefully. Imagine, advertising for a mate for Charley. It took a man who had advertised for a mail-order bride to think of ordering a cat the same way. It also took a male to think of a male's needs. She sighed. She had never thought of getting a mate for Charley. A lady didn't think of things like that. Did she?

Lucas did find Emery at the depot, just as the stage rolled in.

"It was good of you to come see me off, Lucas."

"Don't flatter yourself." Lucas grinned. "I had to bring back a buggy I hired." He helped Emery load his trunk onto the back of the stage.

"I left a letter for you," Emery said, "explaining in detail my meeting with Newcomb."

"Good, but there's something else I want you to do, aside from what you're working on now."

"Anything, Lucas," Emery replied eagerly. "That's what you're paying me for."

"That friend of yours, the detective?"

"Jim?"

"Yes. I want you to find him as soon as you get back."

"I doubt he'll still be in St. Louis, Lucas."

"I don't care if he's on his way back to New York, just find him. I want you to get the rest of the information he has on that Hammond girl. I want her name, description, everything he knows about her."

"Is she related to your fiancée after all?"

"Sharisse isn't sure, but she remembered having some cousins in New York, people her family lost touch with. She'd like to find out more about the girl."

"It will be a pleasure to oblige such a beautiful young woman," Emery said agreeably. "I'm just sorry you didn't bring her to town so I could tell her so myself. I would have loved seeing her."

"You forget that she's spoken for," Lucas said, a sudden cold edge to his tone.

Emery grinned. "A woman like that is worth stealing, Lucas, even from one's friends." His smile widened as Sharisse caught his eye. "Ah, so you did bring her."

Lucas looked down the street. Sharisse had just stepped out onto the sidewalk, and not twenty feet away, Leon Waggoner was making his way toward her.

"Have a safe trip, Emery," Lucas said absently as he walked away.

"But, Lucas . . . "

Emery fell silent, knowing when he'd been dismissed. A strange man, Lucas Holt. Agreeable most times, sometimes coldly indifferent. He had stopped trying to figure Lucas out. It didn't matter what kind of man he was, as long as the pay was good. And it certainly was good.

# Chapter 26

SHARISSE barely had time to shield her eyes from the glare of the sun before the clink of spurs made her turn around. The cowboy stopped as she turned. He was stocky, not young but not old, either. Something about the way he looked at her made her uneasy. Had she met him at Samuel Newcomb's party? If so, she didn't remember him.

"Miss Hammond, ain't it?"

"Have we met, sir?"

He hooked his thumbs in his gunbelt, his stance relaxed yet belligerent, wary. "No, I guess I'm about the only one in town you ain't had the pleasure of meetin'. But that's easily rectified. Name's Leon, ma'am. I'm top foreman out at the Newcomb ranch. And you're even prettier than I been hearin'. Yes, ma'am, you surely are."

Sharisse knew she had heard the name, but where? The very idea of his approaching her like that, let alone his manner!

"Mr. Leon, if we haven't been properly introduced—"

"It's Leon Waggoner," he said. "And I introduced us just now. I would have met you at the boss's party, only I missed it, thanks to your man and the shiner he gave me. I couldn't show my face for nearly a week."

"You're the man Lucas fought with!" Sharisse gasped.

"He told you, did he? I suppose he thinks he won that fight. Well, it was nothin' but a lucky punch. I bet he didn't tell you he caught me when I'd had too many drinks, did he? What'd you do to him to make him come lookin' for a fight?"

"Me? How dare you, sir! I don't approve of fisticuffs."

"What's fisticuffs mean, ma'am?"

"Good day, Mr. Waggoner."

He grabbed her arm. "Don't turn your back on me, woman," he growled. "That ain't good manners."

"I think it was your mother who neglected to impart manners, Leon."

They both started at the sound of that voice. Lucas stood, feet apart, hands at his sides. His face was granite-hard, matching his voice.

Leon released her arm. "Your woman ain't very friendly, Holt."

"Maybe she's just particular about who she talks to."

Leon tensed. Something about Lucas just then gave him pause. The man was too calm, deadly calm.

"It ain't finished between us, Holt. If you didn't have the lady with you . . . "

"Don't let that stop you, Leon. If you want to have a go at me right now, fine with me. If you'd rather go for your gun, that would suit me, too. I'll oblige you either way."

Sweating, Leon shook his head. "You're crazy! You ain't been the same ever since she come. I'll look you up when you're back to normal. I ain't fightin' no crazy man."

Lucas watched Leon hurry away. Perhaps he *was* a little crazy. He knew only that when Leon put his hand on Sharisse, he had wanted to shoot that hand off.

He turned toward Sharisse, ready to calm her if she was upset. But those beautiful amethyst eyes glittering with anger was the last thing he'd expected to see. Hadn't she been afraid?

Sharisse was indeed angry, but it was a nervous reaction to Lucas, not to Leon. Watching him deal with Leon had made her realize what a paradox Lucas was. Had she been misled by his gentleness? Was he made of the same savage stuff as his brother after all?

"How do you do it?" she accused harshly.

"Do what, Shari?"

"You become just like Slade sometimes."

"Do I?" He grinned. "Slade will be glad to know that."

"Why?" she asked warily.

"He taught me all I know. You don't think a tenderfoot like me could make it out here without a few survival lessons, do you?"

"You mean that was all a bluff?"

"Of course. What else?"

She frowned. "Why do I have the feeling that's not the truth?"

When he didn't answer, she asked, "Why do half the people in this town treat you cordially, while the other half go out of their way to avoid you?"

"You're imagining things, Sharisse."

"No, I'm not," she insisted. His expression told her he wasn't pleased by her observation, but she had to know. "Why do they fear you, Lucas? Is there a reason?"

"It's not me they fear, damn it. You know that."

"It's Slade? And it bothers people that you look alike?"

He didn't even bother to reply. "What I'd like to know is why you've got Slade on your mind so much."

"But I don't have him on my mind."

"Don't you? I think my brother made too much of an impression on you."

"If he impressed me with anything, it was that he was an arrogant, cold, heartless—"

"That's a very strong impression."

"Oh, nonsense!" she said in exasperation. "I told you I don't like him. I hope never to see him again. But I can hardly help thinking about him at times when you're acting just like him."

He stared hard at her. What was he thinking? Did he suspect how close she had come to succumbing to Slade's kind of persuasion?

"I *am* just like him in some ways, Sharisse," Lucas told her finally. "Maybe it's just as well you understand that."

Now what the devil did that mean?

# Chapter 27

SHARISSE set down the lunch she had packed for Lucas on the tack chest in the barn. He had told her curtly that morning that he and Billy would be riding up into the hills today to check on the foals. He hadn't asked her to make him lunch, but she hoped he'd appreciate it.

If she had thought, three weeks ago, that she would end up trying to please this man, she'd have laughed at the absurdity of it. She had intended to be disagreeable, to make him dissatisfied with her so he would send her back to New York. Well, he had certainly been dissatisfied ever since that run-in with Leon Waggoner and their argument about Slade. He had barely spoken to her for five days, and he had not touched her once.

It was just as well. Any day now she would be getting a letter from Stephanie and the money to get home. So why was she even bothering with Lucas?

What an impossible situation! Her feelings were so contradictory. She wasn't sure what she wanted anymore. To physically desire a man she wouldn't consider marrying was terrible. What was wrong with her? She had to stop it, ignore the feelings he aroused in her. She had to get a grip on herself.

Lucas wasn't in the barn, but Mack was. He was saddling his horse, and she frowned.

"You're not going up into the hills with Lucas and Billy, are you, Mack?"

He glanced at her. "No, ma'am. I'm headin' into town for a couple things Luke forgot to pick up last week."

"You mean Willow and I will be here alone?"

He understood. "No need to fret, gal. Luke'll be within shootin' distance if you need him. Anyone comes around here you don't recognize, you just fire that rifle he keeps over the fireplace and he'll hear you."

"Oh. Well, I didn't realize he kept the foals that close to here."

"Any farther, and they might end up disappearin'." Mack chuckled. "Indians, you know," he added.

Sharisse ignored that. "I guess there is nothing to worry about, then. But you won't be gone long, will you?"

"Nope. My days of stayin' over in town for certain unmentionable reasons is long past. I got all I need right here in my own whiskey stash."

Sharisse smiled. The old timer was always so blunt. "Can you check the mail for me while you're in town? I'm expecting a letter."

"Sure thing, ma'am."

No sooner did Mack ride out than Lucas came in the back of the barn leading two of the new mares. Billy was right behind him. The horses were only blanketed, and as Billy mounted one, Sharisse realized they weren't going to saddle either horse.

"Isn't it dangerous, riding that way?" she asked, just to break the silence.

"This is their first ride with a man's weight on them. They need to get used to that before we go adding a forty-pound saddle."

He was undoubtedly used to riding like that, so she had no business worrying that he might fall off. She didn't want to talk about horses, anyway. Her single experience sitting alone in the saddle the day they returned from town had been most unpleasant. Her backside was still tender.

"I made you lunch."

She gave it to him and watched anxiously as he put it in his leather bags. He was wearing his moccasins and a fringed buckskin shirt that stretched tautly over his hard muscles. Watching the play of those muscles had an effect on her, and she blushed furiously. If he didn't relent soon, she was going to be tempted to do the unthinkable and make the first move herself.

Sharisse was glad the light in the barn was dim when, finally, Lucas turned and looked at her. Their eyes met, and she waited breathlessly for some kind of statement from him. But his eyes were unreadable. "This won't take all day," he said easily.

Her heart fell. "You'll be back in time for dinner then?" she managed.

"Before then." He started to mount, looked back at her once more, then growled, "Oh, hell!"

He yanked her to him and kissed her long and hard. When he leaned back, his eyes were soft, his emotions obvious once again.

"I haven't been sleeping well lately." The grin curled slowly. "I think maybe I've stewed long enough."

"I think so, too."

He was obviously reluctant to let her go, but he had to. "Don't tire yourself out today," he told her as he pulled himself up on the horse.

"I might make the same suggestion to you."

He laughed delightedly as he rode away. Sharisse stood in the barn door smiling foolishly as she watched him racing to catch up with Billy.

# Chapter 28

SHARISSE had avoided thinking about her father since Emery Buskett had mentioned him. But with the ranch nearly deserted all day and time on her hands, she found herself dwelling on Marcus.

Even if the means to leave came in the next few days, she couldn't go directly home, not yet. If the reward for her return was as large as Emery had said, then her father's rage was still at its height. It was out of the question to consider facing him until his temper cooled. But to be found by one of his detectives and returned to him would be even worse. So she couldn't travel back to New York just yet.

She might be able to stay with her aunt. Surely Aunt Sophie's house had already been checked for her, and was unlikely to be checked again. And her aunt would take her side after she heard how unreasonable her brother-in-law had been about Joel. Aunt Sophie was a romantic.

Another problem on Sharisse's mind was that she would have to confront Stephanie about her jewels. Her sister had ended up costing her dearly, more than she could have known. She could understand the desperation that had made Stephanie do it, though. And what had Sharisse really lost but her innocence? Truth to tell, she didn't miss it in the least.

She smiled as Lucas crept back into her thoughts.

She wished the time wouldn't tick by so slowly. Anticipation was building.

Sharisse strolled over to Willow's house, but a quick look inside showed that both mother and child were taking advantage of the quiet day to nap. She wished she were tired enough to do the same, but she wasn't.

She sighed and headed for the backyard. The garden could always use watering. It was planted in good mountain soil, but it still tended to dry out quickly in the heat, and it was hot today. The sky looked almost white, without a single cloud.

The bucket was down in the well. By the time she got it raised she was ready for a drink herself and set it on the ground to scoop up the water with her hands. In the second before her fingers disturbed the water, a face appeared in the water's reflection, above her face.

Sharisse jumped up so fast that her head knocked his chin. The man grunted, and she gasped, and then they were staring at each other. She was so terrified she couldn't even muster a scream. An Indian— short, dusty—looking at her as if he had never seen a white woman. Was he as startled as she?

Her hair seemed to fascinate him the most. She had let it down after Lucas left, remembering that he liked it that way. But now this savage was reaching for a lock falling over her shoulder. Was she going to be scalped?

Her voice failed her, but her reflexes didn't. She knocked the Indian's hand away, moving just enough to see another Indian on a horse coming around the side of the house. No! There were two others, and there were more coming!

She ran for the house and slammed the door shut. But one look at all the open windows told her it was pointless to bolt the door. The rifle over the fireplace was her only chance. Of course, she didn't know the first thing about using it, but an only chance was an only chance.

The back door crashed open, and she raised the heavy rifle to her chest and aimed it at the door. It took all her strength. The momentum of the heavy thing carried her around in a circle, and by the time she got it aimed at the door again, there were seven Apaches crowding the room, their baleful expressions freezing her.

Panic overwhelmed her, and her finger squeezed the trigger. If she could wound one of them, the others might back off. But nothing happened. She squeezed harder. Still nothing happened. Worse, they could see what she was trying to do and they began laughing at her.

"It might help if you squeezed the trigger instead of the guard."

Sharisse whirled around to face the front door. It had quietly opened, and there he was. "Lucas! Thank God!"

But as she saw how he was dressed, she realized it wasn't Lucas. Still, she'd never been so relieved to see anyone in her life—even Slade.

He strode across the room and took the rifle.

"Damn fool woman," he growled so low that only she could hear him. "Were you trying to get yourself killed?"

Her back stiffened. "I was protecting myself."

He swore under his breath as he put the rifle back in its place. Then he said something to the Indians in their own tongue, and they began to leave. When the last one was out the door, she sank back against the wall, color slowly coming back into her face.

"You knew them?" she asked Slade.

"Yes. I brought them here. A couple of their horses won't make it all the way to Mexico, where they're headed. They wanted replacements."

As his words sank in, her temper exploded. "So

you were here all along! You could have showed
yourself sooner! Why didn't you?"

His brows drew together. "I don't think I like your
tone, woman."

"You don't like it!" she shouted, coming away
from the wall and facing him squarely. "I don't give
a fig what you like! *I* don't like being scared to death.
I think you get some kind of perverted pleasure out
of frightening women."

"You're not making sense, you know."

"I am making perfect sense!" she blazed. "You
scared me intentionally!"

"You're hysterical. If you'd settle down, you'd realize you got scared over nothing. You weren't in any
danger."

"Was I supposed to know that?"

"I might ask you how I was supposed to know
you'd take one look at my friends and go crazy? And
as for your wanting to know where I was, Billy's wife
heard us coming in and called out to me to say that
Luke wasn't here. Not even a minute passed before I
heard you cry out and I ran to investigate. I couldn't
have told you I was here. No time."

"A minute?" she gasped.

Was that all the time that had passed? It probably
was. So he hadn't meant for her to get frightened. It
had just turned out that way. Oh, what an utter fool
she had made of herself, accusing him.

"I . . . perhaps I owe you an apology," she said
lamely.

"Forget it." He walked past her to the backdoor.
After a moment staring at the corral, he informed
her, "They've picked out the horses they want."

"Shouldn't Lucas be asked first?" Sharisse ventured.

"Wouldn't make no difference," Slade replied.
"That's a raiding party out there. You either give
them what they want and let them go on their way,

or they take what they want and someone gets hurt."

*No danger,* he had said. "Nice friends you have there," she said hotly.

He glanced back at her. "Better my friends than my enemies."

"Will they leave now?"

He shouted something out the door and raised a hand in salute, then closed the door. "They've gone."

"But aren't you going with them."

He took off his hat and tossed it on the table. "I only met up with them this morning and rode along with them since we were heading in the same direction. They came here for horses—and I came to see you."

All of a sudden, the Indians were forgotten. "You mean Lucas, don't you?"

"No, I mean you. In fact, it suits me just fine that Luke's not around."

His eyes fixed on hers, a yellow-green so bright they seemed to glow. His gaze held her immobile as he closed the space between them.

"Lucas will be back soon," she told him in a breathless whisper.

"So?"

"So you've wasted your time coming here if it was only to see me." She managed to sound a bit bolder.

"Why don't you let me be the judge of that."

He reached for her, but her hands held him off. "Don't, please. I've made a commitment to Lucas since I saw you last. He and I . . . we've—"

"So he's bedded you." His mouth tilted mockingly. "I told you before that makes no difference to me."

She took a deep breath. "It does to me!"

"Does it? Let's find out."

He knocked her hands away and brought her up hard against him. His mouth came down on hers with brutal force. She squirmed, then gave up after a moment, for his arms were like steel. And then, unbidden, her body began to respond to him. And just as suddenly, Slade shoved her away from him.

Sharisse stumbled back against the wall, bewildered. Hadn't she been through this before? In the mountains, just before they joined Billy? Then, too, Slade had kissed her only to release her. Was all of this just a cruel game he was playing, or did he have a conscience after all?

"Well, I guess the question has been answered, hasn't it?" Slade's voice sliced through her. "You're as fickle as a woman can be. Or is it that my brother isn't enough man for you?"

"What are you talking about?" she demanded angrily. *"You* kissed *me!"*

"But you kissed me back, woman!"

So she had. Lord, what was wrong with her? They were two different men, not the same man. Why couldn't she separate them? Well, when her senses weren't being bombarded, she had no trouble separating them. It was only when they held her close that she couldn't control herself. Did she really desire them both? No! She couldn't accept that about herself.

"Why did you kiss me if you didn't want me to kiss you back?" she asked.

"Did I say that?"

"Oh, will you stop confusing me? You were angry about it. You can't deny that."

"You know me so well, do you?"

His expression closed off, and a nervous chill ran down her spine. How did you deal with a man who could instantly conceal even the most powerful of emotions? He might be in a murderous rage without her even knowing it.

"What do you want from me, Slade?"

"No pretenses. When I make love to you, I don't want recriminations afterward."

"You . . . you don't mean—?"

His laugh cut her off, a most ominous sound. "I didn't come all this way just to talk."

"But I don't want you!"

As soon as she said it, she remembered that he was convinced otherwise.

"If . . . if I did respond to you, Slade, it was only because Lucas has ignored me lately."

His eyes rolled over her slowly. "If you're trying to tell me he's tired of you already, I'm afraid I don't believe it."

"I didn't say that. We had an—argument—because of you!"

She wanted to kick herself.

"I wonder why?" he said thoughtfully. "Maybe he figured out that you've been yearning for me all this time."

"How absurd! Must you always jump to the wrong conclusion? It was simply that he behaves like you sometimes and I don't like it and I told him so. He's as bad as you about drawing wrong conclusions. He assumed . . . oh, I will *not* explain this to you!"

"Why not? I'm fascinated."

His amusement added to her frustration. "I believe you've missed my point," she said with as much haughtiness as she could muster. "I don't like you or anything about you. You're a cold, callous man, Slade, and I despise your arrogance. You remind me of my father, though he's not nearly as ruthless as you are. I would be insane to want you when I have Lucas."

"Even though he ignores you. Even though he might continue to ignore you?"

"Even if he never touches me again," she insisted. "Because he's tender and thoughtful, and he wouldn't try to take what I'm not willing to give."

"But does he excite you the way I do, beautiful?"

In a moment he reached her and wrapped his arms around her. She was prepared to fight him, to prove that she really didn't want him, but he did the unexpected, and once again she was thoroughly confused. Instead of overwhelming her with hard passion, he moved his lips on hers with exquisite tenderness. He reminded her of Lucas so much that she reacted as she would to Lucas.

Slade ended the kiss, but he didn't move away. His eyes smoldered as they pierced hers, making her melt.

"You might think you prefer Luke, beautiful," he whispered, "but your body doesn't care which of us takes you to bed. You and I know that. I think it's time Luke knew it. Your bed is a good place for him to find us when he gets here."

"No!" she cried. He picked her up and carried her toward the bedroom. "Oh, please, Slade, you don't understand. It's what neither of you understands. Will you listen to me!" She pounded on his chest until he stopped and she had his attention. "When you kiss me, when he kisses me, it's the same. There's no difference between you. I don't understand why, unless it's because you're twins. You both have the same power over me."

"So you finally admit it?" His tone was not at all triumphant.

"What I am telling you is that if you stand away from me and let me think clearly, I can say in all honesty that I prefer Lucas. You might be able to get what you want from me, but I hate you for it."

"Is that supposed to bother me?"

"Yes! I'm *not* fickle!" She said this as much for herself as to convince him. "Lucas has made me his— not legally, but his. One man is all I want."

"That's what I came here to find out."

"Do I have to beg you to leave me alone?"

"Would you?" he asked softly.

"Yes."

Now he was triumphant. She saw it in his eyes. He wanted to humiliate her on top of everything else.

She had never met anyone so despicable. She began to cry.

"Is that necessary?" Slade said roughly.

He set her down and moved away. Sharisse couldn't believe what was happening. Had she really found the means to hold him off? She cried harder.

"Stop it, woman!" he demanded.

"Will you leave me alone?"

"Yes!"

"You swear it?" she persisted between sobs. "You won't touch me again?"

"I swear, damn it!"

She quieted down. She had heard all she needed. She straightened her back and walked over to the kitchen for a towel to dry her face. When she looked back at Slade, he was scowling at her.

"You know, beautiful, if I thought for one moment you—"

"You swore, Slade," she quickly reminded him.

"So I did."

He grabbed his hat and moved to the front door, then stood there with the door open, staring out at the mountains.

Impulsively she said, "It's too bad you and Lucas aren't one and the same, Slade. Then I wouldn't . . ." She stopped, amazed at herself. Couldn't she leave well enough alone?

He didn't turn around to look at her, but she heard him laugh. "What? Be faced with wanting us both?"

She didn't dare answer that. But she did feel a little vindictive after all he had put her through. "You know, there is a little of you in Lucas. I've found that out. But there's none of him in you. Go away, Slade. Leave us alone."

# Chapter 29

SHARISSE was sitting at the kitchen table when Lucas and Billy rode in late that afternoon. She had a jug of brew before her, though she had no idea what it was. She had gone to Willow and asked her for something to calm her nerves, and Willow had complied, though with misgivings. Sharisse didn't care what she was drinking, because, with her cup near empty for the second time, she was calm.

When she saw Lucas standing in the doorway, all she could see was those cursed moccasins, and her heart plummeted, as she thought Slade was back. But this was Lucas. No more comparisons.

"You got back early," she commented.

"Actually, I'm late," Lucas replied, his gaze falling on the jug. "Hey, is that Billy's mescal you're drinking?"

Sharisse smiled. "I don't know what it is. It's not bad after the first few sips. And you can't be late. Mack's not back yet, and he said he wouldn't be long."

Lucas frowned. "Are you all right, Sharisse?"

His concern warmed her. "Well, of course. Why shouldn't I be?"

"Willow said Slade was here."

"Yes, your dear brother did pay us a call. But you know, Lucas, I think I might have misjudged Slade. He's not such a bad sort really. Why, he didn't rape me or kill me or anything."

Lucas burst out laughing. "You're drunk!"

"I am not!"

He pulled her to her feet, catching her around the waist. "This is not the kind of reception I was look- ing forward to, honey," he told her huskily. "I've been thinking about you all day, but how can I take advantage of you when you're like this?"

"Take advantage of me?" She frowned, then reali- zation dawned. "Oh, that." She wrapped her arms around his neck. "Well, sir, if you don't, I'll never forgive you."

"Don't what?"

"Take advantage of me. I insist."

"Oh, well, if you insist."

Sharisse squealed as he hefted her up onto his shoulder. He carried her straight into his bedroom and tumbled her onto the bed.

She held on to him as she fell, making sure he joined her. How wonderful it felt to have him there and not to feel guilty about what she was feeling. What she felt was fire in her blood.

"Oh, Lucas, I want you so much."

Lucas tensed. "He does it to you every time, doesn't he?" he asked, eyeing her carefully.

"Don't. Don't mention him," she pleaded. "It's you I want."

His eyes searched hers for a long time before he answered, "Yeah, I guess you do, don't you?"

He began kissing her, and she knew it would be all right. All she could think about was him, the heat of his mouth, the feel of his body pressing against her.

But he stopped suddenly, listening.

"It's only Mack returning," she said as she heard the hoofbeats.

"There's more than one horse, Sharisse."

"Company?" Her spirits sank. "But if we don't go out, they'll leave, won't they?"

"I left the front door open."

"You don't mean that whoever it is will just come right in?"

"Most folks do."

They glanced together at the bedroom door. It was open, too. Lucas swore and got up off the bed.

"Come on." He sighed. "You keep looking at me like that, and I'm going to shoot whoever is out there."

"Well, I wouldn't want you to do that, Lucas." She giggled.

She turned away to straighten her clothes while Lucas went out into the other room. When she joined him, she was surprised to see Samuel Newcomb. Mack was with them, and another man.

Mack held out a letter to her. "Hope there was no trouble, ma'am," he said. "Didn't think I'd be gone so long, but I got sidetracked by an old coot I ain't seen in twenty years. We had us some reminiscin' to do."

Sharisse hardly heard him. She felt funny all of a sudden. Here was what she had anxiously been waiting for, her letter. But all she could think about was Lucas. Here was her escape, but there was Lucas. The sudden thought of never again feeling his wonderful hands bringing her body to life brought on panic.

"Will you excuse me, gentlemen, for a few minutes? I have been waiting a long while for this letter."

"Sharisse!"

Lucas was annoyed at her rudeness in ignoring their guests, but she couldn't wait. "I'll only be a minute, Lucas," she assured him, and fled to her room.

Dearest Rissy,

You can't imagine how difficult it has been for me to find a way to get this letter to you. I have been denied my freedom and denied visitors as well. But Mrs. Etherton has taken pity on me, and she promises to help sneak Trudi into the house for a visit, so I will give this to Trudi to post. I didn't dare ask one of the servants, for they would tell Father.

Rissy, it has been awful here. With you gone, the full brunt of Father's anger had fallen on me, and I'm afraid neither of us realized just how angry he would be. He has cut me off from everything. I can't go anywhere or see anyone. Even the servants aren't supposed to talk to me. And I haven't been able to see Joel once! Not even when Father had him and Mr. Parrington over to explain your "illness." That is what he was telling all our friends, that you were ill and the wedding would be postponed for a while. But that was when he thought he would have you back soon. So much time passed that he's had to tell Joel's father the truth. Doing that made his anger even worse.

Oh, he's been simply horrid, Rissy. I see no hope for me and Joel any time soon. If I even mention Joel's name, Father explodes. But that isn't the worst part. Father now says that if you don't come home within this next week, which is impossible as we both know, he is going to disinherit you.

I could just cry. This is all my fault. I don't know how you can ever forgive me. But please, don't give up hope. I promise I will figure something out. It will just take a little more time. At least I am relieved by your description of Mr. Holt. He sounds like a reasonable man, so you should have no difficulty imposing on him a bit longer. Don't despair, Rissy.

Sharisse put her head in her hands. Don't despair, when there were no tickets and no money enclosed with the letter? Disinherited within a week? It had taken longer than that for this letter to get to her. What did it all mean, that she couldn't go home?

That she could never go home? Was she to be stranded there forever?

She sat, absolutely still, for a long time. After a while she heard Lucas open her door. "I think you better get out here, Sharisse. Sam has brought us a little surprise."

She heard the tension in his voice, but she didn't wonder about it. She was beyond coping with anything further. She rose automatically and followed Lucas into the other room.

# Chapter 30

LUCAS slowed his stallion as the ranch came into view. It was such a pleasant sight, the dawn sky behind it streaked with violet, purple, amethyst . . . all the shades of her eyes, he told himself disagreeably.

A spiral of smoke rose from Billy's house, but from the main house there was no sign of life. Sharisse would still be sleeping. There was no reason for her not to be. When he'd left, he'd gone without telling her he was going.

He wondered what she thought about his desertion six days ago. That was certainly how she would view it, as desertion. That would determine the kind of reception he was in for. If she was angry, or even hurt, well, that was just the way it was. He had considered her feelings before his own when it mattered most. That was enough.

Lucas nudged his horse forward. The sack hanging by his leg moved, and he grunted. The cat was still alive then. He still couldn't figure out why he had bothered with the damn thing. But he had found it on a homestead outside Tucson where he stopped for water, and buying it from the farmer just seemed the thing to do. After all, it wasn't as if he was bringing the cat for Sharisse. It was for Charley, that was all.

Lucas managed to get his horse settled in the barn without waking Mack. Then he let the cat loose and watched her run off to find a dark hiding place. Well,

Charley would sniff her out soon enough. Right now he had his own female to deal with.

Charley growled the moment Lucas entered Sharisse's room, but it didn't take him long to smell the female cat on Lucas, and he changed his tune. Sharisse didn't wake even when he shooed Charley out of the room and closed the door again.

He had time to study her as she lay there unawares, to marvel at her beauty. The effect she had on him was instantaneous, and he didn't try to fight it. But seeing his ring on her bedside table cooled him off just as quickly.

Disgruntled, he sat down on the bed with a bounce intended to wake her. It did.

"Lucas?"

Was that pleasure in her voice? No. That was the voice of an irate woman. Good. Why should he be the only one upset?

"How've you been, honey?" he asked.

"How have I been?" Sharisse gasped. She came off the bed, grabbing her robe, and moved well away from him. "How dare you ask me that after what you did?"

"All I did was take off for a while."

"I wasn't referring to that!" she snapped. "You can take off again for all I care. You tricked me, Lucas. I would have thought that ridiculous ceremony was nothing but a dream if Mack hadn't called me Mrs. Holt!"

"So, that really was panic I detected in you when I introduced you to the preacher. And here I convinced myself you were only surprised."

His sarcasm gave Sharisse pause. Oh, why did this confrontation have to take place now, when she wasn't even fully awake yet? She hadn't meant to reveal her true feelings to him, only to confirm what she suspected—that he had been even more upset than she was when Samuel Newcomb brought them a preacher.

"It *was* only surprise, Lucas," she said in a more reasonable tone. "But I don't like being taken advantage of."

"I believed the word you used was 'tricked.'"

"Well, how else should I feel?" she said defensively. "I wasn't myself that day, for one thing. I had been drinking that foul concoction of Willow's. I'd been frightened out of my wits by half a dozen Indians, not to mention your brother. And on top of that . . . well, never mind," she quickly amended. "Heavens, I can't even remember half of what took place that day."

"What difference does it make? There was little choice involved, what with the preacher standing right there. You do recall that, don't you? Or was the time and place more important than your reputation?" She turned her back on him in a huff, and he said derisively, "No, I thought not."

Lucas glared furiously at her back. She might not have had any reasonable choice, but he'd had one. He could have kicked Sam and the preacher off his land, as he wanted to. But oh, no, he had thought of Sharisse first, Sharisse and her damned sensibilities. He simply couldn't bring himself to shame her in front of Sam by refusing to marry her. What a gentleman he was.

Marrying her wasn't what infuriated him, though. It wasn't a legal marriage, anyway, unless he chose to honor it. She didn't know that, of course. He was enraged because he had lost control of the whole situation.

Damn Newcomb and his meddling. The bastard thought he was doing them both a favor by bringing the preacher out to the ranch, but all he'd done was complicate Lucas's plans all to hell. And after six days of mulling it over, Lucas still didn't know how to handle things. Damn!

Maybe it would be better if Sharisse just stayed

angry with him. It would certainly make it easier on both of them when they finally parted.

"You know, Sharisse, your attitude leads me to believe you didn't want to get married."

His speculation, which was all too true, made her simmering temper boil over. "How can you say that?" she retorted, striding toward him, arms akimbo. "Didn't I come here to get married? Don't I have the right to get upset when sudden changes occur? You did tell me I would have time to adjust, time to get to know you. You told me that. And I had been here a mere five weeks when we were married!"

"I think you got to know me pretty well in that time," he taunted.

Her color rose. "That is not the point," she insisted. "Besides, if anyone's attitude leaves something to be desired, it's yours. You can't deny you were angry that day, Lucas. You were so angry you left right after the preacher did, without so much as a good-bye. And you're still angry. I would really like to know why."

Lucas stared her straight in the eye. He could do one of two things. He could placate Sharisse and put their relationship back the way it was, or he could be honest for a change, which would set her against him completely. The one would benefit him, the other her.

For her sake, there was only one choice. With studied indifference, he said, "If I seem a little out of sorts, it's simply because I never had any intention of marrying you, Sharisse."

She stared at him in utter, silent disbelief.

"What?"

"It's true."

Sharisse felt sick. All the years of feeling unattractive because of her height and coloring crowded in on her.

"I don't understand, Lucas. I . . . I know you thought maybe Stephanie was your bride, but you said it didn't matter. Now you say it does matter. Why didn't you send me back immediately if you found me so unacceptable?"

The pain in her eyes tore at him. She was supposed to be angry, not hurt.

"Damn it, you've got it all wrong," he said quickly. "There's nothing wrong with you, Sharisse. Why, I've never known a woman more desirable than you. I just didn't want a wife—any wife. It's nothing personal."

"But you advertised for a wife."

"So I did."

"With no intention of marrying her?"

"That's right."

"Why?" she cried.

"That, honey, is none of your business."

"None . . . oh!" She turned her back on him again, only to swing back around. "You seduced me without honorable intentions!"

"I didn't hear you complaining."

She slapped him, and she would have again if he hadn't grabbed her wrists. "You're despicable, Lucas!"

"Perhaps," he sighed. "But now let's talk about you and who you really are."

Her heart skipped a beat. "What . . . what do you mean?" she asked warily.

"Think about it. When a woman claims to be a widow, it stands to reason she's no longer a virgin. How do you explain the fact that you were?"

"You knew?" she gasped. "Why didn't you say something?"

Lucas shrugged. "I didn't want to embarrass you."

"Oh, but it's all right to embarrass me *now* because I'm your wife?"

She was too angry to let him turn the tables on her after what he had just admitted. Guilt over her own deception vanished in light of his.

"Let go of me, Lucas," she demanded icily.

"You going to keep your hands to yourself?"

"You deserved that slap."

"What I deserve and what I'll stand for don't always match, Sharisse," he told her brusquely. "And we were talking about you."

He released her, and she rubbed her wrists as she glared at him. Her mind was racing, searching for a way to assuage his curiosity without confessing.

"Lucas," she began with fine hauteur, "if a man is less than honest, he tends to be skeptical of others."

"Given a good reason, he does indeed. Your supposed first marriage is very much in doubt."

"Did it ever occur to you that my husband might have had a problem? That he couldn't consummate our marriage? It was unfortunate, but not all men are as healthy and virile as you. I felt no less married because of that."

Lucas grimaced. Lord, she really was the innocent victim all the way through this. He was going to have to reevaluate the way he thought of her all over again. And damn, he could see it already, the guilt piling up and him doing something foolishly noble to make it all up to her.

"If you want an annulment," Lucas offered quietly, "it's possible under the circumstances."

"Of course I do," Sharisse said stiffly. "You don't think I would stay here with a man who doesn't want me."

He gazed down at the floor. "So be it. But in the meantime, you will stay here. And if it's to be the easy way, annulment instead of divorce, then you better stay the hell away from me, because there was never any question about my wanting you."

There was a silence, and then she said, "Why can't I leave now?"

"I'm broke, Sharisse. I can't afford to send you anywhere, let alone all the way back to New York. New York is where you want to go, isn't it?"

"Yes. How long, Lucas?"

"What's your hurry? You did come here to get married, remember?" he flung at her. "Consider yourself married for the time being, okay?"

"I find our situation intolerable," she said flatly.

"You think I like it? I'd just as soon shut you up with kisses, but I'm not going to add to the injuries I've already done you." He stood up and went to the door. "But the reason I needed you here still exists, and now that we're married, it would cause too many questions if you left right away. You'll just have to wait this out with me, Sharisse."

"You won't tell me the reason?"

"No."

"Then go, Lucas. And please have the decency not to set foot in this room again."

He left, sorry he had hurt her, aching to make love to her, full of sorrow and regret.

# Chapter 31

WANTING to leave and actually gathering the courage to go were two very different things, Sharisse found out. As the morning progressed she dressed to ride and packed all she could manage to stuff into her portmanteau, which would hook onto a saddle. But as she waited, praying for Lucas to leave the ranch so she could go without having to face him, she had time to think about what she was doing.

What she hadn't considered before then was that not only might Lucas try to stop her, he also had the legal right to stop her. Even if she managed to get to town and Samuel Newcomb gave her shelter, Lucas could bring her back. No one could do anything about it, least of all herself, because he was her legal husband.

So where did that leave her? She couldn't stay here, not with Lucas's true character revealed. Oh, if only he had told her how long he wanted her to stay, then she might not feel so desperate. But for all she knew he might want her around for years. And the way Lucas affected her, she knew it would be only a matter of time before she forgave him everything. If they became lovers again, she couldn't annul the marriage. She simply had to go and go now.

Lucas did finally leave, taking one of the new mares out for a ride. Sharisse hurried to the barn to have Mack saddle her a horse. She hid her portmanteau and Charley's empty basket outside the stable.

No point in testing Mack's loyalty. Then she went in search of Charley. She found him in the back of the barn, sitting on the ground staring at a dark corner. When she called him, he wouldn't respond, wouldn't even turn around to look at her. Then she saw that the gold eyes glowing out from under a plank in the corner belonged to another cat.

Sharisse was amazed. Lucas had to have brought the cat to the ranch. What a sweet thing to do. But she couldn't let that change her mind. She had to remember everthing else he had done.

Charley obviously didn't want to leave his new friend, but Sharisse wouldn't consider leaving him. She locked him in his basket and hurried away. Fortunately Mack didn't follow to see her secure her belongings to the saddle. There was only one thing more she had to do, say good-bye to Willow and her baby.

It was a tearful affair. Willow didn't try to stop her. She asked no questions, seeming to fathom Sharisse's feelings.

Sharisse made it to town without incident. She left the horse at Pete's Livery where Lucas could find it some day, then headed for the hotel. Wilber, sitting out front of the mail dispatch, called out to her that she had a letter.

That was surprising enough, but what was inside the envelope caused her to cry out with joy. Money! More than enough to get her home! She couldn't believe such luck, coming just when she needed it most. She wouldn't have to impose on anyone now, or risk asking Sam Newcomb's help. She could leave Newcomb before Lucas even discovered her gone.

Sharisse went straight to the stage depot, not even taking time to read Stephanie's letter. Her only concern was whether there was a stagecoach due. There was, and her luck was holding, for the stage was late and expected any time.

Waiting was nerve-racking. Even when the large,

clumsy stage finally rolled into town, Sharisse had to wait an hour while the horses were changed and the driver was fed.

She waited inside the stage. It was an oven, the leather curtains closing out most of the air, but she was hidden.

She was beginning to relax when the door opened and Slade stepped into the stage and sat down beside her. She was absolutely stupefied.

"How—?"

"Saw you come into town," he told her. "Been watching you ever since."

"But what are *you* doing in Newcomb?"

"I go wherever the mood takes me." His eyes pierced her. "Where are you going, beautiful?"

She clamped her mouth shut, determined that she didn't have to tell him anything.

"No answer?" he prodded.

"It's none of your business," she said stonily.

"Oh, I don't know." He relaxed back into the seat and said in a too casual manner, "I saw Luke in Tucson a few days ago. I guess I didn't believe him when he said he'd tied the knot. I came back this way to find out the truth. Sure enough, I heard from several people that a preacher made a respectable woman of you." He sighed. "I never did like respectable women."

"Isn't it the other way around, that they don't like you?" she said sharply.

He smiled. "Think so? But we were talking about your new status, Mrs. Holt, and whether or not what you do is my business. Seems to me, as long as you're married to my brother, it is."

"Nonsense," Sharisse snapped. "You never cared about your brother's feelings before. Why should you suddenly want to protect his interests?"

"Who said anything about his interests? That name you carry now is mine, too, beautiful. You think I want it said that a Holt couldn't hold on to his woman?"

Before she could say anything, he went on. "You're here alone. That tells me Luke doesn't know you're leaving. And here I thought he was all you wanted. You did tell me that, didn't you?" he asked with pure mockery.

"Leave me alone, Slade."

She turned away, but he grabbed her chin, forcing her to look at him. "Answer me."

"Yes!" Then, "Yes, he was all I wanted. But that doesn't matter anymore, because he doesn't want a wife. I can't stay here, knowing that."

"Maybe he doesn't know what he wants," Slade remarked cryptically. "Did you fall in love with him?"

"Certainly not," she replied, too quickly. "And you needn't concern yourself, Slade. Lucas is quite willing to let me go. He expects me to get an annulment of our marriage. I won't disappoint him. It will be done as soon as possible."

He stared at her thoughtfully, then said, "Well, before you quit being a bride, there's an old custom I want to take advantage of."

She threw up her hands to stop him. "Slade, no!"

His mouth closed over hers in a hard, searching kiss. Ripples of excitement flowed through her. Oh, no, not again, she despaired. But she pressed closer to his hard body even as she tried to move away.

She was breathless and dazed when he released her.

And then he was gone, as abruptly as he had come.

# Chapter 32

BILLY drew up short when he entered the barn and found Lucas readying his horse with more gear than he could possibly need for a long trip. "Willow tells me your wife took off. You going after her?"

Lucas didn't bother to glance up. "Nope."

"Then what's all this? You just got back from being gone a week. Where'd you go anyway?"

"Around."

"Oh," Billy said sardonically.

Lucas chuckled. "Since when did you get so curious about me?"

"Since you took off the same day you got married," Billy replied. "I got to thinking maybe being married didn't sit too well with you."

"It didn't."

"Shoot, Luke, I thought you liked her."

Lucas shrugged noncommittally. "That's got nothing to do with it. I'm not like you, Billy. I just didn't want a wife, that's all."

"Then why'd you let me talk you into sending for one?" Billy's voice rose with agitation. "You're making me feel guilty as all hell, Luke. Willow said I'd end up regretting butting into your life."

"Forget it. I went along with it since it seemed like a good idea. It wasn't your fault. I never planned on actually marrying the girl."

"Did she know that?"

"She does now."

Billy whistled softly. "So that's why she took off."

Lucas nodded. "That leaves you married, but without a wife to show for it. You willing to go on like that?"

Lucas considered explaining the nonlegality of his marriage, but decided against it. "I won't have to, Billy. Sharisse will take care of ending the marriage just as soon as she gets back to New York."

"You sure?"

"I'm sure."

Billy frowned. "You planning on paying your respects at the Tucson graveyard again?" he ventured. "Is that why you're packing so much stuff?"

"I did that a few days ago." Lucas finally looked at him squarely. "I'm quitting this place."

"You ain't!"

Lucas couldn't help laughing. Billy, with round, incredulous eyes, didn't look like Billy at all.

"Why are you so surprised?" Lucas asked. "You knew I'd move on soon."

"Yeah, but not yet. It ain't over. How can you go before it's finished?"

Lucas shrugged. "The last phase is in the works. I'm not needed here for anything else."

"I can't believe it. After all the time you've put in to make your plan work?"

"That's just it, Billy. I've been here too long."

"It's because she's gone, isn't it?"

"Maybe," Lucas hedged. "What's the difference? You can handle the end of it. All those thank-you letters that came in from the different charities we dumped Sam's money into are in my room. All you have to do is see that he gets the lot of them as soon as Buskett sends word that Sam's ranch is sold and the last of Sam's money given to a worthy cause. He's not a stupid man. He will realize immediately that he's been taken for everything he owns. And I bought the bank myself so I could cancel all those mortgages. I'll send an agent in to take care of that."

"Another expense you figure is worth it?"

"I want the folks here to be free to move on to more properous towns if they've a mind to, yes."

"You know they'll go. This town will be dead within a year. But shoot, Luke, I thought you wanted to deliver the blow to Newcomb yourself," Billy grumbled. "What kind of revenge is that, taking off without even seeing the expression when he reads those letters? I just don't understand."

"It was never revenge, Billy. It was justice. And that's been served. And I can imagine how he will look," Lucas said grimly. "I don't have to be there to see it. I've wiped him out. Next to go will be his wife and his small army that made him feel like a king. All he'll have left is a suite in a hotel that never earned any money and never will, and soon there'll be a ghost town to surround it."

"What about this place?"

"Sell it if you can find someone fool enough to buy it. Or keep it, if you like. It doesn't make any difference to me what you do with it. And you're welcome to it."

"I'll probably head back to the reservation. Willow likes it better there."

"I figured that."

"And you?"

"Henri Andrevie wrote that he'll be in New Orleans for a while before he sails for France and the gambling halls there. I think I'll join him."

"Isn't he the rascal who taught you so much?"

"The same. He never did understand why I wanted to give up the gentleman's life to become a horse rancher. Maybe I'll tell him the reason now and give him a good laugh."

"Maybe you better not. He might just figure out how you used him before."

"I guess you're right," Lucas conceded.

He was ready to leave. He looked at Billy one last time. How well they understood each other. He was going to miss this friend.

"Think you'll ever get back this way?" Billy's expression was sad.

"You never know. But there's one more thing you can do for me, Billy. That passel of letters you're to deliver to Sam? Seal them all in a big envelope and write on it 'Compliments of Jake Holt, Boothill, Tuscon.' If that bastard's got any conscience, he'll remember."

"The perfect touch." Billy nodded solemnly.

Lucas wondered about it as he rode away from the ranch and Newcomb. The trouble was, Samuel Newcomb might not remember Jake Holt. After all, Jake was only one of Sam's victims. But he would wonder, and he would try to connect the name with Slade and Lucas. And if he wondered about all of it long enough, he just might remember Jake Holt.

# Chapter 33

"IS this your first trip to a big city, child?" the elegantly clad woman beside Sharisse asked condescendingly.

"New York is my home," Sharisse replied automatically.

"Oh."

The lady looked away, her interest gone at being denied the chance to dazzle a country girl with tales of city life. Sharisse shrugged and stared out the window again.

She did indeed look like she had just come from the country, with her portmanteau at her feet, Charley's basket on her lap, and her poor traveling suit ready for the ragpile. But on this trip, her appearance had not been one of her concerns.

In less than an hour she would be home. What awaited her? The letter in her reticule just didn't make sense. Sharisse had read it so often since leaving Newcomb that she knew it by heart, but she still couldn't decide what it meant.

She took Stephanie's rumpled letter out and tried, one last time, for some insight.

Dear, dear Rissy,
My dreams have come true at last. Joel and I were married last night, secretly. You will think this was terribly sudden after what I told you in my first letter, and it was. Oh, I wish I had waited

before writing that letter, but I didn't think Joel could arrange things so quickly. But he did. And now I have to admit that I lied to you before.

Oh, Rissy, you just have to understand. When you wrote that you wanted to come home immediately, I didn't know what else to do but try to convince you that you couldn't. It was still too soon. Father was worried sick about you, but there was never any mention that your wedding would be called off. He wouldn't talk to me about it at all, and I thought, that when you returned, he would make you marry Joel.

You see, he didn't admit to Edward Parrington that you ran away. I lied about that, Rissy. He hasn't talked to anyone, because being worried for you took the place of being angry. That happened on the second day you were gone. I was the one who made excuses to everyone for your absence. Naturally Sheila or one of your other friends would have wanted to come up to see you if you were ill, so I told them it was Aunt Sophie who was ill and you had gone to stay with her.

They still think you plan to marry Joel, but we can tell them that you changed your mind while you were gone. Then, later, after a reasonable time, it can be announced that Joel and I eloped. That way no one will know you ran away.

This must sound rather complicated, but it isn't really. I would never have lied to you if I hadn't been so desperate, Rissy. And don't think I've been completely heartless where Father is concerned. I didn't tell him where you were, but I did let him know that you had written to say you were all right. I told him you would be coming home soon. Do come home soon, Rissy, before he gets sick from worrying.

Please don't be too angry with me, Rissy. I did try to let you know everything would work out

when I told you not to despair, remember? Surely
you understood?

Sharisse tucked the letter away. It was no good.
She still couldn't decide if Stephanie was telling her
the truth this time, or if her father had found out
that Stephanie knew where she was and had forced
her to write this letter just so Sharisse would come
home. Was she going to face Marcus Hammond at
his very worst, or had he really been so worried
about her that he would welcome her home without
wrath?

She hated to think of Stephanie betraying her in
this letter. But far worse was to accept that first letter as lies. To deceive a stranger with lies, as she had
done, was one thing. But to deliberately deceive
one's own sister! Why, that first letter was indirectly
responsible for her marriage! If it hadn't come when
it did, she might have had her wits about her that
day. It was just inconceivable that sweet little Stephanie could be so unscrupulous, even for the sake of
love.

Sharisse wished that were all that was troubling
her on this journey, but it wasn't. Ironically, going
home was no different from when she had headed
west, for the same three people occupied all her
thoughts. But this time the third person was no
longer an unknown entity.

Sharisse found herself missing Lucas. She wouldn't
have believed it possible, yet she hadn't been a day
away from Newcomb before it became apparent that
what she was feeling was pure melancholy.

He had always managed to affect her in some way,
whether or not she'd wanted him to. He could amuse
her, exasperate her, even frighten her, and of course
thrill her with pleasure. No matter what, when she
was with him, she'd always felt something.

So now, missing him, she had no control over her

emotions. Angry because of her sister, worried because of her father, she was constantly up and down with the feelings Lucas evoked. The strain was getting the best of her, and her nerves were raw.

# Chapter 34

AN intense autumn sun burned down on the quiet avenue, but Sharisse barely noticed, used to a hotter sun. She stood on the curb, looking up at Hammond House, long after the hired driver had gone. It all felt somehow foreign. She had not been away even three months, but it seemed as though years had gone by. And most unnerving was the feeling that she didn't belong there.

Climbing the stairs very slowly, taking deep breaths, Sharisse was tempted to knock on the door. But that would be cowardly, and that was not the impression she wished to convey. She walked right in as though she belonged there, then stopped in the large foyer, overwhelmed. For so long she had taken all this for granted, the marble floors, the rich wall-papering, the crystal lighting; such quiet elegance.

She stood there realizing how easily she would give it all up just to see Lucas's jewel-like eyes again. And then she chided herself. Lucas didn't want her: she had to remember that and make herself stop thinking about him so much.

"Miss Hammond!"

Sharisse jumped as her name echoed in the large foyer. Mrs. Etherton stood at the top of the stairs, as prim as ever, though a little shaken up just then.

"What is it, Mrs. Etherton?" Marcus Hammond called out through the doorway of his study.

Utter silence followed. Sharisse didn't move a

muscle, didn't even breathe. It was only a moment before Marcus Hammond appeared in the doorway. He stopped, staring at her, his blue eyes quickly covering her from head to foot before they settled on her face. If she had expected to see a man exhausted from worry, this wasn't it. He looked tired around the eyes, but otherwise there was no difference.

Sharisse carefully guarded her expression. Was that relief she saw on her father's face for a second before he mastered his own expression? She couldn't tell, for the sound of running footsteps made him frown.

Stephanie had heard Mrs. Etherton's exclamation and come running. She nearly collided with the housekeeper at the top of the stairs. But Sharisse didn't spare a glance for her sister, because she couldn't take her eyes off her father. He glared at both of them, then said to Sharisse, "Put those things down and come in here."

How easy it was to revert to following this man's orders without question. Sharisse set her portmanteau and Charley's basket on the floor and crossed the hall to enter her father's study. A brief glance at her sister showed Stephanie's alarm, which made her own apprehension worse.

The door closed behind her, and Sharisse steeled herself. She couldn't bear the silence. "You're still angry with me?"

"Of course I'm still angry," he said in a rough voice. But even as he spoke he came to her and drew her into his arms. He hugged her so fiercely, he squeezed the breath right out of her. Then he let her go just as suddenly. She could only stare at him amazed. He was frowning, but that didn't alarm her now.

So it was true. He really had worried about her. Her relief was so great that she grinned, delighted.

"I think you missed me, Father."

"Don't you get sassy, girl," he said sternly. "I

should take a strap to you, by God. What you did was
the most irresponsible—"

"I am aware of that." She cut him short before he
could work himself into a temper. "And I really am
sorry, Father. No one regrets my foolishness more than
I do."

His concern revealed itself then. "You *are* all
right, aren't you, Rissy? I mean, nothing . . . happened to you?"

She hesitated. "Well . . ." She didn't want to tell
him about Lucas if she didn't have to. "No. I look
fine, don't I?"

"Have you seen yourself in a mirror lately?" he
asked brusquely.

Sharisse blushed. "I've been traveling for over two
weeks, Father. Once I clean up and change—"

"Two weeks?" he exclaimed. "Just where *were*
you? The men I hired couldn't find you. Two weeks!"

"I . . . I was in the territory of Arizona."

"That's clear across the country! Are you crazy?
The territories outside the states are barely civilized. Whatever made you—?"

"Does that really matter?" she interrupted. "I'm
home."

Marcus clamped his mouth shut. He didn't know
how to deal with this daughter anymore. He'd never
known her to be like this, to be—just like her mother.

Too, Marcus didn't want to risk another demon-
stration of her newfound independence. How did you
explain to your child the agonies you suffered, not
knowing where she was or even whether she was
alive? She wouldn't understand, not until she had
children of her own. Marcus knew he couldn't go
through another disappearance, he just knew it.

"Sit down, Sharisse." He moved behind his desk,
where he felt more in command. "I want your solemn
word that you will *never* leave home again without
my blessing. You are of an age where a certain
amount of freedom is acceptable, but you are never-

theless vulnerable. And your breeding demands proper behavior, Sharisse. Anything less is a disgrace to our good name. Do I have your word on this?"

"Yes."

Marcus was thoughtful after that terse response. Was she truly repentant? If so, this was a good time to see just how repentant she was.

"I'm glad to see you're being sensible, my dear. You will be relieved to know that your misadventure hasn't changed anything. Your wedding will proceed as planned, albeit slightly delayed."

"Father—"

"I won't hear a single word of objection," he told her adamantly.

"You'll hear more than just a word," she said, just as adamant as he was. "I can't marry Joel. Stephanie married him."

He stared at her wordlessly.

"Ask her, Father."

If there was one thing Marcus could not abide, it was to have something sprung on him. His brows drew together darkly as he marched to the door to summon his younger daughter. But as soon as he opened the door, Stephanie stumbled into the room, having failed to hear her father's approach. She stood there, shamefaced at being caught eavesdropping.

"Is it true?" Marcus demanded furiously. "Are you married to Joel?"

Stephanie trembled. She never had been able to cope with her father when he was angry. She couldn't meet his eyes, but she managed to whisper, "Yes."

"How?"

Stephanie gathered her courage. "Joel arranged it. We . . . we drove upstate. We were married in a small church, and . . . and he brought me back home before you returned from the office."

"You call that being married?" Marcus blustered.
"That's ridiculous. I will get an annulment."

"No!" Stephanie cried.

"I will not tolerate any more defiance in this house! Go to your room!"

Stephanie turned a stricken face to her sister. "Rissy, do something!"

Suddenly Sharisse was awfully tired. Tonelessly she answered her sister's plea. "I think I've done quite enough, don't you?"

Stephanie burst into loud wails as she ran from the room and up the stairs. Marcus closed the door and returned to his desk. How he hated interference with his well-conceived plans.

"You see how easily that was settled," he stated autocratically.

Sharisse sighed. Her father was still the ruling overlord, taking no one's feelings into consideration.

Her eyes met his directly. "Why is it so important that I wed Joel? It can't be that you simply want our family joined to his, for Stephanie has accomplished that. And he obviously prefers her. What's wrong with that?"

"You are the one who will inherit the bulk of my businesses, Sharisse. And since your husband will handle your affairs, he has to be someone I feel is capable of the task. I thought you were sensible enough to realize that."

"Then leave it all to Stephanie," she said sensibly.

"No."

"Why not? Why should I get most of it just because I'm older? I hardly think that's fair."

"You misunderstand, Rissy. I am not leaving your sister with nothing. I will simply leave her the properties that don't require constant supervision, that's all."

"So you have a plan for Stephanie? I suppose you have already picked out her husband?"

Marcus frowned. "There's no hurry, she's still young."

"And in love, and married. I don't see why you can't just switch things around, for heaven's sake. Plans *can* be changed. Let her have the businesses you're so worried about and leave me what you would have given her. Then you'll still have Joel to run these businesses, and everyone will be happy. Why can't you agree to that? It's so easy."

"Edward wants *you* for his daughter-in-law, not your sister."

Her gaze deepened with understanding. Bits and pieces of arguments she had overheard as a child came back to her all at once. "It's because Edward loved my mother and I remind him of her, isn't it?" At his shocked expression, Sharisse became angry. Now at last she knew the reason for his obstinacy. "Yes, I knew about that."

"How?"

"You and Mother were never quiet in your disagreements, Father, and I can remember many that involved Edward Parrington. I thought you were jealous because he knew Mother before you did. But now I wonder how many of those arguments stemmed from your guilt, Father."

"That's enough, Sharisse!"

"I don't think so," she continued. "That's it, isn't it? You still feel guilty for winning her away from your best friend. And you were willing to sacrifice both your daughters to make amends for your guilt!"

"That's utter nonsense."

"Then why," she demanded bitterly, "are you stubbornly holding on to a plan that has long since lost its point for Stephanie or me?"

"Because you were perfectly willing to have Joel until your sister said she wanted him. Such nonsense. Did it never occur to you that she only wanted what was yours?"

"You're saying that she might not really love him?" Sharisse frowned. Her father wasn't aware of all the things Stephanie had done in order to get Joel. "No, I can't believe that. She loves him."

"She's a child, Sharisse. She may *think* she's in love at the moment, but she will feel the same way about a dozen men before she's ready to marry, and that won't be for several more years. No, her hasty marriage will be dissolved. I will not have well-laid plans ruined on the whim of a child."

"You won't reconsider?"

"No."

Sharisse slumped in her chair. She had tried to keep Lucas a secret, but it wasn't to be.

"That's too bad, Father."

"What is that supposed to mean?"

"Even if you did manage to annul Stephanie's marriage, I still couldn't marry Joel. I didn't want to tell you this, at least not right away, but you leave me no choice. I already have a husband."

"You're lying," he said flatly.

Sharisse opened her reticule and placed her marriage certificate on the desk.

He picked it up carefully and read it. Then he dropped it back on his desk. "I'll have that annulled, too."

Sharisse shook her head slowly. "You can't do a thing, Father. I don't know about Joel and Steph, but Lucas and I had our wedding night, if you know what I mean." She didn't have to admit that had happened before the marriage. "I don't believe an annulment is possible unless I deny the marriage was consummated."

Her father turned with fury. "Then it will be a divorce!" he shouted.

"And suffer the scandal?" Her voice rose as his did.

Her mouth was set firmly, and her eyes sparkled defiantly. Marcus knew he was beaten. There wasn't a thing he could do, not if her marriage had been consummated. For that matter, he hadn't bothered to ask Stephanie if she and Joel . . . Lord, how had everything gone from bad to disastrous?

Sharisse relented a little as she saw how defeated he seemed. "If you will be reasonable and let Stephanie and Joel stay married, then I will agree to having my marriage annulled. I can find some other man you will approve of. You can do as I suggested earlier and change your plans about the inheritance. To be honest, I'm in no hurry to get married again. Let Joel and Steph inherit what was going to be mine, Father."

"You said you were intimate with your husband. How can you annul the marriage?"

The subject was embarrassing enough without elaborating on it. "He won't contest it. I don't have to be exactly truthful about what passed between us, do I? Can you arrange it with a lawyer?"

"Anything can be arranged," he said hastily. "But let me get this straight. You're saying this Lucas Holt doesn't care what you do?"

"That's putting it rather bluntly, but in essence that's true. You see, neither of us really wanted to get married. It was a matter of circumstances, my living under his protection, people assuming we would marry, the preacher coming along—oh, Father, it's a long story. I would rather not get into it right now," she ended with a sigh.

Marcus would have none of it. "Don't think you're not going to tell me about this man."

"There's nothing really to tell," she said. "He's a rancher."

"In Arizona?"

"Yes."

"What is his standing?"

Sharisse knew the way his mind worked. "He's not rich. He owns a small horse ranch outside the town of Newcomb. It just barely supports him and

the few men who work for him. He catches wild
horses, tames them, then sells them to the Army and
to other ranchers. What breeding stock he has
started is still too young for sale, as I understand it."

"What is he like?"

Sharisse didn't want to be thinking about Lucas
and replied offhandedly, "I guess you could say he's
handsome, if you like the type."

"The type?"

He just wasn't going to leave it alone. She sighed.
"Dark, rugged, excessively masculine. He's tall as
well, and frightfully strong, with a body . . ." She
blushed to the roots of her hair. Whatever was she
doing? "Let's just say his physique might be envied
by some men. As for his character, well, he's like
you. Stubborn, arrogant." Her father said nothing to
that. "Lucas can be roguishly charming, too. He's like
no man I've ever met before."

"How *did* you come to meet him?"

She tried to sound bored. "It's all rather complicated."

Marcus didn't like her evasiveness one bit, but he
had heard all he needed to know for the time being.
"You're sure he's not for you?"

She lowered her eyes, feeling quite dejected all of a
sudden. "That's irrelevant."

"Why?"

"If you must know, he didn't want me. He was furious when we were forced to marry."

Marcus paled, then the color rushed back into his
face. "This man dared reject *my* daughter?"

"For heaven's sake, Father, my being your daughter had nothing to do with it. I never told Lucas my
background. In fact, he thought I was destitute."

"So you weren't good enough for him," Marcus
concluded. "A girl with no money."

"No. I don't think my means had anything to do
with it. He simply didn't want a wife."

"Then he should have had the decency not to bed you before sending you home!"

Sharisse cringed. It made Lucas seem so callous, but how could she explain?

"He didn't send me home, Father. I left of my own accord as soon as I had the means to do so. Lucas won't end the marriage himself. He is leaving that up to me. I have little doubt that if I insisted he remain my husband, he would do so."

"What makes you so sure?"

"We were compatible in many ways."

Her manner became evasive again, and Marcus asked suspiciously, "Are you being completely honest with me, Rissy?"

"What do you mean?"

"Did this man really let you go, or did you up and take off from him like you did from home?"

"I didn't consult him about it, if that's what you mean," she replied irritably. "For some reason that he wouldn't tell me, he wanted me to stay for a while. But how could I stay with him after he admitted he didn't want a wife?"

Marcus was thoughtful for a moment before asking, "Is it possible he might come after you?"

"No," she said firmly. "Even if he wanted to, he doesn't have the money for a long trip. There is no reason why he would want to, anyhow. I really am tired, Father."

"Of course," Marcus conceded. "But there's just one more thing."

She sighed. "Yes?"

"Are you pregnant?"

Her eyes rounded with incredulity. She hadn't thought, had never even considered . . .

"No!" she shouted.

"Then there should be no problem." He gazed at her intently, for she looked alarmed. "Your 'no' was a bit hasty perhaps?"

"Perhaps," she admitted miserably. "It's just too soon to tell."

"So it's possible?"

"Yes!" she snapped. "It's possible."

Considering her reaction, Marcus said reluctantly, "I suppose we should postpone doing anything until you are sure."

"Must we?"

He shrugged. "We could always invent a husband for you if it becomes necessary. But since you already have one, and since you're reasonably certain you won't ever see him again, anyway, I don't see why we need invent a lie. Do you?"

"No, I suppose not. I'll just have to wait and see."

After Sharisse left, Marcus sat back, drumming his fingers on his desk. Both his daughters were married. He had given neither of them away. All his careful planning had come to nothing. Was this a dream? He shook his head.

One daughter was happy. Edward could be talked around. And the other daughter? Well, she had been evasive about her feelings for this man Holt, but it hadn't passed his notice how quickly she had come to his defense. And she had glowed when describing him. Did she love the fellow perhaps without knowing it? Was she only hurt by his rejection?

The rejection rankled Marcus. Who the hell did Lucas Holt think he was? He had a good mind to—no, he ought to leave well enough alone. Still, something Sharisse had said intrigued him. Holt was like him. That was the only thing wrong with young Joel. He was capable enough, but he lacked backbone.

Stubborn, arrogant, she had called Holt. A man cut from the same mold as himself. Marcus smiled for the first time that day. He knew he ought to leave the situation alone. But on the other hand . . .

# Chapter 35

SHARISSE lay back on her bed and closed her eyes. She had just spent two incredibly long hours being fussed over by Jenny. Her skin still tingled from the hard scrubbing she had received in Jenny's vain effort to remove her new skin color. Jenny had done nothing but cluck and *tsk* over the unfashionable dark tan, but it wasn't going to come off with a brush.

Charley had settled right in after sniffing every corner of the room. He had taken up his old favorite position in the center of the bed, watching the bustle around him, yawning every once in a while. He knew he was home.

When Sharisse joined him after Jenny finally left her in peace, Charley curled up against her side. He started purring even before she began stroking him. At least one of them was content with the end of their journey.

His mistress continued stroking Charley, preoccupied. A baby. Was it possible? Of course it was. Her monthly times were always far apart, so that wouldn't tell her much. She had been with a man, a virile, passionate man. She had let him love her, and that was all it took.

Did she want Lucas's child? A boy to grow up like his father—strong, handsome, arrogant. Or a girl. What would his daughter look like? She knew she shouldn't be thinking about it yet, it was too soon.

But she couldn't help herself. Now that the shock had passed, she was filled with a strange kind of wonder. To have created something from that wonderful passion she had shared with Lucas was magical. She did want his baby, just as much as she still wanted him. The despicable man. She still ached for him. Yet he had probably already forgotten her.

"Oh, Rissy!" Stephanie burst into the room without warning, scattering Sharisse's thoughts. "Father just informed me he has sent an invitation to Joel for dinner tonight. It's to officially welcome him into the family. I don't know how you did it! I'm so grateful. I just knew you wouldn't let me down."

Sharisse sat up slowly, her eyes trained on her sister. "I didn't do it for you, Stephanie. I did it for me."

"But—"

"Father still wanted me to marry Joel. Of course that was out of the question."

"Well, of course. It wouldn't be right after Joel and I—well, you know," Stephanie whispered.

"No, I don't know."

Stephanie blushed. "We didn't come directly home after the wedding. There was an inn we went to, and . . ."

"For heaven's sake, why didn't you tell Father that?" Sharisse snapped.

"I couldn't say something like that to him," Stephanie gasped. "You saw how angry he was. It wouldn't have mattered."

Sharisse shouted in exasperation. "Of course it would have mattered. If you've been with Joel as man and wife, your marriage can't be annulled. Don't you know anything?"

"Oh, dear. I believe Joel said that. But I was so upset today, I just didn't think."

"You never think anymore," Sharisse replied angrily. "You don't think of consequences, you don't think of—"

"I don't see what you're displeased about, Rissy. It worked out fine, didn't it?"

"For you, yes. But I had to give Father a reason why I couldn't marry Joel, and it was something I wanted to keep to myself. Oh, I don't know why I'm even speaking to you after everything you've done!"

"Oh, Rissy, don't be like that," Stephanie pleaded. "I can explain everything."

"Can you?" Sharisse demanded. "Then begin by telling me where my jewels are. Because I didn't have them, I was forced to go all the way to Arizona. Why did you take my jewels?"

"You know how impetuous you are, Rissy. I was afraid you would change your mind and come right back. And I was right, wasn't I? You wrote immediately that you didn't want to stay in Arizona."

"There is. A monumental difference. Between staying alone. In some quiet town. And staying *where I was.*" Sharisse ground out the words. "Do you have any idea what it was like? Indians still raid. Men wear guns on their hips and think nothing of shooting each other. And the sun does this to your skin, Stephanie." She pointed to her face. "This is not theatrical makeup I'm wearing. It will take months for it to wear off."

"Well, goodness, Rissy, why didn't you mention any of this in your letter?"

"Because I was thinking of your feelings! I thought that if you knew my true plight, you would be so upset about me that you wouldn't be able to work rationally on our situations. But I can see now that it wouldn't have made any difference. You're not at all sorry."

"That's not true. If there were any other way—"

"Oh, shut up, Stephanie! I have heard enough."

Sharisse crossed to her vanity, dismissing her sister. But Stephanie was reluctant to leave. She stared at Sharisse's stiff back and said peevishly, "You said you gave Father a reason why you couldn't marry

Joel. Why didn't you just use that excuse before? Then you wouldn't have had to go away in the first place."

Sharisse glared at Stephanie in her mirror. "Obviously my reason is a fairly new one, or I would have. I can't marry Joel because I already have a husband—thanks to my stay in Arizona."

"What?" Stephanie felt sick. "You married him? But you couldn't have!"

Sharisse turned slowly in her chair. "Couldn't?"

"You weren't supposed to. Why did you?"

"You don't just live in the same house with a man and then refuse to marry him when the preacher comes around," Sharisse said dryly. "I had no choice."

"Oh, this is just terrible, Rissy. I didn't want anything like this to happen to you."

"I know," Sharisse sighed.

"What did Father say?"

"He wasn't exactly pleased."

"But you're not going to stay married to Mr. Holt, are you?"

"No."

"Can you get out of it?"

Sharisse nodded. "He didn't want a wife."

Stephanie gasped. "Yes, he did. He—"

"—was as deceitful as I was. He never had any intention of marrying me or anyone else."

"Why, that's despicable!" Stephanie gasped indignantly. After a moment, a new realization dawned. "Oh, dear! If you married him, that means you had to . . . make love with him. Without loving him. How awful for you, Rissy. With Joel, it wasn't at all what I expected, but at least I love him. You must have been so unhappy."

Sharisse smiled. She couldn't help it. "That was not one of my complaints, Stephanie."

"You don't mean you liked him?" The younger girl was aghast.

"Lucas is a devilish rogue, handsome, exciting all the time. He has more faults than saving graces, but as a lover, he was superb, Steph. I was very happy."

Stephanie didn't know what to say. She was shocked by her sister's candor. And she was also envious after her own disappointing experience with Joel.

At last she said petulantly, "I don't know what you're so angry with me for. Why, you had a wonderful time during your stay with Lucas Holt."

Sharisse had no reply.

# Chapter 36

LUCAS was beginning to think that if you'd seen one gambling club, you'd seen them all. The one Henri had found in the south of France was more opulent than most, and spacious, with ample room for tables to be set wide apart. The late April climate allowed them to leave the long windows open, and the perfume of pink laurels filled the air, vying with the fragrances of the women. And there were many women in the room.

"That one is married," Henri said as he noticed Lucas staring at a statuesque brunette. "But it is good to see you finally taking an interest, *mon ami.*"

Lucas grunted. "I take it you can tell me a little something about everyone in the room, as usual?"

"Of course. I did not waste my time today as you did, walking on the beach. I found a waiter who loves to gossip. He was very informative."

One of Henri Andrevie's special talents was knowing the people he gambled with. He never failed to learn something about each of them before he sat down and proceeded to take their money away from them. Information of a personal nature was his edge, and Henri managed to support himself very well.

He was a little man, and he and the tall Lucas made quite a pair. Blond, with dove-gray eyes that twinkled mischievously, he looked younger than thirty-nine. He was a devil-may-care rascal who could talk his way out of any situation and could charm the ladies with just a smile. Lucas had seen, in the months they had been traveling together again, that Henri hadn't lost his touch.

"You will find the English play together, as you see there and there," Henri pointed out. "They come here to gamble, not to decipher languages, and there are many different languages represented here. That graying fellow is a duke. He plays seriously, but he never wins."

Henri chuckled here, and Lucas couldn't help grinning. He knew Henri so well. "You will have all his money before the night is through."

"I think you are right, *mon ami.* Now those two, the *messieurs* Varnoux and Montour, are brothers. But they do not wish this known, so they use different names. They send each other signals, clues, so stay away from their table. That fellow there you might enjoy playing against." Henri pointed out a well-dressed man who was so good-looking as to be almost feminine. "He knows nothing at all about cards, but he is a gambler at heart and he will bet on anything. By the way, that was his wife you were staring at. Pretty, no?"

"Very."

Henri sighed. "As much as I have been trying to get you to enjoy yourself, I must warn you against trying that one—unless you wouldn't mind having the husband watch."

"I think not."

"Yes, they are a decadent pair. I was told his specialty is seducing virgins, and he takes wagers on how quickly it can be done. His wife knows all about it. Isn't that charming?"

"But is he never challenged by an irate father or brother?"

"Occasionally. For that very reason, he and his wife never stay too long in one place."

Lucas scoffed. "You can't believe everything you're told, Henri."

"Ah, but there is always a grain of truth in every lie."

A memory nagged at Lucas. "His name wouldn't be Antoine, would it?"

Henri shrugged. "Gautier is their name. I do not know the first. Why? Do you know of him?"

"It would be too coincidental if I did. I don't know why I even thought of it."

Only he did know. He had been alone too long that day, and as usual when he was alone, he had thought about Sharisse without stopping. All of their conversations were recorded in his mind as if they had happened only yesterday, not last summer. And today he had remembered about Antoine. Antoine had wanted only one thing from her, just as this Gautier wanted only one thing from his victims—sport.

It couldn't be the same man, but damned if Lucas didn't wish it were. He felt so bad over his own treatment of Sharisse that he wouldn't have minded exacting a little revenge for her sake. Trouble was, she would never know about it. As impossible as it had been to forget her, it would be disastrous ever to see her again. He was still hoping time would make the memories less potent, ease some of the pain, put an end to this ridiculous longing he still had for her.

Undoubtedly, she had had no trouble forgetting him. She would have got her annulment a long time ago. Maybe she was even married again. Even if he had wanted to see her, he didn't know where to find her. The money he had deposited for her in a New York bank was still there, uncollected. Four months of inquiries had produced no results. The only John Richards to be found was an immigrant hat maker without daughters. There was no Mrs. Hammond that fit her description, no Miss Richards, either.

Henri continued telling Lucas a little something about each person in the room, but Lucas listened only sporadically. They finally parted, Henri going to the Duke's table.

Lucas continued to watch the dandified Gautier. After a while he quit his table and joined two gentlemen, apparently acquaintances. From their conversation, which soon became animated, and their many covert glances at a pretty dark-haired girl across the room, Lucas imagined a wager taking place.

Curiosity drew him to the bar where the three men were just finishing their conversation. Thank heavens he had learned French well, mostly through Henri.

"Two weeks?"

"A week and a half, Antoine, no more."

"Agreed."

*Antoine.* Was it the same man? It was a common French name, and there were no doubt many men who found it amusing to seduce young girls on a dare. Or a wager.

Gautier seemed well pleased with himself after his two companions left him. He ordered a drink, then turned to stare at the dark-haired girl across the room.

"Allow me." Lucas paid for the drink and handed it to the shorter man.

Gautier accepted, eyeing Lucas speculatively. "Do I know you, *monsieur?*"

"No, but I believe I've heard of you. Antoine Gautier, isn't it?"

"Yes."

"So I thought, after that interesting wager I just overheard."

Gautier chuckled, relaxing. "Perhaps you wish to join my friends in losing some money?"

"Not if you already know the girl." Lucas played along with him.

"No, I have not had the pleasure yet," the dandy assured him. "Claude has been rebuffed by her, which is why he made the wager."

"Claude is one of those men who just left?"

"Yes. He hopes to soothe himself by seeing me fail as well. But if you doubt me, *monsieur,* pick any girl in the room. I would enjoy a double challenge."

Lucas barely managed to conceal his disgust. The man's eyes were gleaming in anticipation. With those dimples and that eager look, he was downright pretty. Were women actually attracted to this peacock?

"You seem confident of winning," Lucas pointed out. "I wonder why."

"Because I never fail."

"Never? Ever?"

Antoine flushed. "Ah, yes, you did say you had heard of me. I suppose you have met Jean-Paul and he told you? It has been three years, but he still likes to brag to one and all that he is the only one who has collected from me on a wager like this one."

"The girl eluded you?" Lucas's voice turned very casual.

"Yes, she did. She was a sweet innocent. Eighteen. How naive they are at that age. And I almost had her. Just another few moments and my record would not have been broken."

Eighteen three years ago? That wasn't Sharisse. Lucas was going to be terribly disappointed if he had no reason to bash the bastard's face in.

"What happened?" Lucas asked.

Antoine clucked in disgust. "My wife was impatient for my company. She had to walk in and ruin everything, revealing that she was my wife."

"Your wife doesn't mind your conquests?"

"Not at all, which is why I cannot understand why she deliberately ruined my chances with the American. And it *was* deliberate, although she still will not admit it."

"Jealous?"

"Perhaps." Antoine sighed. "If the girl had been only an ordinary beauty, Marie would not have interfered. But the Hammond girl was different, vibrant—"

"Hammond?" Lucas cut in smoothly. "I know a Mrs. Hammond. An American, too."

Antoine stepped back from him. "You . . . you need not fear I have trifled with . . . an acquaintance of yours. I do not bother married women."

"Sharisse." Lucas threw the name out viciously and watched the Frenchman pale. "Sonofabitch!" Lucas growled, dropping the French they had been speaking.

Antoine was shocked. "You are an American, too?"

"Right. I think you and I better take a walk."

"I do not understand."

"Outside, Gautier, now."

Antoine understood perfectly. His stomach turned over. The American's incredible size had not gone unnoticed.

*"Monsieur,* I deplore violence. Be reasonable. I did the girl no harm."

"I doubt she feels that way." Lucas propelled Gautier toward the doors. "Don't make a sound, *mon ami,* or I will break your arm," he added in a deadly whisper.

"What . . . what is she to you?"

Lucas walked him into the garden, well away from the building. He let go of the Frenchman, who stood facing Lucas. What was Sharisse to him? The rage Lucas felt said it all.

*"She's my woman."*

"But you know I failed with her!"

"Only because of your wife's interference. It was your motive, Gautier, that sickens me. To go after a woman because you want her is one thing, but to seduce her on a wager! Did she find out?"

"What?"

"Don't push me, Gautier," Lucas growled. "Did she know you pursued her over a bet?"

Antoine was too frightened to lie. "My wife did mention it in her presence, yes."

"So she was humiliated as well as hurt."

Lucas said it softly, so softly that Antoine was taken by surprise when he felt his nose break. He staggered back from the blow, falling into the bushes, clutching his face in agony.

"Please . . ." he moaned.

Lucas yanked him to his feet before he could finish. "Give this your best effort, pretty face, because I'm going to show you the same mercy you show your victims."

Antoine did try, but there was never any question as to who would walk away the winner. Lucas was heavier, taller, in better shape, and furious enough not to care that it wasn't a fair fight. He showed no mercy. Every punch was calculated to do as much damage as possible, especially to that pretty face.

It was over in a very few minutes, the Frenchman groveling on the ground, barely conscious. Lucas stood over him, wrapping a handkerchief around his bloody knuckles. He was still churning with anger.

"You can thank your wife that all I did was rearrange your face," Lucas said. "If you had succeeded with Sharisse, I might have killed you. But I don't think you'll have such an easy time winning your disgusting wagers now, Monsieur Gautier. Next time you look in a mirror, remember me."

Lucas walked away, his stride quickening with a new anger. She had lied to him, lied about her age, her name, her supposed marriage. He recalled her reaction the day they were married. Surprise? Bullshit! She had panicked. That meant she'd had no intention of marrying him. It also meant that he had been torturing himself with guilt all these months over nothing. She'd undoubtedly been delighted to hear he didn't want a wife, and even more delighted when he told her an annulment was possible. Hadn't she left immediately? And where the hell had the money to leave come from? Was her being destitute also a lie? Was any part of Sharisse not a lie?

His anger had reached a dangerous level by the time Lucas arrived at his hotel. But he hid his feelings expertly as always. The desk clerk didn't suspect at all as he handed him a letter. It was from Emery Buskett and had taken five months to reach Lucas.

Lucas waited until he was in his room before he opened the travel-worn letter. Anything that would take his mind off Sharisse, even for a few moments, was welcome. The bottle in front of him was welcome, too.

Lucas,

It's a good thing you finally got around to letting me know where to find you. I didn't know what to think when Billy Wolf wired me that you had left Arizona. I didn't know if you still wanted that information from my friend Jim or not. Jim had returned to New York and was off on another case, so I couldn't find him. But he found me about a month ago, and you'll never guess why.

Jim has been hired by the same Marcus Hammond . . . to find you. He had already been to Newcomb and talked with Billy, who told him vaguely that you might be found in Europe somewhere. But Billy did give him my name. I suppose he figured you might contact me and would want to know about this. By the time Jim tracked me down in Chicago, where I have moved to, he was pretty annoyed by all the runaround. And of course I had nothing to tell him about you, which didn't help the poor man's disposition any.

As for the information you requested, I find it very curious that you would need me to verify that your fiancée is Marcus Hammond's daughter. You must have known that all along—same name, same description. It just couldn't be coincidence.

Jim tells me Miss Hammond came home on her own as he'd suspected she would do. And now here her father is looking for you. Was she really your fiancée, or were you only helping her hide from her father? Oh, well, I don't suppose that's any of my business.

I heard by way of Jim that Newcomb is fast becoming a ghost town. There were few people left for him to question about you, except for one Samuel Newcomb who raved that you were responsible for ruining him. Jim didn't credit anything the man had to say since he couldn't find Newcomb sober long enough to get any decent answers out of him.

If you ever need me again, you know where to find me.

Your servant,
Emery Buskett

Lucas read the letter one more time before he crumpled it and threw it across the room. So Sharisse was back home with her father. A runaway, not estranged, not destitute. Was there no end to the lies she'd deceived him with?

The conclusion he came to damned her entirely. The spoiled rich girl angry with her father, seeing Lucas's advertisement as a way to disappear for a while, thinking nothing of the harm she was doing. She had no way of knowing he wasn't serious about wanting a wife. Why, he might have been some lonely fool who'd have fallen head-over-heels in love with her and been heartbroken when she took off. Had she considered that? Did she care? Of course not. Her type never thought of anyone but herself.

No wonder he hadn't been able to find her. No doubt those incompetent bankers he had left the matter to didn't have the sense to check out all Hammond households. Either that, or Marcus Hammond had paid them off.

Was that why Hammond was looking for him? Did he know about the money Lucas had deposited for Sharisse? A man of his stature might take that as an insult. Then again, Sharisse might have confessed his treatment of her to save her own skin. Hammond might be an enraged father wanting retribution. No doubt she had painted an innocent picture of her own part in everything.

Lucas sat back, his mouth turning up into a caricature of a smile. Set the hounds on him, would she? He shook his head and reached for the bottle. She ought to've left well enough alone.

# Chapter 37

SHARISSE returned her friend Carol Peterson to Carol's home on Lafayette Place, one of the older residential areas still occupied by the upper crust and still holding out against the advance of commerce. Sheila was supposed to have joined them, too, but she hadn't, so Sharisse and Carol had spent an enjoyable afternoon walking between Union and Madison Squares, Sharisse's driver following slowly behind. Of course the girls couldn't resist stopping at the great retail houses of the Tiffanys, the Arnolds, and the Lords and Taylors.

Sharisse was tired, but not anxious to get right home, even though she did have an engagement that evening. She told her driver to take his time, wanting to enjoy the sights of the city she loved so much.

They drove past the two-hundred-foot-long multi-columned Custom House, up Broadway and along Park Row, and by Printing House Square, which took its name from the large number of newspaper offices in the vicinity. Between lamp posts were the tall utility poles with as many as nine crossarms. Organ grinders were playing on the streets, and candy men were pushing their carts next to vendors of ice cream and ices. A penny would buy a small cup filled with one or another delicious concoction.

The streets never quieted. Horsecar railways operated on many streets, as did the elevated railroad, but the older horse-drawn omnibus was still the only means of transportation besides private carriages on Broadway south of 14th Street. They were brightly colored vehicles with large lettering above and below a long row of windows. The driver, up front, was exposed to the elements and kept an umbrella ready for an unexpected shower. Riding on them was an adventure for children. Sharisse hadn't been on one for years.

Park Place revealed many shops advertising rattan furniture, fireworks, glass shades, polishers, and printers. Past City Hall many of the older structures had been replaced by buildings with stone and cast-iron fronts. There could be found manufacturers of safes, firearms, and scales. Curb trees diminished there and then vanished altogether. Ready-made clothing stores offered hats, gloves, flowers and feathers, corsets, shoes, and furs.

Up near Bleecker Street, Sharisse smiled as they passed the Grand Central Hotel, thinking of her father getting red in the face every time the "eye sore" was mentioned. It really was monstrous, towering above the other buildings around it, yet stylish with its marble front and mansard roof. In 1875 when it opened, an incredible eight-stories high and having six hundred thirty rooms, it was reported to be the largest hotel in the world.

When she arrived home and took off her hat and gloves, her father appeared at his study door.

"I would like a word with you, Rissy."

"Can't it wait, Father? Robert is taking me to a play tonight, and I don't have much time to get ready."

"Then you should have finished your shopping sooner," he said disagreeably. "And it's about your recent purchases that I want to talk to you."

Sharisse sighed and followed him into his sanctum. "You're not going to chastise me for spending too much, are you? It was only a few dresses, Father."

"A few? I believe a dozen boxes were delivered here last week, and more arrive every day."

"Well, the full bustle is becoming popular again. You can't expect me to make do with last year's fashions when they have changed so drastically. And besides, you've never begrudged me a good wardrobe."

"That is not why I called you in here, Rissy. I don't care if you purchase a hundred new gowns. I just want to know who's paying for them."

"Paying? Why, you are, of course."

"Am I?"

Sharisse frowned. "I don't understand."

"I happened to be on Broadway this morning, in the midst of that infernal 'Ladies' Mile,' as you girls call it. I thought I would stop in at your dressmaker, as long as I was there, to settle your account. But the lady tells me your bill has been taken care of."

"But how—?"

"That's what I would like to know. She couldn't tell me anything except that a boy had come around with the money and said it was to take care of your bill. She assumed the money came from me, including a large tip."

"It must be Joel seeing to Steph's gowns."

Her father shook his head. "Your name was specified by the errand boy."

"Well, it must be a mistake then."

He shook his head again. "I went to three other shops where I know you trade."

Sharisse knew by his look. "They were paid up, too?"

"Yes."

She sat down next to his desk, thoroughly confused. "I don't know what to tell you. You know I never carry cash when I go shopping. Everything is charged to you. But if neither of us paid those bills, then who did?"

"Robert?"

"Certainly not! I barely know him. I wouldn't be seeing him at all if Joel and Steph hadn't kept pestering me about it."

"I know he's a close friend of Joel's, so I thought . . . You haven't been seeing anyone else, have you?"

"Father, really! Are you suggesting I'm some man's mistress?"

He cleared his throat uncomfortably. "No, of course not. But you apparently have a generous admirer, although his approach is certainly unusual. Who could it be?"

"I've met several gentlemen recently who are new in town, but none impressed me as showy or extravagant. No, I can't imagine anyone I know doing this. It's intriguing, though. Those bills you mentioned weren't for trifling amounts."

"Your bills never are, my dear."

She ignored that. "It is an unusual way to bestow a gift. Flowers or trinkets could be returned, but I'm not going to give back my new clothes after all the time I spent in fittings. I hope you will have cash available so that I can give the money back when I find out who this man is."

"Why don't you let me handle that. I don't like the idea of a stranger paying for your necessities. Buying you little gifts to win your favor is one thing, but paying your bills is downright audacious. It must be a foreigner. They have funny ways of doing things."

Sharisse grinned at his conclusion. "Well, whoever it is, I'm sure he will reveal himself soon enough. Now I really must go and get ready, Father.

Will you be going to your club tonight? I hate to think of you being at home alone."

"Don't you worry about me. I think I'll wait up for you, just in case you learn anything this evening."

# Chapter 38

THE first act of the play was already in progress when she and Robert arrived at the Academy of Music on the east side of Union Square. Its plain exterior, next to the more impressive Tammany Hall, failed to prepare one for its lovely interior. Balls were held there, as well as operas and amateur theatrical performances like the play that night.

Carriages lined the street, but not everyone was there for the play. Across the street couples strolled in the square or took advantage of the benches enclosed by grass and foliage. Mornings and afternoons would find the benches and walks crowded with white-capped nurse maids and children, idlers from the tramp to the overcome tippler, and pedestrians seeking the quiet shelter of trees in that "bit of country in town." At night, lamps hung from the trees gave one a cozy, sequestered feeling. At night it was a place for lovers.

Sharisse didn't know why she was gazing at it with such longing as she entered the Academy on Robert's arm. Robert certainly didn't tempt her. Oh, he was attractive enough with his light brown hair and blue eyes, and attentive enough. And he made it clear that he wanted to be far more than just as escort. But if she were going to take a lover, she would want someone taller, darker, a little wider in the shoulders, more like . . .

She cleared her mind of annoying thoughts and

tried to concentrate on the performance. It worked for a while, but then her ring caught her eye, the large peridot surrounded by brilliants that matched her necklace and earrings. She had done it again, automatically chosen those jewels to wear tonight, just as she had chosen them for every formal occasion she had attended since her return to New York. Pearls would have looked better with the new silver-gray gown, or even her emeralds. But the large oval peridots were exactly the right color, with just enough yellow to make it seem that a fire was banked in their depths—just like his eyes.

*Why* couldn't she forget him? A year had passed, a whole year since she'd seen Lucas Holt, yet his image rose in her mind as clearly as if she'd seen him only yesterday.

"Sharisse! I thought that was you!"

She looked up to see Sheila Harris squeezing through the crowd to get to her. The intermission lights were on, and most of the audience was heading for the lobby. Robert excused himself to do the same, and Sheila sat down in his seat. She looked exceptionally colorful in a dark blue gown with gold brilliants running through the bodice. Sheila never conformed to fashion modes, but she always looked beautiful no matter what she adorned herself with.

At the moment, her blue eyes were wide with curiosity, and she leaned forward as soon as Robert was well out of hearing. "Whatever are you doing with him?"

"Hello, Sheila," Sharisse grinned. "It's nice to see you, too."

"Oh, yes, hello," Sheila said impatiently.

"We missed you today."

"Today? Oh, no! Was it today I was supposed to meet you and Carol? I forgot. You will forgive me, won't you?"

"Of course." Sheila never failed to amuse Sharisse.

"Well? Answer me about Robert."

Sharisse shrugged. "Robert has been my escort for some time. You know that. You see me with him all the time."

"I know. I didn't mean it that way. I only thought . . . well . . . why would you be with Robert now that he's back?"

"He? Make sense, Sheila."

"Don't play coy with me, Sharisse." Sheila narrowed her gaze. "I behaved like a perfect fool when I met him, and it's all your fault. I was just so surprised that I was speechless—and you know I've never been speechless in my entire life."

"Sheila, if you don't explain yourself this minute!" Sharisse warned in exasperation.

"It was completely unfair of you to give me so little warning. I begged you for details, and all you told me was 'he's different.' Now if that isn't an understatement! 'Different!' He's gorgeous. Why didn't you just say so?"

Sharisse sat back, shaking her head. It wasn't possible.

"You say you met . . . him. When?"

"Last night, at the Stewarts' soiree. Donald introduced us. You know Donald."

"Yes, yes, the man you've been seeing, I know Donald. Get on with it, Sheila."

Sheila continued, and Sharisse prayed she wouldn't ask why she wasn't in touch with Lucas. "Well, Donald didn't associate his name with you and only introduced him as Mr. Holt. Of course, how many Holts do we know? I simply had to ask him right out if he was your husband. I didn't expect him to be, not after your careless description of him. You can imagine how surprised I was when he said yes."

"What . . . what else did Lucas say?"

"Well, not much. He's not much of a talker, is he? I asked him about his ship." Sharisse looked upset, and Sheila asked anxiously, "What's wrong?"

"Nothing. Go on."

"I asked about his ship and if his trip to the Orient was successful, but he was awfully evasive. And of course I asked why you weren't with him, and he said you weren't feeling up to it. But you must be better, or you wouldn't be here tonight with . . . oh, dear. He asked a lot of questions, mostly about Robert."

"What? You told him about Robert?"

"*I* didn't tell him," Sheila said in a wounded voice. "I assumed you already had, since he knew Robert's been escorting you recently. He wanted to know what Robert was like, but I couldn't tell him much since I only returned to the city two months ago, and before I went away you were still upstate with your aunt. But your husband certainly was curious about Robert. I suppose that's only natural, though, with him being away on business for so long. Such a long separation wasn't an ideal way to begin a marriage, but it couldn't be helped, could it?"

"What?" Sharisse could barely think at all.

"Will he be around for a while now before he has to leave on another voyage? I did wonder how you could marry a ship's captain, even if he did own his own ship, but I can certainly understand why now! He might be away for long periods, but when he's at home, oh, I do envy you."

Sharisse heard herself blurting, "I . . . I don't know when he is leaving again, Sheila. We . . . ah, we haven't got around to discussing that yet."

"But where is he now?"

"Busy," Sharisse snapped, then quickly smiled and said casually, "Just because he's home doesn't mean I get to monopolize his time. He has a lot of business to take care of. Things that were neglected while he was away."

"Is that why you're with Robert?"

"Yes. And now I really must go and see what's keeping him," she said firmly.

She rose to leave, but her friend grabbed her arm.

"What about your sister's party this Saturday? Surely you can get your husband to take you to *that*. After all, who among our friends has met him besides me?"

Oh, no! "I don't know, Sheila. We'll just have to wait and see," Sharisse muttered, desperate to get away.

She found Robert as quickly as she could and asked to be taken home immediately, using the throbbing headache she was fast developing as a legitimate excuse. She hardly said a word to him on the way home and left him with a quick, distracted good-bye. Mrs. Etherton met her in the foyer and took her cloak and gloves, worrying over Sharisse's pinched expression.

"Where is my father, please?"

The housekeeper sniffed disapprovingly and said stonily, "In the kitchen, miss."

"Raiding again?" Sharisse grinned.

"I believe so, miss."

Sharisse was still grinning as she went to find her father. She liked to think of him upsetting the servants by entering their domain. It was so like him. She found him alone in the kitchen, a cold chicken and a loaf of bread before him on the kitchen work table. Well, he wasn't quite alone. In the corner was Clarissa, the cream-colored female cat it had taken Sharisse weeks to find after she got home. Clarissa was suckling her litter of three. And there was Charley, never far from his little family, curling his way around Marcus's feet. Sharisse was astonished to hear her father say, "Damned cat. I suppose you want some of this?"

"Why, you old softy!"

Marcus jumped, turning around to glare at her. "I'm too old to be startled like that!"

"I'm sorry." She sat down near the work table and picked up a piece of chicken.

He eyed her curiously. "You're back early. Did you find out who your secret admirer is?"

"No. Well . . . maybe. Oh, I might as well tell you right out and see what *you* can make of it. Sheila was at the Academy, and she told me she met Lučas last night at the Stewarts'."

"Lucas? You mean . . . *Lucas?*"

"Yes."

"Well, well, isn't this interesting."

"Alarming is more like it. Couldn't it be someone else pretending to be Lucas?" Sharisse asked hopefully. But she knew it couldn't be, not with Sheila's adoring description.

"What did you tell her?" her father asked.

"I couldn't very well tell her that I didn't even know he was here. How would that look? But she did have one thing to say about him," she added testily. "She thought he was gorgeous."

"What kind of way is that to describe a man?" Marcus asked.

"Sheila's way. She found him quite attractive," she said nastily.

"As I recall, you did, too. All right, let's assume this man is your husband. He's here. What are you going to do about it?"

"I'm not going to do anything," she said flatly. "I'm certainly not going to see Lucas."

"You may have to, my dear. I can't very well deny him access to this house if he demands to see you. He is still your husband. He might not have been aware of that fact when he arrived here, but he's obviously found it out. And he's also made sure that you are aware of his rights as your husband."

"What do you mean?"

"He paid for your purchases. I doubt that was simply a matter of owning up to his obligations. I would call it an extravagant message. A message to you."

"In other words he wants me to know that if he wants to play the role of my husband, he can?"

"Exactly."

"I don't know, Father. Lucas is more straight forward than that. He would just barge right in here and—"

"Then why hasn't he?"

"Oh, how should I know what's on his mind!"

"I'm sure you can guess. He's going to want to know why you're still married, Rissy. Are you going to tell him?"

"No," she replied adamantly, "absolutely not."

"Then you better think of something pretty soon, because I don't think it'll be much longer before you meet Lucas Holt again."

# Chapter 39

SHARISSE was just finishing lunch when her sister came into the dining room, moving faster than Sharisse had seen her move in a long time, though slowly by any normal standards. Stephanie, five months pregnant, was barely showing yet, but from the moment she'd learned of her condition, she'd begun to pamper herself, just as their mother had done. No matter how often Sharisse tried to tell her it would be healthier if she wouldn't treat herself like an invalid, her younger sister wouldn't listen.

Today Stephanie was downright animated as she made a quick glance around the room to be sure she and Sharisse were alone.

"What brings you here, Steph? I'd have thought you'd be riding roughshod over your servants all day in preparation for your party tonight."

"Honestly, Rissy, wherever did you pick up such funny expressions? 'Roughshod' indeed." Stephanie sat down, making an elaborate show of getting comfortable before she said, "Father isn't in the house, is he?"

"On a Saturday? You know he always has lunch with your father-in-law on Saturdays."

"I just wanted to make sure. I wouldn't want him to overhear this."

"I don't keep secrets from Father anymore, Steph."

"You didn't tell him about my part in—"

Sharisse hastened to calm her. "No, no, relax. But I have nothing to hide from him now, anyway."

"Not even that Lucas Holt is in New York?"

Stephanie believed she was delivering monumental news, and her face fell as Sharisse said, "We know that."

"You do? Well good heavens, why didn't someone tell me? I had to hear it from Trudi today. She heard it from Barbara Stewart, and you know what Barbara—?"

"I get the picture, Steph," Sharisse cut in dryly. "I think Sheila is making sure everyone knows. She met him, you see. At the Stewarts'."

"Well?"

"What?"

Stephanie waved her hands impatiently. "Well, what's he doing here?"

"I don't know."

Stephanie was reaching the boiling point. "You're just not going to tell me, are you?"

"I'm not hiding anything from you, Steph. I really don't know why Lucas came here. I haven't seen him."

Sharisse wouldn't admit how vexed she was that Lucas hadn't come to see her. What did he mean by playing this hide-and-seek game with her?

"I thought I heard my girls," Marcus called as he walked into the room.

Sharisse was surprised to see him. "Didn't you have lunch with Edward?"

"I cut it short. Something came up. And what brings you here, my dear?" he asked Stephanie, giving her a kiss.

"I needed a breath of fresh air. All the cleaning going on at our house, you know. Will you be coming to my party tonight, Father?"

"Heavens, no. That's for you young people. I'll be spending the evening at my club."

"Well, I really should get back and see how things are going," Stephanie said, reluctant to leave.

"If you hurry, my carriage should still be out front. It can take you home, Stephanie."

Sharisse groaned. "You're as bad as she is, Father. Her house isn't a block away. She needs the exercise."

"Nonsense, Rissy," Stephanie said cheerily as she hoisted herself up to go. "It never hurts to be careful."

When they were alone again, Sharisse chided her father, "You shouldn't encourage her."

"I know. But right now she reminds me so of your mother. You certainly didn't. All the way to the end you acted as if nothing special was happening."

"I was fortunate. Someone once showed me . . . oh, never mind. What interrupted your lunch?"

"This was delivered to the restaurant." He dropped a folder on the table. "I've been waiting for it for two days. It's a report on your husband."

"You didn't!"

"Of course I did. He's staying at the Fifth Avenue Hotel and has been for a little over a month."

"That long? But that's a luxury hotel. Where is he getting the money? I wonder if he sold his ranch?"

"Oh, his ranch was sold all right, but not by him. It was sold last year by a Billy Wolf. Lucas Holt had left the area long before the sale."

Sharisse stared at her father wide-eyed. "How on earth do you know all that?"

"I sent someone out there last year. It was only reasonable that I should have him investigated."

"You knew these things all this time and you never told me?"

"There was no point in mentioning it, and I didn't want to upset you. Besides, once Holt disappeared without a trace, I was forced to call off the search."

"Disappeared?"

"An old timer who had worked for him said he left

his ranch the same day you did," Marcus replied. "No one saw him after that."

She thought about that for a while. "Do you think he tried to follow me?"

"No. He could easily have caught up with you."

"Of course." She couldn't quite keep the disappointment out of her voice. "Why should he try, anyway?"

Marcus gazed at her thoughtfully. "There were reports that he was responsible for ruining the founder of Newcomb. If that's so, then maybe he *had* to leave. Newcomb is destitute. Do you know anything about that?"

"Samuel Newcomb? But they're friends . . . or something. No, I can't believe Lucas would do such a thing. Not Lucas."

He cleared his throat. "Well, as I said, they were only reports."

"What else did you find out?"

"Mr. Wolf—my man tracked him down—suggested your husband was on his way to Europe."

"Europe! But he had no money."

"Well, he does now," her father said. "He's staying in one of the most expensive hotels in the city, and he's bought the old Tindel mansion."

"He what?"

"There's something that puzzles me," Marcus said. "I thought you might be able to explain it."

"Only one thing?" she asked sarcastically. "Good Lord, I can't believe we're even talking about the same man I knew!"

"Maybe we're not."

"Father," she began wearily, but he interrupted. "The man is registered at the hotel as Slade Holt, not Lucas Holt."

"Slade! Oh, no!"

Marcus was alarmed by her color. "What is it, Rissy?"

"Slade is Lucas's brother!"

"But why would Lucas use his brother's name?"

"It might not be Lucas," she gasped. "It may be Slade."

"Nonsense. This man claims to be your husband. You would be able to expose him if he's not your husband."

"Would I?" she laughed humorlessly. "They're twins. I can tell them apart only because Slade dresses like an Indian. If he dresses inconspicuously here, as he would, I wouldn't know the difference, I swear."

"Then this might not be your husband?"

She bit her lip, then cried, "Oh, I just don't know what to think!"

"Well, I'll have to go and question the man," her father said resolutely.

"No!" Sharisse came up out of her chair like a shot. "You can't do that."

"Why not?"

"If it *is* Slade, well, he's . . . difficult. He's different from Lucas. Slade grew up alone in the wilderness. He's a gunfighter. He's blunt and kind of raw. He's not civilized. You don't talk to Slade, Father, not easily."

"Does he have an interest in you?" her father asked.

"He did, yes," she admitted reluctantly. "He's just not the kind of man you can confront, Father, so please don't do anything."

"Something has to be done, Rissy. We can't just keep waiting and wondering."

"Yes, we can," she insisted. "You said yourself it probably won't be too much longer before he calls on me. I'd just as soon delay that meeting if it's Slade." She gazed down at the table, then explained, "At least I know how to deal with Lucas. But Slade? My God, if he has it in mind to impersonate Lucas in order to force me—"

"He wouldn't dare," Marcus growled.

"Oh, yes, he would, Father. I've been trying to tell you. He's unscrupulous. He would think it amusing to pose as my husband for a while, to have me right where . . . Well, as I said, he did pursue me before."

"Perhaps you should stay with your aunt again for a while."

"Then how will I ever resolve this situation? No, I should continue to live as I normally live. I refuse to hide from him. What I should do is see a lawyer on Monday and get this marriage over with. Then it won't matter whether it's Lucas or Slade."

"It's too late to end it easily, Sharisse. You need your husband's cooperation now. You know that," he reminded her gently.

"Well," she sighed, ruefully, "there is one thing. His attitude about a divorce will tell me who he is. If he doesn't want a divorce, I'll know it's Slade."

Her father stood there looking at her sadly, then turned and left the room. He needed a chance to think, alone in his study.

# Chapter 40

"YOU were supposed to get here early, Rissy, not late," Stephanie complained as she took her sister's arm and walked with her toward the parlor.

"Don't scold, my dear. I almost didn't come at all. Robert sent his regrets, and if I hadn't already been dressed when his note arrived, I wouldn't have come."

"But it doesn't matter that you're not escorted. You know everyone here."

"That's why I decided to come anyway." Actually, she had needed the distraction, needed it desperately. "And I'm not really late." They stopped at the entrance to the large parlor where twenty or so guests were gathered. "Sheila hasn't arrived yet, I guess."

"Well, she's the only late one besides you. And you can never depend on Sheila to do anything when she says she will."

"Now don't be so sulky, Stephanie. It doesn't become you."

"I can't help it," the younger girl hissed in a low voice. "I've been a bundle of nerves ever since I heard about you-know-who."

"I wish you wouldn't bring that up." The front door sounded behind them, and Sharisse pulled away from Stephanie. "There now. Go and greet the last of your guests. I'll go in alone. I'll be . . ."

"What is it, Rissy?" Stephanie followed her sister's gaze and gasped, "Is that him? It is, isn't it? Oh, what should I do? Should I have Joel ask him to leave? Rissy?"

It took a hard shake before Sharisse was able to reply at all. "Don't . . . don't do anything, Stephanie." She swung around, closing her eyes to try and calm herself.

"What should I do?" Stephanie whispered frantically. "I can't very well welcome him to my home. Joel should be told."

"Stephanie, you have no sense!" Sharisse snapped. "You don't get a man like that to leave if he doesn't want to leave. You're only going to cause trouble if you involve Joel. Just pretend everything's all right."

"Well, how am I supposed to do that?" Stephanie gripped Sharisse's arm. "Oh, God, he's seen you! He's coming over, Rissy! I think I'll go."

"Don't you dare leave me alone with him!" Sharisse hissed.

She turned around. Her eyes locked with his. And suddenly she went all funny inside. It was those eyes, that clear golden-green, so bright and so disarming.

Warm or cold, his gaze affected her, and apparently that hadn't changed. His skin was not so heavily bronzed now, but he was still darker than any other man in the room. His black hair was shorter, his clothes more sophisticated. But he was still the man she could never forget.

"Hello, beautiful."

The husky voice sent shivers through her.

"I believe you know several of my friends already, but you haven't met my sister," she said as steadily as she could. He glanced briefly at the flustered blonde and nodded curtly, then looked back at Sharisse. His face might have been carved from granite.

The two of them continued to stand there, eyes locked, unmoving.

"Well, we finally see the newlyweds together," Sheila called out, striding toward them quickly, Donald on her arm. "You'll never believe where we found him, Sharisse. Clear across town. I just knew he'd never get here on time unless we offered him a ride."

"How thoughtful of you, Sheila," Sharisse replied tightly.

"Well, we'll talk to you later, darling," Sheila said cheerfully. "I must say hello to everyone first. Mustn't be rude."

Sheila went on into the parlor and Stephanie followed, leaving Sharisse alone with him.

"Is there somewhere we can talk, privately?"

"No!" She blushed, hearing how emphatic she sounded.

"You afraid to be alone with me, beautiful?"

"No, I . . . I just don't see any reason why we can't stay right here."

"Have it your way," he growled, "But I can't wait any longer."

He drew her fast against him, and his mouth came down hard on hers. The shock of his body pressing hers was like a lightning charge, his lips hungry, demanding. Powerless to resist him, her hands moved over his shoulders, around his neck, into his hair.

He raised his head, wondering whether she would draw away from him, but she didn't. Her eyes glowed, darkly amethyst.

"I'm afraid I couldn't help myself," he said softly.

"What?"

He grinned at her bemused condition. "Look around you, beautiful."

She did, and blushed scarlet to the roots of her hair. Stephanie was staring at her in amazement. Sheila was grinning. Trudi Baker and some other girls were giggling. The men in the room were trying hard to pretend they hadn't seen anything. She wanted to die.

She looked back, saw her hands wrapped around his neck, and pulled them back, stepping away from him. "How could you?" she hissed furiously.

"Very easily, and with pleasure," he replied, taking her arm and leading her a little distance away from their audience. "Why don't you ask yourself that question? You have just acknowledged me as your husband to everyone present."

"Well, aren't you?" she snapped.

"No."

Her eyes opened wide. "So it *is* you! How despicable you are, Slade. I'm only surprised that you admitted it."

"Slade?" He raised a dark brow in that infuriating way. "Now why would you think I'm Slade?"

Sharisse shook her head. "Don't try to confuse me. You're registered at your hotel as Slade Holt."

"So your father has been checking up on me—again." His voice turned cold.

"Again?" she asked hesitantly. "You know about the man he sent to Newcomb?"

"That's why I'm here. I want to know about that. That—and a few other things."

"But he was looking for Lucas, not you. Oh, I could just scream!"

He chuckled. "Then I guess we'd better find somewhere private. How about your sister's bedroom?"

"As if I would trust myself in a bedroom with you," she said. "The garden will have to do."

She led him outside to the enclosed garden in back of the house. There were benches and a small fountain nestled among the roses. Light from the house softly illuminated the garden, and it was pleasantly cool. After closing the doors, she turned around to face him.

"If you don't start explaining yourself, then we have nothing to discuss," she told him plainly.

"Me? Honey, you're the one who has the explaining to do."

"Not until you tell me who you are."

His eyes narrowed. "I'm the man you married in Arizona."

"Then why did you deny you're my husband?"

"Because that paper you have that says we're married is worthless."

She stared at him, open-mouthed. "You mean the preacher wasn't—"

"Oh, the preacher was real. And you and I know I married you. But can you prove it? If I go by another name, am I your husband?"

"I don't understand. You can't get out of a marriage just by changing your name."

"I can. And you know I can . . . if the other name I use is 'Slade'. Having a twin brother has some advantages."

"I have never heard of anything so preposterous! That can't be possible."

"I'm not going to tell you exactly why it's possible, just believe me, it is. That paper that says we're married is valid only if I admit to being Lucas Holt."

"But you have admitted to being Lucas!"

"To you." He grinned. "Not to anyone else."

"That's not true. Sheila thinks you're my husband. You haven't denied it to her or to anyone else."

He shrugged. "Lots of couples pretend to be married so no one can accuse them of immorality. I wonder what your friends would say if they thought you had been pretending all this time?"

Sharisse took a long, deep breath. It would mean scandal, and he knew that.

"But there was a ceremony and—"

"—And you have no witnesses to that ceremony. Your friends would only think you were trying to save your reputation. It's human nature to believe the worst of someone if there's enough gossip. You know that."

"You can't do this to me," she told him firmly. "We have to be married!"

"Why?" His voice rose. What was behind this?

"Lucas, I know you must have been surprised to find that I'm still your wife."

"Surprised is not what I was."

"If you'll just let me explain. I had every intention of getting that annulment, but when I returned home, my father still insisted I marry Joel."

"Your sister's husband?"

"Yes. You see, Stephanie loved him. Didn't I tell you that before? But my father wouldn't listen, and he would have forced me to marry Joel. If I hadn't told him I was already married, I would be Mrs. Parrington now. He didn't like it, of course. He tried to find you, to find out what you were like, I guess."

"Didn't you tell him I was a bastard?"

She was stung. "I didn't tell him what a deceitful cad you were, if that's what you mean."

"Me?" he exploded, and grabbed her shoulders in a rage. But one look at her wide, frightened eyes, and he didn't shake her, just pushed her from him.

"Let's talk about deceit—yours," he said coldly. *"Mrs.* Hammond, wasn't it? Daughter of John Richards? Eighteen years old, you claimed to be. Destitute—a widow—estranged from your father. Have I forgotten any of your lies?"

She cringed. "Lucas, I can explain."

"Can you?" He was shouting now. "What if I had really been some poor fool who wanted a wife? Did you even think about that when you answered my advertisement? Did you?"

"I didn't answer it!" Sharisse shouted back. "My sister did!"

They stared at each other in surprise. Then he

said, "Sit down, Sharisse, and start from the beginning."

She did, explaining again about Joel, and Stephanie. "She was so heartbroken that I was about to marry Joel that she didn't know what she was doing. You can't blame her, Lucas. I had intended to send back your tickets along with a letter from Stephanie. But after I left New York, I found that my jewels were missing." She didn't explain why, but hurried on. "I had no choice but to use the tickets, because I had no money."

"Why didn't you tell me all this when you arrived? Hell, I would have made a deal with you. We could have helped each other without all these lies."

"I would have, but you were so formidable. I was afraid. I had hoped you would simply disapprove of me and send me back East." He laughed, but she ignored it. "What deal would you have made? Why did you need me there, Lucas? Did it have something to do with Samuel Newcomb?"

"Your father found out about that, did he?"

"Only rumors. Did you really ruin Sam? On purpose?"

"That's why I was there in the first place," he said, unashamed. "Sam was too well-protected to kill, but breaking him was just as good. Well, after a while, Fiona started messing things up for me by making Newcomb jealous. I didn't want him hostile at that point, so I figured my having a fiancée would put his mind at ease. It did."

It dawned on her as he was talking. "He's the man who paid to have your father killed, isn't he?"

Lucas nodded. "I couldn't prove it, but yes."

She shook her head in amazement. "Slade got the one man, and you took care of the other. You Holts don't wait for the law when it comes to righting wrongs, do you?"

He grunted. He could tell her all of it, but he didn't

see any point to that just then. He still didn't know what he was going to do about her. He hadn't expected that his first sight of her after all this time would cause a pain that was eating away at him. She was just as beautiful as he remembered, even more so, and damn, he wanted her so badly. Even thinking she was a heartless baggage, he couldn't turn away.

He was thoughtful too long, making Sharisse uncomfortable. What was he thinking? "Look, Lucas, I know you don't want a wife, and I'm sorry I didn't take care of that sooner. But I will. I'll get a divorce just as soon as possible."

"You can't divorce a man you're not married to," he replied absently.

"Lucas! You're not still angry because I lied to you, are you? You have no right to be." She was losing her temper again. "You lied to me just as much. What if *I* had really wanted a husband?"

"You would have been amply compensated for your disappointment. In fact, I deposited a small fortune in a bank here for you. But of course, no Mrs. Hammond could be found to collect it." He shrugged. "Now that I know you don't need it, I've put it to another use."

Sharisse's eyes sparked. "You had money all along, didn't you? You could have sent me back when I asked you to! You . . . oh!"

"I'm rather glad I didn't." He grinned.

"Why were you living that way if you had money?"

"My father's gold mine made me wealthy, but I was playing a role in Arizona, for Sam's benefit, and throwing money around wasn't part of it."

"But you said the mine was never found."

"I said Newcomb couldn't find it. My brother and I knew where it was."

"So you really are wealthy?"

"Are you disappointed?"

It infuriated her, the way his eyes were twinkling. "It makes no difference to me, I'm sure."

"Doesn't it?"

"No. Wealthy or not, you're still despicable."

He laughed outright. "And here I thought you would be pleased to know I can buy you all the little luxuries you're accustomed to. You could use a restraining hand, though. You spend too much."

She gasped at his meaning. "No one told you to pay my bills, Lucas! Why did you?"

"You wear my name. That gives me license to do what I want to where you're concerned."

She shot to her feet. "But you said you're not my husband!"

"I haven't denied it publicly—yet. Have I?"

"But you intend to, don't you?" she snapped. He didn't answer, and the storm went right out of her. She sat down slowly. "Oh, Lucas, why do you want to do this to me? I can bear the scandal of a divorce if I have to, but not that I was never married to begin with."

"You created this mess, Sharisse."

"I told you why!" she cried.

"Because of your sister," he replied, "but she's been married a long time. What excuse do you have for not correcting this situation sooner?"

Sharisse looked away. To tell him the truth would be to force him into something he didn't want. She wouldn't do that. She couldn't.

"I . . . I didn't think there was any harm in leaving things the way they were, Lucas. My father might have found another husband for me, and I didn't want another husband." How true that really was, she began to realize.

"And what if I wanted to get married one day?"

"But you said we're not married."

"You didn't know that."

"Well, I would have done something about it

eventually. I just didn't think there was any hurry. What difference does it make to you, Lucas? Why can't you just let me pretend to get a divorce? That would solve everything. I swear you'll never have to be bothered with me again, never have to see me again."

His eyes narrowed. Never see her again?

"If you want a divorce, Sharisse, you're going to have to marry me again."

"But that's ridiculous!"

"Take it or leave it," he replied curtly.

"But, Lucas, it doesn't make any sense to go through all that trouble if we don't have to."

"I'm through with pretense. We either do it my way, or I'll be honest enough to admit to that crowd in there that I'm not your husband."

"Don't!"

"Well?"

"Oh, all right then, Lucas, but I swear you're crazy."

"Maybe I am." He smiled engagingly, infuriating her further. "I'll pick you up in the morning, around ten. Be ready. And don't worry, no one will have to know that you're marrying me again just so you can divorce me. It's only the divorce that will have to be made public."

"You're being very unreasonable," she said stoutly, "but you never were a reasonable man, Lucas."

"I'm just tying up loose ends, beautiful. You can't object to that."

She didn't know what he meant by that and she didn't ask. She was suddenly exhausted.

"I don't think I'll return to the party," he said. "You can make my excuses for me. I don't care for the idle chitchat of parties. We seafaring men don't, you know." She blushed at the reminder, and he asked, "Was that necessary, making me a ship's captain?"

"It seemed appropriate for a husband who was never around," she said tartly.

"Well, I suppose we can always say I've given up the sea."

His grin enraged her. "You can say anything you want—as I'm sure you will. You always do."

She turned in a huff and left, and he stood there grinning as he watched her march away.

# Chapter 41

SHARISSE dressed sedately in a cashmere dress of cobalt blue with a matching cape. Nothing fancy for this ludicrous outing.

Lucas arrived on time, and she didn't even give him a chance to get out of his carriage, but hurried out to meet him. He was amused by that.

"One might think you were eager to see me," he commented as he pulled her inside beside him.

"I just didn't want you meeting my father," she said crossly.

"But I was so looking forward to that. You've said how alike your father and I are. Didn't you tell him about our getting married again?"

"Certainly not. You did say no one would have to know," she reminded him.

"So I did," he sighed.

"Have you changed your mind?" she asked hopefully.

"Ah, beautiful," he said roguishly, "what's the difference if you marry me twice, as long as the end result is what you want?"

"You mean what *you* want!"

He chuckled, and Sharisse sat back stonily, determined to ignore him. The rest of the ride progressed in silence, with Sharisse fuming and Lucas absorbed in watching her. He took her outside the city, to a small church. He had made arrangements beforehand, and the minister was waiting, along with two parishioners who would act as witnesses.

Sharisse went along with it all in the same stony silence until, halfway through the ceremony, the minister addressed Lucas by a name she hadn't expected to hear.

Before she could protest aloud, he whispered to her, "Don't worry. An oversight, but it makes no difference."

"But—"

"If you don't want to go through with this, there *is* the alternative."

Sharisse clamped her mouth shut.

Lucas anticipated further objection over the signing, but Sharisse surprised him. He didn't know it, but she didn't remember signing her first wedding paper, so the fact the minister hadn't yet written in their names didn't alarm her. She didn't comment, either, when he insisted she sign her maiden name. She just did it, then stalked out of the church to wait for him in the carriage.

When he joined her in the carriage, he dropped the completed document in her lap and sat back and waited. He didn't have long to wait.

Sharisse read no further than Slade's name and glared at Lucas. "You said his saying the wrong name was an oversight. But you signed 'Slade,' too!" She threw the paper at him.

He looked at her but said nothing.

"How could you do this to me, Lucas? You have married me to your brother!"

"No. I have married you to me, legally this time. Isn't that clear to you yet?"

She allowed all her questions to run through her mind, then came up with some answers. "You really are Slade, aren't you? You only pretended to be Lucas to trick me! And what the devil do you mean *this time?*" He smiled, and she cried, "Oh, it was *you* who married me before. You came back that day and let me believe you were Lucas so you could . . . If the preacher hadn't arrived when he did, then you would have—no wonder Lucas was so furious. You married me to him without his knowing!"

"You have some of that right, beautiful, some. You want to hear the rest of it or do you want to keep on sputtering?"

"What can you tell me that will excuse what you've done?" she said, furious. How dare he be so high-handed? "I'm not married to both of you, am I?"

"No. Your first marriage wasn't legal."

At least she wasn't a bigamist, though that was a small relief.

"I don't know what you think you've accomplished by all this trickery, Slade. *You* I will divorce—with pleasure. You've got nothing."

"Will you divorce me, beautiful?"

"Immediately," she assured him.

Sharisse turned away. The matter was settled. They returned to her house in silence, as they had left it, and then he amazed her by saying, "Go and pack some of your things, Sharisse. You're moving in with me."

"Don't be ridiculous, Slade." She moved to step out of the carriage.

"I didn't marry you just for the hell of it. I had no legal rights over you before, but now I do, and I intend to keep it that way. Do what you're told."

She was horrified. "But I won't stay married to you! I won't!"

She ran into the house, slamming the door behind her, but in a moment he threw the door open.

"You didn't think it would be that easy, did you?"

She faced him, enraged. "Get out!"

"What the hell is going on in here?" Marcus stepped into the hall and stared at the tall, dark-haired stranger.

Sharisse turned to her father and said in the same furious voice, "He thinks that because I married him he can tell me what to do. But he tricked me, Father. He's not Lucas. He's Slade! *You* tell him he can't get away with this, because *I* don't ever want to see him again."

With that she ran up the stairs, leaving the two men staring at each other across the long hall. Marcus was stunned. Was this his son-in-law then, this formidable looking young man whose unflinching gaze meant cold determination?

"I was hoping we might meet under easier circumstances, Mr. Hammond, but now I must warn you not to interfere." Marcus drew himself up to speak, but his son-in-law said, "She might be your daughter, but a husband has undeniable rights. You know that. I'm not leaving here without her."

"Then you really are her husband?"

"You heard her admit it."

"But she was married to your brother. You're not Lucas Holt."

"Mr. Hammond, it's a long story. In all fairness, Sharisse should hear the story first. All you need to know now is that I love her, and I believe she loves me."

Marcus smiled. He couldn't help himself. "Oh, I have no doubt that she's in love, though she's never owned up to it. I knew she was in love when she came back from Arizona. But it's Lucas she loves. She doesn't like you at all, believe me."

"She might have given you that impression, but I can assure you her feelings will change before the day is through. Now, I am going to collect my wife— with or without your permission. It would be easier for both of us if you gave it. Getting off to a bad start is a bad idea for both of us. But nothing is going to stop me from taking her out of here, not the fuss she makes, not any objections from you. Do you see?"

"By God, she was right," Marcus blustered. "You're not an easy man to deal with. Am I supposed to just take your word that Sharisse won't be unhappy being married to you?"

"Yes, that you are."

Marcus shook his head. What an outrageous situation. But Sharisse hadn't been able to disclaim this man as her husband. So what choice did Marcus have?

"Go on then," Marcus sighed. "Her room is the second door to the left. But I damned well better not regret this decision, Holt. Remember that. Treat her well, you hear?"

A black brow rose. "Is that a threat, Mr. Hammond?"

"No. Yes, by God, it *is.*"

"Fair enough." The younger man chuckled, and he started up the stairs.

# Chapter 42

SHARISSE had locked her door, of course, but it opened as he forced his shoulder against it.

She stood in the middle of her room, refusing to be intimidated. "What did you do to my father?" she accused. "Why didn't he stop you from coming up here where you're not wanted?"

"He was smart enough to realize that you belong to me. You might as well accept that fact, too." In two long strides he took hold of her shoulders. "Now, do you walk out of here with dignity, or do I carry you?"

"You wouldn't!" He tossed her over his shoulder. "Put me down, Slade! I won't stand for this!" That didn't stop him. "You might be able to force me to live with you, but I will never let you touch me. I love Lucas! Do you hear?" He kept right on moving. "I hate you!"

He deposited her in his carriage, and she scrambled to the farthest corner of it.

"What about my things?" she demanded.

"We'll send for them."

"I hope you know how despicable you are."

"I believe I do, yes." He had the audacity to grin at her. "We will be at my hotel in a few minutes, so I suggest you calm down and think about how you're going to enter it. I don't mind carrying you inside."

She walked into the hotel, his fingers clamped firmly on her elbow. They made no scene as they passed the luxurious public rooms on their way to the elevators.

Slade's room was on the fifth floor. She noticed the rich appointments as she jerked away from him and took a seat. She intended to remain glued to the chair. He stood in front of her, though, his legs spread out and his arms folded.

She regarded him resentfully. "Don't think you can intimidate me, Slade Holt, because you can't."

He gazed around the room. "These rooms will be comfortable enough until the house is finished. Another week ought to do it."

"Don't you think you're taking a lot for granted?"

He smiled. "Is there still some question about our marriage? Your friend Robert understood when I told him he wasn't needed anymore. Yet you still need convincing, don't you?"

"So that was why Robert . . . oh! What are you doing in New York, Slade, really? You don't fit in. You're a gunfighter, a product of the uncivilized West. You can't mean to live here."

"I think I've proved I can fit in just about anywhere."

"But you're not really going to settle here, are you?"

"Why not? I always wanted to see more of the world, but I've traveled enough. I'm afraid it wasn't as exciting as I thought it would be, but maybe that's because I couldn't get you out of my system. We'll have to see Europe together some time."

"Europe? Then you went to Europe with Lucas?"

"You might say that." He grinned. "By the way, Lucas met an acquaintance of yours in France, a disgusting little peacock who makes wagers involving naive virgins."

"Antoine?" she gasped.

"I'm afraid Lucas took exception to the man's sport. He wiped the ground with Gautier's face, which isn't so pretty anymore."

Her eyes lit up with amazement and unmistakable pleasure. "Lucas did that for me?"

"I did," Slade answered softly.

"You? But you said—"

"When are you going to realize the truth, Sharisse? Don't you see? There is only one of us."

The color drained from her face. "That . . . that isn't possible," she said shakily.

He knelt down beside her so his eyes were level with hers, and said as gently as he could, "You're not frightened of me. You were before, but now you're not. Haven't you wondered why?"

Her eyes scanned his face. It was true. He just wasn't, well, dangerous anymore. If she hadn't been so angry, she'd have realized it sooner.

"Then, you have to be Lucas," she concluded.

He sighed and stood up. His expression hardened. The gentleness was gone—just like that. The change was abrupt and startling, leaving her no doubt. He was Slade.

"Sharisse, Lucas is dead." His voice was tinged with bitterness. "Feral Sloan killed Lucas the same day he killed my father. I didn't know that until the day I shot Sloan. For nearly ten years I thought Lucas had got away, that he was alive somewhere and I would be able to find him some day. I had blocked his death from my mind because, you see, I saw it happen, just before I lost consciousness."

Slade turned away from her to hide his grief. "Lucas didn't ride on when I fell from my horse to the bottom of a gorge. The fool kid stopped to try and help me. I suppose I would have done the same thing. We were just too close, being twins, too much a part of each other. That closeness gave Sloan the chance to catch up with us and put a bullet in Luke's back.

"There was so much blood covering me from a gash on my head, I guess Sloan assumed I was dead. He figured taking one body back, along with my horse, was enough to prove there were no more Holts alive to claim that gold mine. He took Luke's body." There was a long silence. "I was nineteen when I found my brother's grave beside my father's in Tucson."

Sharisse stared at his back, pain welling in her chest.

"You killed Sloan. Why didn't you kill Newcomb, too? I would have!"

He faced her, surprised by the fury in her voice. "I told you. He was too well-protected. I would have been a hunted man for the rest of my life, and I already knew what that's like. There was only one way Newcomb could get what he deserved. I took away what he valued most, his wealth. His ill-gotten gains."

"But you waited so long to do it."

"It took that long, Sharisse. It took planning. And besides, I never could have got away with it as myself. You saw how the people of Newcomb regarded me. You were frightened of me yourself."

"Your manner was brutal, Slade."

He grinned at her. "Honey, I've been a saint compared with how I was eight years ago. After living half of my life with fear and hate as constant companions, I knew no other way to be. There wasn't any friendliness in me. How could I get Newcomb to trust me when he saw me as a killer? I had to change myself completely, to create a different man.

"I went east to do it, to civilize myself. It wasn't easy. I am reserved by nature, but I had to train myself to be more open and friendly. Meeting up with a French gambler helped. Henri Andrevie was everything I wasn't, a devil-may-care fellow with a roguish charm and an exasperating sense of humor, just the sort of man you fell in love with."

Sharisse blushed at his knowing smile.

"Instead of going to all that trouble to change yourself, why didn't you just hire someone to take care of Samuel Newcomb? You had the money. Wouldn't that have been easier?"

"Yes, but not at all satisfying. I don't believe in getting someone to do my work for me. It was something I had to do myself. It took five years before I felt I was ready.

"But when I returned to Newcomb, a completely changed man, it wasn't good enough. The people all remembered me. And to try and convince Samuel Newcomb that I was reformed just wouldn't have worked. So I became my own twin, pretending to be Lucas in order to fool Newcomb." He sat down across from her, a little of the tension going out of him. "No one suspected there weren't really two of us. Showing up as myself occasionally in town helped, because we were so completely different."

"No one knew? No one at all?"

"Only Billy."

"Of course." She nodded, understanding. "He made a point of telling me stories when I first got to the ranch, stories about you and Lucas and him tracking horses together."

He chuckled, and she said, "I'm surprised he never slipped and called you Slade by mistake."

"To avoid any mistakes like that, I had to insist he keep Lucas and me separate, even when we were alone."

"So all that business about you, or rather Lucas, living with an aunt in St. Louis was lies?"

"Oh, there was an aunt, but she was a bitch. Luke and I hated her as much as our father did. There was never any thought of going back to her."

"You could have told me before now," she said, trying to take it all in.

"No, I couldn't. There were too many discrepancies in your own story for me to trust you."

"But you let me leave Newcomb thinking I was married, when all along my husband didn't exist. How could you be so cavalier?"

"There was no need to tell you. You were supposed to get an annulment. Remember?"

"Why was it necessary for me to ever meet you as Slade?" she demanded. "You know how he terrified me."

"I'm afraid that was pure selfishness on my part. I wanted you so much, but you were playing hard to get. I couldn't think of anything except you. I figured, as Slade, I could send you running to Lucas for protection. It worked."

"Well, of course it worked," she snapped. "Lucas wasn't nearly so frightening after Slade. Who could be?"

"That was the idea," he admitted. "I couldn't understand your fear of Lucas. You were supposed to be a widow, for one thing, and your response to his kisses contradicted your protests. You put him off, yet I knew you wanted him."

She blushed and looked away. Did he have to be so blunt? "It was only afterward that I realized your reaction would have been extreme with any man who threatened your virginity. You really should have told me you were a virgin."

"So you simply changed places that night on the mountain? Of course, Billy played along with it, making me think there were two of you." It all came back to her in a rush. "No wonder Slade let me go so easily when we got there. You just assumed you would bed me later, as Lucas!"

"True. You can't deny that I made it easier for Lucas. You wanted us both. He was your choice, but the harsh Slade you feared could also have made love to you, and you know it."

Oh, how she wanted to deny it. But she couldn't. And he knew she couldn't. It infuriated her.

"Pure selfishness is not a good enough term for your actions," she said bitterly.

"You can't make me feel guilty at this late date for making love to you! I could have gone to Rosa's place in town and had my pick, but I wanted only you. Hell, I wanted you even before you got there, just from your damned picture. Do you have any idea how ridiculously delighted I was when you showed up instead of your sister?"

She was absurdly pleased to hear him say that. And, truth to tell, she didn't regret for a minute giving herself to him. But it wasn't him—it was Lucas. She'd made love only to Lucas, and he wasn't Lucas.

"Oh, I'm getting so confused."

He kept silent, letting her sift through her thoughts. "Why did you show up that second time at the ranch? It was bad enough that I suspected you had the same power over me as Lucas did. Did you have to prove it and make me feel even worse?"

His mouth hardened. "I was hoping to disprove it. It didn't sit too well with me that you wanted us both. I thought you would forget about me after Lucas made love to you, but you didn't, did you?"

Her eyes widened at his sharp tone. "You can't be jealous of yourself, Slade."

"You didn't know we were the same man, Sharisse. In your mind we were completely different men."

"In my mind you were an extension of him, the dangerous, unpredictable side—" She stopped as he began that infuriating grin. "What is so amusing, please?"

"You just admitted that you love me, honey."

"I most emphatically did not!" she said indignantly. "I fell in love with Lucas, not you." His cool look flustered her. "Oh, you know what I mean!"

"And what makes you think I'm not the man you fell in love with?"

"You don't act the same. You're not nearly as nice."

"There's only one man, Sharisse—me. Now I can be myself. No more acting, no more having to be cautious every time I do something."

"But you always frightened me as Slade."

"That was intentional, honey. You don't think I wanted you giving in to both of us, do you?"

She remembered the first two times she had almost succumbed to him, that first time at the ranch, and then again at the mountains. Not almost—she *had* succumbed. And she recalled her confusion as he set her away from him both times. She remembered his look of triumph when she said she would beg him to leave her alone. She had thought at the time it was because he enjoyed humiliating her, but now she realized it was because she had made the choice—she didn't want them both.

"But why did you show up at the ranch again?" she asked him. "You had already accomplished your purpose. Lucas and I—"

"That time wasn't intentional, Sharisse. The fact is, I was heading home early that day because, after the way we had parted, I couldn't wait the whole day to be with you again. But then I ran into those Apaches, and I knew I couldn't show up with them as Lucas. You might have wondered why I could communicate with them so easily."

"But you didn't have to make advances again."

"No, but after I got there, I remembered what we—or you and Lucas—had fought about, and it was an impulse to get that settled once and for all. And you made your choice. But you certainly enjoyed rubbing it in, didn't you?"

She couldn't meet his knowing eyes, recalling her vindictiveness once she had been assured he would leave her alone. "What if I hadn't started crying? Would you have made love to me?"

He shook his head. "I would have found some other way of making you fight me. You were never in any real danger of my ravishing you, beautiful."

"I wish I had known that at the time," she said tartly.

"You know I always let you go. It wasn't easy," he

said. "Every time I got near you I got carried away, no matter which role I was playing. And they were both roles, Sharisse. I'm not like the Slade you met in Arizona, and I'm not Lucas, either."

She frowned. He was a combination of them both, and he was neither. Well, hadn't she once wished they could be the same man? Whatever else he was, she knew one thing. This was the man she had fallen in love with, despite her firm resolution never to lose her heart.

But what did he feel? She would be able to get used to him as he truly was. But what did he feel toward her?

She gazed at him for a long while, and then she asked, "Why did you follow me to the stagecoach that day?"

"I saw you leaving the ranch and figured you'd try to leave town."

"But why come as Slade?"

"If you were upset enough to leave Lucas, then I figured you'd cause a scene in town if Lucas showed up."

"But you could have caught up with me before I got to Newcomb. Why did you let me get to the stage?"

"I felt I'd done you enough harm, Sharisse. If you were set on leaving, I wasn't going to stop you. That wouldn't have been decent. But I had to say good-bye to you, or say something. I could manage that as Slade without making you panic. I couldn't just let you leave without doing something."

"Why not?" she asked.

"For God's sake, woman, haven't you realized yet that I love you? Why the hell else would I be here? And why would I be standing here answering these fool questions when all I really want is to take you in my arms and show you how much I love you?"

"Well," she said quietly, "what's stopping you?"

Slade stared in surprise, then burst out laughing.

"You truly are amazing, Mrs. Holt. Is that all it took to win you over?"

Smiling, she came into his arms.

"I love you, beautiful," he murmured. "I want you. I need you. Now let me show you."

# Chapter 43

THE carriage moved along Fifth Avenue at a brisk pace, but it couldn't be fast enough for Sharisse. She was in a fine rage, and it was all her father's fault. Slade, on the other hand, sat nonchalantly gazing at her from the other seat, looking as if it hardly mattered that they had been interrupted just as he lifted her in his arms to carry her to bed.

It was more than a girl should be asked to bear. She had waited a year for this man to come back into her life, a whole year of dreaming of him, yearning for him, and just when she discovered that he loved her as much as she loved him, her father ruined everything by sending over two strongarms who insisted they return to Hammond House.

Sharisse glared at Slade. "How can you just sit there? Aren't you the least bit angry?"

Slade smiled at her display of temper. "Their timing wasn't appreciated, but I expected them. I knew your father would do something. He was just too agreeable about my taking you. I'm sure he's been worried about you."

"But—"

"Once your father is assured you're all right, we'll find a way to be alone."

"You promise?"

He laughed, delighted by her frankness. "Come here, you." He pulled her across the carriage onto his lap. "I can't make love to you right now," he whispered, "but at least I can hold you. Would it embarrass you to be fondled in an open carriage?"

"Let's find out." She grinned, entwining her arms around his neck as he captured her lips in a searing kiss.

Slade ended the kiss while he still could, taking a deep breath. He set her back on the seat across from him. "That wasn't such a good idea, Sharisse."

She smiled at his discomfort. He wasn't sitting there so calmly anymore. And there was a light glowing in his eyes just for her. She sighed, silently urging the horses on.

She tried to think of a distraction, anything to calm her racing heart. "I don't know if I want you living in New York, Slade. There are so many beautiful women here—"

He shook his head. "When are you going to accept the fact that no other woman can compare with your beauty?"

She glowed. "Shall we settle here, do you think?"

"For now, though I'm partial to the West. I thought about starting another horse ranch, seriously this time. What would you think of spending half the year here and the other half out West? Of course, you wouldn't have to do the cooking and cleaning this time."

"I think I might like that—if you relent and buy me a carriage."

"I suppose I could tolerate one carriage. By the way, how's Charley?"

She laughed. "He's not jealous of me anymore, if that's what you're thinking. He has his own little family now."

"He might not be jealous anymore, but I sure as hell used to be, watching him curled up on your lap being petted and coddled. You don't know how many times I used to wish I could trade places with that cat."

They arrived at Hammond House, and the two

large men who had ridden up front jumped down quickly to escort them inside the house. But no sooner were they standing in the hallway than Slade laid a fist to the jaw of one man, then landed a punch to the gut of the other. Two more fast jabs sent both men to the marble floor.

"What the hell—?"

Sharisse turned toward her father, who was watching Slade. Slade casually straightened his clothes and said, "Just so you see that I'm not here because you decreed it, Mr. Hammond."

Sharisse giggled nervously. "I wish you had done that back at the hotel."

She moved into Slade's arms and hugged him. Her eyes locked with his, and she felt a jolt of desire that forced her to move away before she forgot where she was.

"It was rather high-handed of you to interrupt our honeymoon, Father, but I appreciate your concern for me. You can see that I'm fine now." To Slade she whispered, "I'll wait for you in my room. You won't have to break the door down this time."

She ran up the stairs, leaving the men eyeing each other. Slade was surprised to see that the older man didn't look displeased. He would have been amazed if he'd known just how delighted Marcus really was. At long last he had a son-in-law capable of taking over his businesses, capable of handling Sharisse. If not Slade, then one of the fine sons he would have would run Marcus's empire. He had little doubt there would be sons, lots of sons. And Marcus was just stubborn enough to live long enough to train his grandsons himself.

"Do you still have doubts, Mr. Hammond?" Slade asked simply.

Marcus chuckled. "Not a one, my boy, not a one. And since your wife is waiting for you upstairs, I think we should put off our talk till later. Don't you agree?"

Slade relaxed, his yellow-green eyes lighting up. "I do indeed."

Sharisse lay back on the bed, her eyes dark with passion. Her lips were sore from Slade's fevered kisses, but it was a pleasant soreness, and she was eager for more. He stood looking down at her as he began to undress, and she felt the familiar constriction in her chest as those green eyes moved over her. This was not the roguish charmer, Lucas. Slade's very seriousness filled her with a thrilling excitement that bordered on fear.

She began to remove her gown, but Slade stopped her, joining her on the bed, his voice deeply persuasive as he took hold of her hands.

"Let me, Shari. I have dreamed of this so often it seems like forever."

She gave herself up to his ministrations, moving only as he directed her to, until she was naked. She could not keep her hands still, needing to touch him, to feel the virile strength that was him. It had been too long.

"You've had a baby."

Stunned, she followed his gaze to her bare breasts. The telltale stretchmarks were revealed. She looked away from him and lay back with a sigh. The time had come, hadn't it? There was nothing she could do but tell him.

"Yes," she said evenly.

"Were you thinking about informing me—ever?" he asked icily. "Or did it perhaps escape your attention that I didn't know?"

She looked him in the eye and said calmly, "Slade, you emphatically didn't want a wife. How could I force you to stay in a marriage you didn't want? If you'd known about the girls you'd have felt obligated to stay married, and I have some pride, you know." Her voice rose as she felt all the tiredness, the secrecy of the last year overwhelm her. It took her a while to realize that he was staring at her with complete incredulity.

"Girls?" he repeated. "More than one?"

"Twins," she said. "And thank you for warning me that twins were a possibility. It might have helped to've had a little warning."

"Twins? Daughters?" he asked, stupefied, and she threw her arms around his neck and pulled him down for a kiss.

"I will be more than happy to fill your ears with every little detail about your daughters, but *not now!*"

"All right, beautiful." He smiled down at her. "But remind me to tell you later how wonderful I think you are."

He kissed her soundly before she could say anything, and very quickly there was nothing to think about except the tremors and the fire being rekindled. It was going to be all right, she told herself as the flames rose within her. No, it was going to be better than that. It was going to be wonderful, wonderful. And it would last forever. They would go on and on together, consumed by their love as she was being consumed by passion right then.

She wrapped her arms around him fiercely, holding her love with all her might, and he answered with a passion as great as hers, leading her from one peak to another until they blazed together into a glorious, never-ending white-hot flame.